I0557066

Heartbeat by Stacy Aumonier

Stacy Aumonier was born at Hampstead Road near Regent's Park, London on 31st March 1877.

He came from a family with a strong and sustained tradition in the visual arts; sculptors and painters.

On leaving school it seemed the family tradition would also be his career path. In particular his early talents were that of a landscape painter. He exhibited paintings at the Royal Academy in the early years of the twentieth century.

In 1907 he married the international concert pianist, Gertrude Peppercorn, at West Horsley in Surrey. A year later Aumonier began a career in a second branch of the arts at which he enjoyed a short but outstanding success—as a stage performer writing and performing his own sketches.

The Observer newspaper commented that "...the stage lost in him a real and rare genius, he could walk out alone before any audience, from the simplest to the most sophisticated, and make it laugh or cry at will."

In 1915, Aumonier published a short story 'The Friends' which was well received (and was subsequently voted one of the 15 best stories of 1915 by the Boston Magazine, Transcript).

Despite his age in 1917 at age 40 he was called up for service in World War I. He began as a private in the Army Pay Corps, and then transferred as a draughtsman in the Ministry of National Service.

By now he had four books published—two novels and two books of short stories—and his occupation is recorded with the Army Medical Board as 'author.'

In the mid-1920s, Aumonier received the shattering diagnosis that he had contracted tuberculosis. In the last few years of his life, he would spend long spells in various sanatoria, some better than others.

Shortly before his death, Stacy Aumonier sought treatment in Switzerland, but died of the disease in Clinique La Prairie at Clarens beside Lake Geneva on 21st December 1928. He was 55.

Index of Contents

BOOK I

DIASTOLE

I

Outside the window a starling uttered a long deep note, then fluttered away. In the twilight of her mind some chord of gratitude responded. She was conscious of the pleasant sense of delightful coming things.... Something tremendous and moving occuring deep down within herself, and she enjoying the cosy contemplation of it. They say this is the hour when people usually choose to die, when the vitality is at its lowest; perhaps it is only shifting from one plane to another. The vitality of Barbara was certainly very pronounced, long before it shifted to the plane of actual consciousness. Rich and full were the anticipations and visions which crowded upon her. When the daylight came, and she had washed and dressed and gone out into the sun, you could see the reflection of them in those profoundly questioning, profoundly vivid eyes. The young are so closely in touch with their inner selves that it is only the external things they question, the things which threaten to re-act upon themselves, to harden them.

The starling did not come again; doubtless he had other sleepers to warn of the miracle of the sun's approach, and they in the exact measure of their true or false visions would welcome or execrate him. Her father, that man of almost unfathomable dignity, the holder of high office under the Crown how would the warning of the starling affect him?... Barbara was too far away to concern herself with such an imponderable question. She had the genius of happiness.

Several hours elapsed before the chain of visions snapped abruptly, caused by a maid opening the door quietly. She had come to awaken the young mistress. In a flash Barbara was awake in every living tissue. A crowd of definite facts leapt to the fore-front of her mind. They took somewhat this order: Yesterday had been her twentieth birthday. It was over, but there were crowds of things to look forward to. Billy Hamaton and the Stradling girls were coming to spend the day. Daddy was going to town after breakfast, and wouldn't be back for a week. She had a pony, a real live pony of her own, given her by her father yesterday. Its name was Tarbrush. These thoughts crowded upon each other while she was speaking.

"Good morning, Sally."

"Good morning, miss."

"Is it going to be fine, Sally?"

"I shouldn't like to say, miss. Ij;'s all right at present a bit misty."

Sally was a born pessimist. She could always find a cloud or a mist about somewhere. "When she had retired, Barbara assured herself with regard to the dubious weather forecast, by leaning out of the window in her nightdress. She knew by experience that it was the kind of day likely to be fine. A slow-moving day, with a thin white mist that would lift later, and leave a scorching sun to do its worst. Poor Daddy! "What a curious idea for Parliament to sit in August, when all the schools and colleges and everything else of the kind were shut! Surely those old gentlemen, who were mostly like her father, well-to-do, comfort-loving old gentlemen, could make what times they liked! If I was Parliament I should break up in early July, she thought. And then well, after all, July is very jolly, and so is June, and May. Why not sit in the winter when it's wet and foggy? How jolly the lavender smelt in the bed beneath her window, and yes, there was Beal already rolling the tennis-lawn while the dew was upon it....

II

There was something about the tenuous lines of the girl's body as she darted about the room immature, like the quivering bud of a plant that has never seen the sun except through glass. Her movements were eager and vital... epicene, indeed almost boyish. She might have been a boy of seventeen rather than a girl of twenty. Even the face was boyish, a pretty, effeminate boy. Her dark hair was caught tight back from the forehead and hung in a long plait down her back. The business of bathing, undoing the plait, brushing out the hair, donning a rather shapeless print frock, was all done in the manner of a boy late for school. Some of the boyishness may have been due to the fact that in her curiously detached life she had many people to spoil her and no one to spoil.

She was her own mother, and sister, and brother. Her father was so much away. Mrs. Tollboy, the housekeeper, and Miss Eidde, her tutor, were kindness itself, but for neither of them had she any deep affection. She lived for herself. She had no recollection of her mother at all; neither did her father ever mention her.

Between her father and herself there were strange little chasms of reserve. Many years previously, when quite a little girl, she had been taken by Miss Ridde to the House of Commons to hear her father speak. He was a very important man. Miss Bldde said he was a Chancellor, whatever that was. He had charge of all the money in the country millions and millions. The knowledge had impressed her enormously. She deducted the fact that if he had charge of all the money in the country he must be the one man that everybody trusted most. If he had millions and millions to look after, it would be so easy to help himself to a little say, a pound, or perhaps half-a-crown. No one could surely ever find out. She had no strong moral bias about these things. She had been brought up to take anything she wanted.

But if the knowledge of his position and power impressed her, the sight of him in the House was a thing she would never forget. The memory of it was one of the causes of the little chasms. There were rows and rows of middle-aged and elderly men solemnly listening to her father as he stood by a table, holding a sheaf of papers in his hand. He looked exactly the same as he did at home. It was the setting which made him appear more impressive. A loose, badly fitting frock-coat hung in pendulous masses about his vast person; chains and signets dangled between the crevices in his waistcoat. His heavy, melancholy face, with the deep bags beneath the eyes, and the great dome of forehead, gave an atmosphere of complete immersion in his subject, of complete aloofness from his surroundings.

The deep boom of his tired voice filled the great hall with effortless ease as he developed the scheme of his ponderous economies. Sometimes a ripple of applause would run round the hall; at other times from odd corners would come murmurs of dissent; but he seemed to be quite unconscious of either interruption. Once a thick-set man with a grey beard addressed a long remark to him in a strident voice. Her father placed one of his large fat fingers on a certain place on the sheet of notes before him, and turned his gloomy face in the direction of the speaker. His face expressed neither annoyance nor approval. He was apparently carefully weighing the value of the interruption. Satisfying himself that the remark was not "germane to the subject," he continued his discourse in the same imperturbable accents. At moments he became husky and wheezy, and he blew his nose in a languid tornado of sound, in identically the same way she had seen him do in the dining-room at home after breakfast. The speech seemed interminable, and quite incomprehensible. Occasionally he would put the papers down and, leaning heavily with one hand on the table in front of him and the other thrust into the sleeve-opening of his waistcoat, he would wander off into a maze of figures, and averages, and percentages, all quoted from memory.

Barbara felt a great desire to call out: "That is my father!" but she dreaded the vision of all those bald-headed and solemn-faced men looking up at her. It was not exactly pride she felt, but an instinct to enlarge the claims of her possessive sense.

III

Curiously enough, this experience did not tend to augment her sympathy with him. At the time he appeared sufficiently impressive, but afterwards, when she beheld him in their own home behaving in the same way, talking to the same kind of men on the same or similar themes, she could not shake off the effect of some overpowering and passionless fate. In his attitude towards her he expressed an enveloping affection, within the confines of an elaborately thought-out code. She knew that he took infinite pains working out the meticulous program of her welfare. He looked far ahead, and allowed for every conceivable eventuality. He protected her from the buffets of worldly friction by a wide fortification of considered training and physical detachment High Barrow, where they lived, wag thirty miles from London; their neighbours were families of gentle birth and culture. He kissed her night and morning. He called her brief, endearing names. He humoured her follies and her wilfulness. In spite of this, she did not know her father at all. She doubted whether anyone knew him. He never upbraided or scolded her; and yet at times he had a way of regarding her through half-closed eyes, as though he had observed her for the first time, and was considering whether she herself was really "germane to the subject." The sensation made her feel like an interrupter who: has hazarded a foolish remark.

It was probably partly due to this attitude and partly to her environment that at the age of twenty she was like a boy of seventeen, a rather selfish, very wilful, impressionable, not very well-informed schoolboy. For it must be observed that as an instructress Miss Eidde was not very convincing. Thomas Powerscourt's instructions to her had been to "teach his daughter all the elementary subjects, but under no circumstances to teach her music, or to allow her to attend concerts or theatres."

As Miss Ridde knew no music and her knowledge was essentially elementary, she found no difficulty in following these instructions. She often cogitated upon the queer embargo upon music and drama, but it was not her business to question. The situation was a well-paid sinecure, and, except for wilful moods, Barbara was a pleasant companion, one who preferred games and amusement to work. In any dispute Miss Eidde always gave in to her pupil. She had not attempted to give her lessons for years. Occasionally they read something together, or discussed safe subjects in a pleasant, tentative way. Miss Ridde was a very useful person. She had quite a genius for self-effacement.

The character of Mrs. Tollboy was more assertive, but it was one of her proudest boasts that "she knew her place. "Her respect for Thomas Powerscourt amounted to reverential awe, and Barbara was his daughter.

Her aunts, Jenny and Laura, paid fugitive visits. They, too, were under the spell of their brother's astounding reputation, and they appeared to adopt towards her a similar attitude of reserve. She felt that she would never get to know them. Both rather fragile old ladies, they made no attempt to influence or interfere with her way of life. And the girl had a great capacity for living. She crowded her day with pleasant occupations, riding, walking, games, lying in the sun, dreaming. She quickly acquired the social habit. Among the numerous friends who lived near by she soon detected a kind of herd-instinct for doing a certain thing in a certain way, and she herself acquired this habit. There was a strong convention of thought and behaviour never openly acknowledged, but nevertheless (relentless. In these circles she even found the figure of her father, in spite of his distinguished attributes, somewhat gauche. He was not assimilable. These people visited him, and on occasions he visited them; but in either case the visit was a Dead-Sea-fruit adventure. His manners were courteous, and his conversation irreproachably correct, intelligent; but he had that faculty of listening without hearing, and of talking as though his mind were actively engaged elsewhere.

In spite of a certain ingrained affection for her father, therefore, it was always with a slight feeling of relief that she heard, as on this morning, that he was going away. His presence acted more as a check upon her freedom of thought than on her freedom of action. When at home he left her entirely to her own devices, but she could not avoid the pervading consciousness of his unexpressed critical perceptions. Sometimes she wished he would get angry with her, order her to do this or that, display some evidence or disapproval of her numerous delinquencies. His passivity dulled the flow of her quickly-moving thoughts. Like all young and healthy people, she conceived! happiness an affair of escaping from the actuality of her environment. She saw herself objectively, a creature participating in the delights of a thousand romantic episodes, her mind coloured by the chromatic tissues of fiction. She and Miss Ridde read a great deal of fiction Dumas and Charles Reade, Victor Hugo, Stevenson, Daudet and Thackeray. Her tendencies were not neurotic. Love with her was essentially an affair of chivalry, brave deeds and self-sacrifice. Her tastes were masculine. Stevenson's pirates and Dumas' adventurers meant more to her than erotic imaginings. She admired those aristocratic women who overthrew kings and cardinals and married some simple fellow in the end. At the back of it all there lurked the ever-recurring impulse to probe experience, to thrill with the responsibility of quick decision; above all, to have a good time. She was not unaware of the good times to be had surreptiously in her father's house. Sometimes she felt an interloper, as though she were there under false pretences.

IV

Her father was eating kidneys and bacon a favourite dish. She kissed him lightly on the brow, and he wiped his mouth with his napkin, mumbling:

"Well, my dear—"

On the other side of the table was a young secretary, a beautifully groomed, rather supercilious young man, who said alertly:

"May I fetch you something, Miss Powerscourt?"

She said: "Yes, you can, please, Mr. Thornley. I'll have some bacon no kidneys."

It gave her a sense of satisfaction to be waited on by this well-dressed person. Whilst he dived about amongst the silver dishes on the side table, she said:

"All right after last night's depravity, Dad!"

"Yes, my dear, And you?"

She was all right, of course. But she had asked the question because she could see that her father wasn't. He ought not to be eating kidneys and bacon now. It was a very curious thing about her father. In spite of his aloofness from the ordinary distractions of social life, he was peculiarly attached to the good things of the table. He drank moderately, but he ate to excess. All the doctors told him the same thing. He was always being unwell, and then he liked to visit well-known specialists. He would listen absorbedly to what they told him. He would order an array of bottles of medicine. When they came he would hold them up to the light and examine them. Sometimes he would take a cork out and smell the medicine, but he never drank it. Neither did he ever take the doctor's advice. He went on just the same as usual. But the visit seemed to give him some kind of satisfaction. When on occasions Barbara remonstrated with him about not obeying the doctor's orders, he would look at her with mild surprise, and murmur a dim acquiescence. It was as though he simply had not the power to resist. It seemed strange that a man who had shown such strength of character in his public life, and was adamant about the nation doing the wise thing for itself, could not resist the oleaginous appeal of a slice of fried ham.

V

Cicely and Jean Stradling were her chief fellow conspirators in this enterprise of robbing the orchard of experience of its choicest fruit. Both pretty, companionable girls about her own age, daughters of a wealthy Justice of the Peace, incorrigibly high-spirited, quick and clever, they brought her the satisfying friction of social contact, the narcotic of adulation. She revelled in their society, adored, schwärmed, and smothered them with embraces, but, as there was nothing she could give them, they touched her less profoundly than she imagined. It was with them, however, that she formed the great conspiracy. It came about through an occurrence at their house which had happened when she was seventeen.

She had been in a sullen mood one day, unreasonable and quarrelsome. It was July, and the air was humid and enervating. She had quarrelled with Mrs. Tollboy and been very rude to Miss Ridde, and, to cap all, she felt that the Stradling girls didn't love her. They had some sort of party on, and they hadn't asked her, although their gardens adjoined. She took a book, and went and lay under the mulberry tree. But even Dumas bored her on this sultry afternoon. She wandered further afield. On the other side of the hedge was a green slope fringed by a clump of larch trees. Thither she drifted, and stretched herself luxuriously under their shade. A little later there was a sound of laughter. Cicely and Jean and the boy, Billy Hamaton, came out into the Stradlings' garden. Their high-spirited fooling annoyed her more than ever, and she was about to vanish further amongst the trees when she heard one of them say:

"Hullo! there's Barbara!"

She could not pretend she was not there when they called to her. Cicely and Jean were perfectly friendly. It was probably only by chance that they had not asked her in. Jean cried out: "Oh, do come in, Barbara. We're having a rag." She did not want to go. She was not in the mood, and she was feeling slightly aggrieved. Nevertheless she answered politely enough, and in a few minutes time found herself wandering on the Stradlings' lawn. One or two elderly people came out through the French windows and talked together in groups. No one was particularly interested in Barbara. She sat on a deck chair on the edge of the lawn. The boy wanted to talk to her, but Cicely and Jean were in one of their giggling moods, and they dragged him to the croquet-lawn, where a game of clock golf was in progress. And then as she sat there in idle dejection, there occurred to her one of those little experiences which sometimes affect one's whole life. Through the open doors came the sound of a song. A French girl was singing "La Pauvre Innocente." As she listened to the notes of this delightful song, something stirred within her. Her whole nature responded to the melodic appeal. Deep, inexplicable yearnings found their partial solution. She felt intensely happy... elated. She dimly realised that during all these years one side of her nature had been starved. And it was her father who was responsible. He had lavished upon her every luxury and comfort except the one thing she needed most profoundly. She began to wonder what was the secret of this deprivation. Why? Why this terrible embargo? She was not conscious of her loss till that moment, for the reason that she had never before heard music of good enough quality to be moved by it. But on that afternoon she became abruptly aware that it was a necessity of existence. When the song was finished her eyes glowed brightly, her breath came in little stabs. She arose and walked away quickly into the woods, her senses tingling with the thrill of her experience.

When the party was over she went back and visited Cicely and Jean. She had forgiven them for their haphazard invitation. She was affectionate and discursive; she told them the exact truth of her experience. In her father's house there was no piano at all, no musical instrument of any kind; music was forbidden.

"I will never rest," she concluded, "till I can sing like that girl or better."

Cicely and Jean were appropriately sympathetic. Jean was having music lessons herself from a Miss Trent, who came to her once a week. Why should Barbara not come across and have a lesson at the same time? She could use their piano whenever she liked. But surely, if her father were approached properly, he would only be too delighted such a kind, generous, easy-going man. Well, Barbara would make one attempt, but she had an ominous presentiment of the result.

And she was right. He listened puffily to her appeal, moved into the shadow of the window recess, unnerved her with the implication of a long, critical silence, then boomed in the impersonal voice of an oracle echoing through the hollow gloom of a forgotten temple:

"No; I don't wish you to learn music. Why not paint flowers?"

There was something thin, almost callous, in this latter phrase. Paint flowers! Like the oracle, too, it carried with it the weight of ambiguity. What did he mean? Why should she paint flowers? What kind of spiritual substitute was this? It was like offering a nosegay to a tiger, and the man was dismally aware of it. It was the idle, evasive remark of a prisoner fencing for time.

Barbara would not paint flowers; she would learn to sing.

VI

That was four years ago. During those four years she had worked secretly at the piano, and at singing. She was no musical genius, but she had a clear, light soprano voice, a good sense of rhythm, an adequate technique for simple, melodious ballads. She could now sing "La Pauvre Innocente" as well as the girl who inspired her to do it. It had been a great struggle to conceal her little accomplishment from her father. It was such a temptation to sing about the house, such a necessity to sing in the bath-room. But on those occasions, when some phrase escaped her, she had always repented it. He would speak sharply and angrily to her, and to this she was not accustomed. Once he had surprised her in the garden, and exclaimed:

"What is that song? Where did you learn it?"

She had replied perfunctorily:

"Oh, I don't know. I heard someone singing it."

She was frightened by him, frightened by his silences and the heavy weight of years which lay between them. And something in her had hardened a little. The deception over the singing bred other little deceptions. As she developed, some inner voice kept repeating: "A girl has got to look after herself. I'm not going to be browbeaten."

As she could not cope with him directly she employed other methods. She went to concerts and theatres, and made up lies to account for her absence. She learned to flirt. It was Billy Hamaton who first initiated her into this intriguing form of pastime; and she enjoyed it enormously, until she found, one day, that Billy Hamaton was no longer flirting. The boy was in dead earnest. It was very disconcerting, and dangerous, and well, what does a girl do in a case like that? It was a great pity; it would spoil everything; and yet there was a grim joy in adventure behind her father's back.

Once she had been very ill: a fever which lasted several weeks. Her father had been alarmed. She knew this by his restless movements and furtive visits. Old Dr. James, the local practitioner, had been in daily attendance. One day he brought another doctor, older than himself, a great specialist from London. She had overheard them whispering together when she was supposed to be sleeping. One had said:

"By Jove! yes, she's the spit and image of Kitty."

"Did you know her?" asked the other.

"Well enough. I don't envy the child her heritage."

They had moved away, whispering interestedly.

Oh, so that was it! Her mother's name was Kitty, and she had left an unhappy heritage. Barbara stored the memory of this incident in her mind. Poor mother! Where was she? What had she done?

Throughout the house there was no portrait of her, no memento, nothing to indicate that a woman had ever been its mistress. She had been told that her mother died when she herself was a baby, but nothing else had been said at all about her.

Sometimes the house appeared a playground of distressing memories almost insupportable. Well, there it was! Her secret music absorbed her, and she was not the kind to indulge in maudlin retrospection. The past was dead: young people were calling to her in the sunlit garden. The beautiful secretary was stuffing papers into an attache case, her father was mumbling:

"Well, my dear, look after yourself!" The great car purred at the door with a noise like the stomach-rumbles of an animal at feeding time. Mrs. Tollboy was very much in evidence. The last instructions were given. The car devoured its victims, and with a satisfied toot as it rounded the drive glided away in the silence of repletion. Phew! what a relief! A week of freedom, and fun, and... music.

VII

Billy Hamaton and the Stradling girls were already there, pink-coloured and bright-eyed, playing an improvised game with a stick and a straw basket on the upper lawn.

"You must come and see the pony," she yelled.

Tarbrush was certainly an engaging little beast, with a shiny mane, a long black tail, and a great sense of humour. He gave the impression that he was used to children and young people and their ways, and he preferred them genteel and well-dressed. For the stable-boy he showed a profound contempt, but he allowed Barbara to ride him bareback up and down the yard. He appeared to say:

"This is quite all right. This is my mistress. She has bought and paid for me, and I was very, very expensive. My pedigree would make you sit up."

He allowed himself to be hugged, and called a darling; he condescended to eat handfuls of crisp white sugar.

They then went down to the little stream on the other side of the coppice, and Billy performed impressive feats of leaping by the aid of a pole. He was agile and neatly-made; he excelled at games that did not require great strength or endurance. They lunched under the mulberry tree, a joyous meal of pies and fruit and lemonade. The afternoon was devoted to tennis, the only thing they did that day that was conducted with grim earnestness. Then followed tea at the Stradlings', with large iced cakes, endless if not very profound jokes, joyous banalities, and laughter all the time. Oh, it was great fun; the kind of day that brings out the best in one. They were in that humour when everything is outrageously funny the angle of a tea-cosy, the colour of Billy's socks, an inane remark about cook's young man anything and everything. Just when the progression of these pleasantries might have begun to pall, the position was vitalised by an unexpected visitor. At the very sight of him the quartette screamed with laughter. It had been one of the assets of George Champneys' career that people laughed directly he came on the stage. At the same time, you could not exactly tell why. He was a man between forty and fifty, with a droll, fat, cleanshaven face. He was not particularly ugly, certainly not grotesque but he exuded a kind of contagious appreciation of the grotesque. You knew that he knew that you knew how intensely comic some aspect or attitude appeared to him. He had you in his pocket, as it were; and so must it always be with a good comedian. After meeting the outburst of his reception with an appropriate display of facial contortion, he exclaimed dramatically:

"This won't do, old boy, you know. It won't do! It won't do! It won't do!"

Now, why on earth was that funny? Barbara laughed till the tears streamed down her cheeks. He then turned to Cicely and Jean and said quite simply:

"Is the guv 'nor out, my dears?"

"Yes; he's up in town, George."

Barbara whispered to Jean:

"Who is he?"

And Jean whispered back:

"Don't you know? It's George Champneys. He's head of the Frolics awful clever. Sends companies out. You'd love him on the stage."

In the meantime George was calling Billy "old boy," much to the latter's delight. Suddenly he turned to Barbara and said:

"Who is our young friend here?"

"This is Barbara Powerscourt," said Jean.

George took Barbara's hand and held it. Then he searched her face keenly with his protruding grey eyes, and suddenly muttered "Fine!" There was nothing objectionable or over-familiar in the way he did this. Barbara merely felt that she had been approved of by a friendly and critical being, and she blushed accordingly with extreme pleasure. She was excited moreover. She was suddenly in touch with the sentient, moving, forbidden world. An actor! indeed a famous actor, one who made the multitude kneel to him. A real comedian! What would her father think? Cicely was exclaiming:

"Oh, George, do tell us some stories."

And Jean was clasping her hands and saying: "Yes, do, do!"

"No," said George; "I can't tell you any stories, but I'll give you an imitation of the Lub."

"Whatever 's the Lub?"

"Don't you know the Lub? the half-brother to the Chunt? They make a noise like this: 'F'rrh! F'rrh!" You feed them on peaches and straw-hat dye. Wonderful old sportsmen. I had one that died of tennis elbow at the age of ninety-seven. Of course, they are not so intelligent as the stoofs these are surprising beasts. As far as I know, there's only one left, and that belongs to a tramcar conductor in Manchester."

He leaned towards Barbara and said very earnestly:

"Do you know that the Stoof can add up eight columns of figures while thinking out the menu for next Monday week's breakfast?"

George Champneys was merely adapting himself to the atmosphere in which he had happened to drift. Young people were food and wine to him. It was from them he drew the spirit of spontaneous fooling and adapted it to his own ends. But probably those burlesques of his, which were famous throughout the country, would not have been so good had it not been that in the presence of youth he felt not only gaiety, but a deep sense of bitterness a kind of savage hunger.

He fooled to some purpose on that afternoon; was extremely droll, high-spirited, in his heart utterly lonely; and was about to make his departure when Jean said:

"Let's make Barbara sing."

The making of Barbara sing was a protracted and keenly fought struggle, but at length she sat at the piano, and sang "La Pauvre Innocente."

Oh, la pauvre innocente! Champneys lay back in the comfortable Chesterfield, and his grey eyes mellowed. There was something clear-cut and incisive about Barbara, her dark hair silhouetted against a malachite damask curtain. Directly she began to sing she became immersed in her job. She accompanied herself with point and discretion. Her voice was flexible and expressive. By Jove! she had everything except training. George could see exactly what he could make of her. She would make a splendid "Frolic," and she was young, young—ah! so wonderfully young. She also sang "Le miracle de Sainte Berthe" and a little song by Strauss.

He was solemn when he rose to go. He took her hand and smiled.

"If ever you want a job, Barbara, you come to me."

That, of course, was another enormous joke! What a jolly ripping person was George Champneys! He lighted his pipe, gave the girls a friendly pat, and ambled away.

VIII

The day was beginning to draw in. Long deep shadows crept across the lawns. Bees were working overtime among the lupins. A flock of rooks cawed noisily up in the elms. Everything appeared to become accentuated... tense. Oh, how vital and moving was this day of days! Barbara had never been so happy, never so in touch with the big moving spectacle of life. She, she was the pivot of it all. She saw herself the heroine of breathless movements, quickly changing and developing. The world loved her and wanted her. She would triumph and succeed. They loved her, but they didn't know how much she had to give. She was something special; she knew that. Restrictions and limitations which applied to ordinary humanity did not apply to her. Up, and up, and up, the rest worshipping, and she wanting to be so kind. Ah, yes, she would always be that. That perhaps was the greatest joy of all... out of her great powers, to give.

Billy was looking at her dolefully and saying, "I shall have to go."

"Oh, no," she cried, "not yet. It's too lovely. Let's climb the mulberry tree in our garden?"

"It makes your flannels so beastly dirty," said Billy. "Besides, I promised the mater I'd be home at seven."

"Coward!"

"I'm not a coward. Do you dare me?"

"Yes, I do. I'll climb higher than you."

"Oh, Barbara, don't be absurd. You'll tear your frock." This from Jean.

"I've had enough sports to-day," echoed Cicely.

But Barbara was already through the gate dividing the gardens.

"Come on, Billy; I challenge you."

Before he had reached the tree, Barbara was swinging on the first branch. It was a very old tree, and not difficult to climb. Up and up she went, and where she went Billy, of course, had to follow. She was there chasing the elf of adventure, and Billy was there to show that he was not going to be beaten by a girl. Indeed, he knew he was committed further than that, for when Barbara had reached her limit, he must manlike go a bit further. They panted and swung and hugged the thick branches.

"Now," said Barbara, at last. "This is my favourite spot. Look; you can't see the ground. One might be miles and miles up in the sky."

The boy pulled himself up beside her, panting.

"I love it like this, when you float in a pattern of leaves and sky, the sun dancing through. You can imagine there is no earth at all, nothing below you, only this going on till you reach Heaven, the birds bringing you messages now and then from the people you love. It's all so near, so near, Billy."

The sun made patterns on his jolly, freckled face. He put his arm round her.

"I love you, Barbara."

"Do you, Billy!"

For a moment she was sustained in an altitude of surrender. If one must be loved, where more appropriate than the top of a tree? There appeared to be nothing more to desire. He kissed her cheek

"You'll marry me one day, Barbara?"

She did not answer. Why shatter the spectrum of this supreme illusion? How did she know? How could she tell? Let us go on up. Suddenly his lips were pressed against hers, and she exclaimed:

"Oh, no. Don't do that, Billy. You'll spoil everything."

She was sorry for him then. He looked so foolish and self-conscious as he muttered:

"I'm sorry."

They sat side by side in an awkward silence. Then Billy roused himself and said:

"Come on, then, my flibbertigibbet."

He wriggled upwards towards the next branch. He was out to excel himself, to accomplish by a gesture what he had failed to do by declamation. By this means have pioneers established great colonies, captains and kings succeeded or failed.

She watched his lithe body wriggling along a branch, his brown hair all awry, spotted with little leaves and fronds. They were alone up in this enchanted place. She suddenly felt strangely disturbed, as though the forces of her life had reached a climacteric.

"It's no good," she thought. "I believe I want him; I want Billy for my very own."

The branches were shaking above her. She could only see his legs, the rubber shoes pressing against the bark.

"Careful, Billy!"

Why this sudden cold transition to foreboding? Why this fear of the unseen ground beneath? She remembered that the tree was very, very old... hundreds of years, people said.

"Billy! Billy!... not too high! Please!"

Then she shrank against the stem, paralysed with horror. She felt it all almost before it had happened. That sudden snap of a branch like a pistol-shot. the body hurtling through the leaves, which seemed to whistle as it passed through them; the thump upon a branch below, a gasp of pain, a thousand years, filled by a scream from Cicely, and then that awful dull thud upon the soil beneath. How she got down she had no recollection. Cicely and Jean, white to the lips, were leaning over the boy. He was curled up sideways and his face appeared quite green. He clutched the grass convulsively with his left hand, but he uttered no sound.

Cicely kept repeating: "O God, he's hurt!"

Jean seemed unable to move or think. It was Barbara who raced into the house. Where would everybody be? She wanted everybody. Mrs. Tollboy, Miss Ridde, Beaver, her father's man, Mrs. Warner, the cook, Sally, the three house-maids anybody who could run or do anything. An inspiration flashed upon her as she entered the hall. She snatched up the stick and beat the dinner-gong with the fury of despair. Heads and bodies appeared from various part of the house.

"Come! Come quick, all of you. Billy Hamaton's hurt!"

They carried him in and put him upon a bed in a spare room. He was semi-conscious, still groaning, still suffering pain. Beaver rode off on a bicycle to fetch the doctor. The three girls stared disconsolately at each other.

'I dared him to do it," said Barbara, in the toneless accents of dismay.

IX

It was exactly a week later, on the day of her father's return, that they told her the truth about Billy. He had been taken away to a hospital on a stretcher. He was alive. He might live for years; he might even live to old age. But he would never, never be able to walk again; neither walk, nor run, nor play tennis, nor climb trees. His spine was damaged. The case was incurable, and there was even the dark menace of insanity. When she heard this, she stared dry-eyed into the garden which to her had once appeared so beautiful. She had called him a coward.

"Come on, Billy. I challenge you." She wandered out into the country. Her primal instinct was to avoid her fellow-creatures, like an animal stricken with disease. She dreaded her father's return. If she could only escape from it all, persuade herself that it had never happened. She heard him arrive in the early evening, and she went to her room and sent word that she had a headache, and didn't require any dinner. But after a time she heard his heavy footsteps on the stairs, followed by three familiar taps upon her door. He entered without her calling out.

He made a few solicitous enquiries about her assumed illness: an impossible man to deceive. Then he perched himself upon a chair that appeared to be inadequately constructed for such a diversion, and wheezed:

"A bad business this about young Hamaton."

"I don't want to talk to him about it," she kept on thinking; and then quite irrelevantly: "He looks absurd in that small chair."

Her father regarded her with his heavy, dog-like scrutiny.

"Better eat something, my dear. Will keep you going. Mustn't give way."

She answered almost crossly:

"I don't want anything."

After he had gone she cried a little, and then lay quite inert, staring at the wall.

The sun went down. She heard the distant sounds of servants movements, waiting on her father. The distraction kept breaking across her mobile reflections.

Now he is having his fish... now he is having his grouse, done in that (special way he makes so much fuss about... now he, is telling Beaver to warn cook not to overdo the cayenne pepper in the savoury... now he is drinking his one glass of port, smacking his lips and holding the glass up to the light... now he is lighting his cigar.

And all the time Billy is suffering... terrible agonies. If he should go mad!

The night came, with its inchoate imaginings, passages of suspended animation, troubled dreams, swift awakenings, an untiring and relentless progression of self-analysis, whether dreaming or awake. Upon the question of her responsibility for Billy's condition she had no illusions, and it did not help her to know that the world would not agree with her self-imposed sentence. Young people playing together... these things will happen... no one responsible. Who was to know that the branch was rotten? These logical conclusions would not satisfy her; they jarred her sensibilities. She wanted to suffer more directly. If only she could be punished, sent to prison, beaten, treated as they used to treat a witch in olden times! She was a witch. Her witchery had destroyed Billy. Almost his last words were:

"I love you, Barbara."

Up and up he had gone, pandering to her witchcraft. And then

In that pattern of sunlight and leaves she had decided that she loved him, that he was necessary to her. The confession had been trembling upon her lips. She was not committed; at the time she was even a little uncertain. But now the stark reality of the position came home to her. If she were pledged in her heart to Billy at that moment, she was even more pledged to him now. She would have to marry him and nurse him to the end of his days. This was the least she could do, the humblest atonement. The realisation shocked and thrilled her. She was frightened. Marriage in its happiest aspects had terrifying features, but a marriage haunted by the spectres of suffering and remorse was an almost unendurable thing to contemplate. Her mind became active with a visualisation of all the restrictions and inhibitions, the setting up of different standards, the cleavage from the old order of carefree enjoyment. Her spirit would be freed and quickened by the grim consciousness of sacrifice. She would lose everything; at the same time she would gain something which the world could not take from her. But, dear God! would that it had not happened!... She lay there, trembling, in the darkness.... Did she really love Billy so much as all that?

She heard her father go to his room; the usual sounds of the large house closing down for the night. How solemn and distant it all seemed. She felt that she would never be part of it again. After a time she sighed and passed into a gentle sleep. Strange, very, very strange, but her dreams were not about Billy at all. It was very curious... everyone was so kind. And there were thousands of them, thousands and thousands, and they were stretching out their hands and smiling at her; and there were flowers and bouquets, and George Champneys was leaning back in an easy-chair and looking so kind and friendly; and he was saying:

"That's right, my dear; sing "La Pauvre Innocente."

She sang it, but at the second verse she broke down and cried. Oh, dear! why was she crying? The crying awakened her to the utter stillness of the house.

"It's the least I can do," she flung into the darkness.

And suddenly her heart was filled with a great pity, not only for Billy, but for herself, her father, the whole world.... She ached for human contact. It's all so empty without each other. She thought of her father, lying there alone in the darkness. What anguish and sorrow might he not have endured in his life, so remote from hers. Perhaps at that instant he was lying there, wide-eyed and unhappy, yearning for her mother.... The stillness of the house seemed suffocating. With a sob she arose, slipped on a dressing-gown, and crept out into the passage. Very gently she turned the handle of her father's door, and whispered:

"Daddy."

The dull reverberation of stentorian breathing greeted her. She called a little louder:

"Daddy! Daddy!"

The noise only increased in violence, accented by the explosive crises of nauseating snores. She shut the door quickly and withdrew, her heart filled with bitterness.

"One gets old, and forgets," she thought. The reflection angered her; at the same time she felt that old hardening process working in her spirit. "A girl has got to look after herself." How was it that this phrase sometimes came to her like an admonition from some far-off friend! She hated her father. "He's nothing to me; nothing, nothing. I'm hungry," she thought savagely. It was not that she could not have eaten dinner; it was only that she could not watch her father eat. She went quietly down into the larder. She cut herself a thick slice of ham and bread. She sat on the kitchen table, eating it and swinging her legs.

Then she drank a glass of water, and went back to bed.

She felt better now, more contained, more mistress of herself... and very, very sleepy.

"I don't know what I'm going to do," she thought drowsily. "But I'm not going to make a fool of myself.... Tomorrow I'm going to learn that new song by Roger Quilter. I wonder whether Mr. Champneys would like it."

When the dawn came, and the starling fluttered against the window, her heart responded gratefully as it did on that morning a week ago, and her slumbering senses quivered with the prescience of delightful coming things.

XI

The weeks that followed marked a period of suspense. Her critical faculties were sharpened. The revulsion against her father became accentuated in the glow of a rebellious judgment. She began to watch him closely, his goings and comings, his remoteness, the complete concentration of his; centralised outlook. She no longer accepted him as a passionless fate; he was a creature to be dissected and analysed, like other creatures. Her thoughts darted round him like fireflies trying to illumine some mysterious object in the, dark. Their light was not powerful, and she observed more by the glimmer of her intuitions than by the direct light of her observations, above all things she became acutely aware of his inordinate capacity for cruelty. It must be so. Not the ordered cruelty of human passion, but the cruelty which emanates from a complete inability to acknowledge any point of view other than one's own, a kind of perverted egoism. So secure was he in the sanctity of his tradition, in the power of his mental equipment, that he would regard any infringement of the code he represented in the way that he had regarded the interrupter in the House, as a thing of so little consequence that it could hardly be said to exist. How terribly cruel such a man could be!

Barbara had always been an initial safely deposited within the letter of the code. She took her place, carefully tended and appraised. But if, if she should ever revolt! The reflection naturally acted as a challenge to her militant self-respect. She had already revolted over the matter of the music. She had revolted in many! little way he knew not of. But was this enough? The upheaval of her whole moral and spiritual outlook, caused by the accident to Billy, reacted upon her provocatively. She pranced within a vicious circle of despair. Her training and environment left her unprepared to face a serious disruption indeed, to face trouble of any kind. She was in the mood to lose her head. The instinct of untrained people in a struggle is to strike wildly. She could not by any stretch of the imagination hold her father responsible for Billy's fall. But his aggravating impassiveness appeared to her as the proper target for her blows. It was perhaps a small thing that he snored on the night when Billy was suffering so after all, why should he care about Billy Hamaton? but it was a spark which seemed to her to light many x of the 'dark spaces of his character. Immediately she thought of a thousand other little incidents in her life things which had not impressed her at the time, but which now seemed charged with significance. Her mother?... What had her mother suffered, when, perhaps, she too revolted against the letter of the code?

XII

She had seen Billy, and the sight of him had racked her heart. Not that he was suffering now; he had been gay enough, and had chaffed her for her mournful face. The cruellest thing seemed to her that he did not know. He believed he was soon to be well again, and his naive optimism increased her sense of responsibility a hundredfold. She wanted to tell him, to feel the torture of his condemnation; but she went away with the vision of his eyes filled with love, and longing, and gratitude.

And yet, as the days went by, another little voice kept repeating:

"You don't really love Billy. You never did. You liked him, and you liked him loving you. You were flattered, elated, in a kind of ecstasy like a bird up there in that pattern of sunlight and leaves. It was the singing of that song, the approval you got, the glamour of George Champneys all these things excited you. A glorious day, wasn't it? Oh, you fool!"

She hardly dared listen to this voice, so consumed was she with the passionate desire for sacrifice, and the craving for revolt.

One evening her father arrived home very late to dinner. He had been addressing a political meeting in his own constituency. He was tired, a little flustered, and preoccupied. She heard afterwards that he had been severely heckled by some Labour people. She watched him closely as h$ took his seat at the table. In this duel she meant to have with him she knew that she must seize every advantage of time and position. All the heavy weapons were on her father's side. She had dined earlier in the evening, but she thought it advisable to sit with him, and be patient and amiable. She knew that to question him about the meeting would only anger him. She was allowed no place in his political preoccupations. So she inquired about his health, and talked placidly of local events. His eyes were concentrated on his plate as he rumbled vague acquiescences. The succession of dishes nauseated her. She was waiting for Beaver to retire, and to leave the master alone with his decanter of port. Would the meal never end? She thought:

"How awful it is that one gets old, insensible to all the finer shades of feeling! Is it like that with all old people that they become material and crusted and careless, making horrid little noises when they eat... fiddling with a toothpick between the courses, because there is no one present but myself? How revolting it all is!"

The inevitable savoury came and went. She watched Beaver remove the last traces of crumb and disruption, place the jardiniere of fruit within reach, also the decanter of port, and the small case of liqueur-bottles (which her father never touched).

"Coffee, sir?"

Beaver had asked that question every evening for twelve and a half years ever since he had been in the service and he had always met with a refusal, but he still persisted to ask hopefully and to retire apparently crestfallen and dispirited on receiving a negative reply.

Barbara landed her first blow.

"Daddy, I want to marry Billy Hamaton."

Thomas Powerscourt was holding a glass of port up to the light, and regarding it critically. When his daughter said this his face showed no general disposition to change. He seemed more concerned not to spill the port than anything else. His hand was trembling, and he hesitated; then he brought the glass up to his heavy lips, and took a deep sip.

He spluttered lightly as he set it down, and blinked across the room at the girl. In spite of the perfect control of his features she could detect the swift reflection of disturbed surprise. He spoke very slowly and languidly:

"You can't, my dear. His spine... Sir Alfred tells me he can never recover."

Barbara had got her opening, and she knew that now was the time to strike quickly. Her voice was eager and tearful.

"I know. I know all about that, but I can't help it. I owe it to him. I love him, and he loves me. Can't you see? it was all my fault that he climbed the tree. He didn't want to. I dared him. I called him a coward. It's all through me he's lying there helpless. I can't desert him just because of this because he's ill. It would be too mean. I shall have to go to him, nurse him as long as he lives. I will do it whatever anybody says."

She was on the verge of tears her most powerful weapon. But Thomas Powerscourt had now complete control of himself. He was very gentle, almost sympathetic.

"It's very unfortunate, my dear; very regrettable. You take an exaggerated view of your responsibility. A mere accident young people playing together. Why, he might have challenged you; the position might have been reversed—"

Barbara was lying in wait for that. She exclaimed fiercely:

"If the position had been reversed, do you think Billy wouldn't have married me?"

It seemed to take a long time for this to sink in; then he said judicially:

"I should say most certainly no. He would not have married you. "

Barbara went white with anger. She could hardly gasp:

"Then you don't know him. It shows what a low ideal you have—"

The big man stood up and walked to the fireplace. He too was angry, and this was evident only by the slightly increased clearness of his diction, making his voice sound utterly toneless:

"There is perhaps one aspect of the case you do not understand."

What was coming? Why didn't he rage at her?

"You probably have not considered, Barbara, or you do not know if you married young Hamaton, your married life would perforce have to be childless—"

"Well, that can't be helped. Many women are childless."

"M'm, m'm." He purred at her, nodding his head like an imitation Chinese god. For a moment he appeared about to overwhelm her with some cyclonic outburst; then he paused, as though regarding the delicate ground between them.

"I am thinking of your good," he said deliberately. "I want you to be happy and to have children." Quite as an after-thought he added: "I have no son."

Barbara rose at him.

"Ah, I see! You have no son, so I am to bear a son for you. He won't carry your name, but the stock will survive, I suppose. You're thinking of me and my good, and my happiness! Well, I'm capable of thinking of my own happiness, thank you.

I'm not always going to do just what you tell me. You wouldn't let me have music, which I crave for; you wouldn't let me go to theatres or concerts, the one kind of thing which appeals to me more than anything else. You give no reason, no excuse. Well, I tell you straight out, I'm going to marry whom I like."

The surprise upon his face was of peculiar quality. He appeared not greatly moved, not, indeed, greatly surprised at what she said so much as surprised by some inner recollection. It was the face of a man passing through an experience which he is vaguely conscious of having passed through before. And the realisation causes him to doubt his own identity. Barbara and her little affair with Billy seemed far away. He sighed, took out a handkerchief and mopped his brow. Then in his normal voice he mumbled:

"We are on the eve of a great political crisis.... I am very tired, my dear. Let us discuss this some other time."

XIII

Barbara was beaten. As the days passed her forces became diffused; time was against her. Her weakest point was that she did not love Billy enough. If she were really fighting for her own happiness, she knew quite well that to marry him was not the way to attain it. The day would come when she would bitterly rue it. It angered her to know that her father was right. It doesn't do to give way to a sentimental whim. The shock had unnerved her. Poor Billy! she could give him her pity, even her love, but it would be foolish to marry him. She had loved what he represented, the life they had passed together. She associated him with sunny days and gay, irresponsible fun. Together they had built a little edifice of happy days, buttressed with understanding, familiar jokes and sympathetic appreciation of each other's genius for life. The accident had shattered it, and it would become necessary to reconstruct. But she could not build upon the site of the other. Games and follies would be haunted by the ghost of Billy. She would have to alter the whole tenor of her life. Her protective instinct told her that salvation lay in work. She must have something to do that would absorb her. Work! But what work? If her father would not let her work at music, what was she to do?

Her aunts Jenny and Laura shared a. small flat at Ashley Gardens, Westminster. It contained two spare bedrooms, one of which was always reserved for the important brother. He sometimes occupied it when the House was sitting late. Barbara had occasionally paid brief visits there, but she did not like it. The rooms seemed cramped, the air was cramped; above all things, the lives of her aunts were cramped. They were timid old ladies, very patriotic and religious, and their lives seemed one long plaint about what things were coming to. They were like two autumn leaves blown along in a gale. In a shiftless and unstable world nothing seemed secure except their brother Thomas Powerscourt. Without the solid weight of his intellect and character England would perish; even the other members of the Cabinet he adorned filled them with suspicion. It was not an atmosphere, therefore, which Barbara felt would be likely to spell freedom from her father's silent tyranny; nevertheless it was the only place she could think of as a temporary refuge. It had the advantage of being in a centre of vivid distractions, and a visit there would not be likely to arouse suspicions. She wrote to her Aunt Jenny, and received a pressing invitation by return of post. Her father fully approved, and took her up to town himself.

"I'm very busy, Jenny," he panted, as he deposited his daughter in the hall. "The political situation is serious, very serious indeed. I may have to take advantage of your hospitality quite a bit just now. This Shipping Bill... Eaynes is trying to fog the issue. Take care of Barbara. She's been she's had a bit of an upset. I shall probably be in to-night."

Oh, yes, a capable diplomatist. What a lot he could crowd into a few commonplace sentences. Hinting at the aunts hospitality, when he was paying all the time. The absorption in the political situation giving him excuse to be ever on the watch. The remark about the "upset" playing upon the sympathies of all concerned, whilst probably on the stairs on the way down he would chuckle inwardly over his victory in the affair of "that young Hamaton."

The abrupt cleavage from her normal associations bewildered and stimulated her. She felt like an explorer in a dangerous and untrodden land. The more she suffered from the loss of Cicely and Jean and their environment, the more alert did she become to the flavour of her own independence. There was a fierce joy in missing things and being ever on the watch. The pursuit of what she manfully called work was fraught with difficulties. The mild activities of her aunts, mostly connected with Church charities, did not appeal to her. Reviewing the occupations of her fellow-civilians, she quickly realised her own amazing ignorance and lack of training. There was nothing, absolutely nothing she could do to satisfy her instinct of service. To be a nurse required years of training; clerical or office work demanded a type of mind she had not got; the way of the Arts was long and steep; science was an unopened book. It seemed strange to think that if she had had to earn her living she would surely have starved. The reflection caused her to nurture a further dull resentment against her father, but, strangely enough, it did not depress her. It is something to know that one is ignorant. Besides, there was something she could do. She kept circling round the subject, pretending to herself that she was looking for something else, but in her inmost heart knowing all the time she meant to do it. One morning she told her aunts that she was going to South Kensington Museum. She dressed herself with care and taste, and started forth. She did indeed go to Kensington, but not to the Museum. She turned off into a quiet square near Addison Road. She rang the bell of a corner house; a maid opened the door, and Barbara said:

"Mr. George Champneys?"

"Yes, miss."

She found the comedian in a large studio at the back. He took her hand, and for a moment she could tell that, although her face appeared familiar, he could not remember who she was. She smiled at his indecision. Then suddenly he gave her hand a little jerk and exclaimed:

"Ah! La Pauvre Innocente!"

They indulged in no further formalities. Barbara felt curiously at home with this man. He was entirely different from the kind of people who constituted "the set" down at High Barrow. She felt she belonged to his world. He said:

"Well, old girl, what can I do for you?"

Barbara leant across the back of a grand piano and poured out her soul.

"It's like this, Mr. Champneys. I want you to tell me how I can get training. You were awfully sweet to me when I sang, but I know quite well I really know nothing about the job. The point is, I've got to do it secret. Daddy objects to my singing at all, let alone anything else, like dancing or acting. But it's no good; I know it's the thing I've got to do. I'm an awful fool, really. I know nothing; but I have got a bit of a voice, and I feel I could do well, the kind of thing you go in for. I'm living with two aunts at Westminster, and they mustn't know either. But I could always visit anyone in the daytime and possibly in the evening. I'm a splendid liar. I'm crazy to begin. Please, dear Mr. Champneys, you must help me."

"Well, well, well, well!"

George Champneys regarded her thoughtfully, then threw back his head and laughed

"A splendid liar, eh? Oh, la pauvre innocent'e! I don't want to get into trouble with your father, though. He'd get an Act of Parliament passed and have me executed in some special, protracted way. Oh, dear! this is awful!"

"Don't let him worry you. I can manage him easily. I can pay fees, too. I've got nearly a hundred and fifty pounds in my own name."

It appeared to George to be the funniest joke he had ever heard. He could not control his laughter. Dear me, what a child! But eventually, of course, he agreed.

His friend, Birtles, the; composer, was; a very good teacher of singing. Madame Katie Shaw could teach her all there was to know about dancing. As a matter of fact, his own studio was nearly always in use for rehearsals and experiments. She could go there whenever she liked. He would help her in any way he could even at the risk of his life.

XV

Then followed the happiest period of Barbara's life. It is, perhaps, a regrettable fact that she thought very little about Billy, lying in a nursing home in the country. Her brief, endearing notes occurred at longer intervals. She never wrote to Cicely or Jean at all. She became absorbed, elated, tremendously excited about herself. She met other girls at George's studio, brilliantly clever, fascinating girls. And Barbara copied their mode of dress, their mannerisms, their point of view. Oh, this was a life indeed! She felt free, strong in her natural powers. As she said, she was a splendid liar. It was necessary to make up a rather elaborate lie, not only to cover her absences, but to account for her long stay in London. The story she made up was that she was studying old lace. Fortunately, she had always been interested in lace, and she knew a little about it, and there was a magnificent collection in South Kensington Museum. But the idea was prompted by the discovery on a bookstall in the Brompton Road of a sketch-book containing pencil sketches of lace obviously a student's work. Barbara bought the book and smuggled it home. She tore out the pages and cleaned them up. Every few days she would produce one of these sheets and show it to her aunts, explaining how she had drawn it herself that afternoon. It was circumstantial evidence of a most convincing kind. Her aunts were greatly impressed by dear Barbara's industry and skill. Besides, it was such ladylike work, and so interesting and refined. Thomas Powerscourt was also impressed, but the political situation was such that he could not devote much attention to his daughter.

XVI

In the early winter this question of a political situation began to force itself on Barbara's mind. For one thing, contact with her professional friends had broadened her outlook; she even took a mild interest in politics itself. The government were having trouble with a Shipping Bill. It was an unpopular Bill, but one which would strengthen their hands in dealing with dockyard labour. Important questions of principle were at stake. Thomas Powerscourt had been the framer of that Bill, and he was considered its protagonist. The trouble centered round a certain Clause 37.

On the surface the minister appeared as imperturbable as ever, but Barbara knew that he was very worried. He slept badly and his digestion was all wrong. She could tell this by his eyes. Sometimes they motored down to High Barrow for the weekend, but Barbara always returned with him on the Monday. His remoteness seemed more pronounced that ever. He took little interest in her actions or appearance. He was strangely absent-minded and vague, and inclined to be querulous. Her subterfuge about the lace studies seemed almost superfluous. He asked no questions, and was completely indifferent whether she stayed in the country or came to town. This attitude naturally added fuel to the fires of her resentment. They were as the poles apart. She was beginning to fear him no longer. In a perverse mood she thought: "One of these days I'll give him the surprise of his life."

A malicious joy crept through her veins. Flattery went to her head like wine. She had heard George Champneys praising her to a colleague. Madame Katie Shaw had declared her a natural dancer, one of the best pupils she had had for years.

Meantime, the governing body perspired with the weight of its unfortunate Shipping Bill. A crisis occurred one afternoon in the aunts "flat. Her father had come in to lunch. He tore at his food savagely swallowing great quantities of mayonnaise and game-pie. He looked like an old bear that had been worried by dogs. He was sullen and morose. The attitude of the aunts annoyed her more than anything. They spoke in hushed whispers, they hung upon his slightest) word, they soothed and coaxed and petted him. The position became unendurable. Barbara had been following the idea of the Bill as well as she could, and she felt convinced that her father's principles were wrong. Her sympathies were naturally with the dock-people and she felt their case was being side-tracked. Without any preliminary warning she suddenly launched a criticism of his pet Clause 37. What she said was neither clever nor penetrating but it clearly showed that she knew something about it.

It was an awful moment. Her Aunt Laura exclaimed:

"Really Barbara dear!"

She had expected that her father would regard her with his usual sleepy indifference and not deign to reply but to her surprise his eyes glowed with malevolence. He spluttered over his food, and suddenly barked at her:

"Leave the room!"

The tactics were unfortunate on both sides. A few months ago she would have slunk away, gone to her bedroom and wept. But on this occasion she did certainly leave the room—she had finished her lunch. She stood up, folded, her napkin, walked quietly out. She crossed the passage and entered the drawing-room opposite. There, there was an old upright piano. She sat down and opened the lid. She ran her fingers lightly over the keys, and then began to sing "La Dame Mariee a un Puant."

She had completed two verses quite successfully when she heard the door open and the heavy stamp of her father's feet. His hand came down heavily on her right fore-arm. He pulled her from the stool.

"What is this? How is it you sing and play against my instructions?"

Barbara broke away from him, and exclaimed defiantly:

"Why won't you let me sing and play? What is your reason?"

"You've done it; you've been working at it behind my back!"

"Why shouldn't I?"

The aunts were already in the room, hovering agitatedly like birds whose nest has been disturbed. Suddenly he put his hand up to his head and complained of dizziness. They led him to the bedroom and he lay down. The telephone rang. The Prime Minister's secretary was wanting to know if he could be at a committee-room at four o'clock.

"Yes, yes!" he shouted from the bedroom.

But he never got to the House at four o'clock. He fell into a kind of coma, and complained of pains around the heart. A grey-bearded doctor arrived shook his head prescribed physic, and a complete rest.

"He's very ill," he said sternly to Barbara, as though aware of her responsibility in the matter.

XVII

In the days that followed the flat became a hive of fevered activities. Various important personages called. Telegrams and despatches accumulated in the hall. The telephone was never silent. It became evident that the Ship of State or perhaps it was only the crew was heading towards its or their doom. Barbara could not help being impressed by these outward manifestations of her father's importance, neither could she quite understand her own indifference to his welfare. When her Aunt Jenny had said:

"Your behaviour, Barbara, has made your father very ill."

She had replied: "Perhaps it was the game-pie. "Later in the day Aunt Laura had said: "Of course, Barbara, we cannot expect you to leave while your dear father is so ill. You will remain to help to nurse him. But Jenny and I both feel that when he is well again it would be better for you to return to the country. We were both exceedingly surprised that you should have used our flat in this way taking secret lessons in singing and playing, against your father's expressed wishes."

To this she had replied:

"All right, Aunt. We'll talk about it later on." She began to take an avid interest in the newspapers. Far from subsiding, the excitement over the political situation was becoming more intense. As is so often the case, there was more behind the Government Bill than appeared on the surface. It also became evident that some of the members and newspapers those in opposition to her father's party were hinting that Thomas Powerscourt's illness was assumed. They did not believe in it, or him. He was afraid to face the criticism of his precious Clause 37. The fight went on for days. Mr. Bream, the Under-Secretary of State, was howled down. Unpleasant things were hurled across the floor of the House. On the third day, when Mr. Bream was trying to speak, a small body of members kept up a kind of chant: "Sit down, Bream. We want Powerscourt."

XVIII.

In order to give him as much air as possible, some of the furniture had been moved out of his bedroom. Among other things a small chest and a few boxes were placed in Barbara's room. On that night when Mr. Bream had been howled down for the second time, the Prime Minister had called late and had an interview with her father. The excitement in the little flat had been intense. The aunts were dreading that their incomparable brother would be persuaded to get up and go down to the House, whatever condition he was in. Specialists had been called in to endorse the verdict of the other doctors. Barbara could not sleep. She never slept very well in Westminster. The night seemed weighted with congested lives. It's all struggle, and struggle, and struggle... even in their sleep the struggle goes on. The struggle for air, food, wealth, love, power. How insignificant we are! Whether we gain or lose in the struggle, we pass away. Others come, fight for the same things. Do things just exist to be fought for? A hundred years ago different people were sleeping in these same dark houses and struggling for these identical things. How queer that was! The things remain to be struggled for, but the people pass on. She peered out of the window and saw the cupola of Westminster Cathedral looking as old and mysterious in the darkness as the religion which gave it birth. And yet the Cathedral was almost new. So some things pass away, too buildings, and power, and wealth. What was she thinking of? What is it that remains? The idea? The spirit? But even before the idea of the Cathedral there were other ideas. Christianity was not so very old. There had been hundreds of religions before Christianity, hundreds of civilisations before this, hundreds of dead worlds swinging in the sky. Nothing remained then: neither air, nor food, nor wealth, nor love, nor power.... She shivered and turned on the light.

"I want something frightfully, and I don't know what it is," she thought.

She took up a book and began to read, but her eyes were tired. She examined the old chest of her father's. It was stuffed with papers and letters and odds and ends. "I've no right to probe into his papers," she said to herself, but she continued to do so. At the very bottom of the chest she came across an old play-bill. It was very crinkled and torn. It was dated October 24th, but there was no year mentioned. It looked very, very old, so she gazed idly at the announcement. It appeared to be of some sort of vaudeville entertainment at the Royal Theatre, Croydon. There was a sketch called "Mr. Ingles Takes the Town." A famous clown was starred the Great Hannifan. Then she came across an announcement which caused her heart to flutter. "Miss Kitty O'Bane, the comedy star from London, in song and dance."

Kitty O'Bane! A strange thrill went through her being. It was almost as though the old play-bill were an answer to her doubts... nothing remains, then? She found herself sobbing as she turned it over reverentially. Something remains. mother, dear!

She searched the chest again more eagerly. In a corner where the play-bill had lain was a packet of letters. The ink had faded and the writing was not very legible. It was what they would call an uneducated person's writing.

"O God! I have no right to read these letters."

Her heart was beating rapidly. She felt she must read just a few words, a sentence or two. It would mean so much to her. It was the thing she had been wanting so much. She peeped into the envelopes without taking the letters out. Endearing terms and disjointed sentences jumbled before her tear besmirched vision. "Your loving Kitty." "My beloved Tom, don't be unkind to me of course I am bound to do as you wish. You led me to think it would be otherwise...." "Oh, how lovely it was last night. It seemed cruel you had to go."

"Tommy dear, what are we going to do?"

"We travelled all night by coach to Edinburgh. I looked up at the stars and thought of you. Your little Kitten was very lonely. O, send me! some message."

No, no; she couldn't go on. It wasn't fair. Whatever he had done, whatever had happened between those two, the letters were sacred to them. Even she the child of that union had no right to intrude.

She put them back and turned out the light. One fact impressed itself upon her disordered mentality. Her father had kept the letters. Whether he was right or wrong, whether he had behaved badly or well, he had kept her mother's letters all these years.

XIX

To Barbara the day that followed was a phantasmagoria, as, indeed, it was to many other people in England. It was November, overcast and cold; a turgid wind moved the fog and heavy moisture up and down the streets as a policeman will move an ugly tramp. In after years she tried to piece together the emotions and experiences of that day, but in vain. She could never be certain as to what she had observed and what she had imagined; as to what part in the story she had taken herself and what part she had pieced together from the records of others. She observed the events of that day, a goddess suspending judgment; strangely alert to the approach of impending tragedy she felt no great desire to avert. What must be, must be. She shrugged her shoulders and prepared to defend her own interests.

The morning papers reflected the cumulative effect of political pressure. The public was in an ugly mood. "The issues involved were too obscure to be closely followed by the layman, but he was angry with the law's delay, the insolence of office." What he wanted was a man, someone to point the way and lead him. In such a mood vast bodies of people will swing from one side to the other, like swallows manoeuvring in the sky. In politics it is the leader's business to anticipate. He pretends to create, but in effect he only interprets.

Observing this larger drama through the reflection of her own, Barbara thought:

"Is he thinking of the people or of himself? Is he a vast abstraction existing for the public good? Or is he a man with follies and tenderness? Why does he live at all? Why don't I know him?"

She sat at her window looking into the dim streets.

The hungry clamour of public importunity began.

"If it were not so very urgent, so very, very important "A tall, fair young secretary in the hall, the younger son of a duke, bowing and apologising. Mr. Bream again: "Just one word." Another specialist. O, God! that telephone! The morning was hustled away. At one o'clock the doctor returned, accompanied by a man with electric batteries.

"I know what that means. He's going down to the House. It will kill him."

The aunts were scared, but slightly flushed with the importance of the occasion. Barbara went out for a walk. "No 'old lace' to-day for me," she thought ironically. She pushed her way through the drifting fog. People's faces looked pink, rather jolly. people, people, how lovely you are! The walk invigorated her. In the years to come she would meet all sorts of people. What people? Who would come out of the fog to be her friend? How queer it seemed to think that at that moment, walking about the world, were people who would be very important to her... perhaps a lover. Perhaps at that identical moment he was walking down the next street, quite unconscious of the happiness she meant to bring him. joy! She sang quietly to herself as she passed the railings of Green Park.

XX

It was half-past three when she got back to the flat. A carriage was drawn up outside. Two men in bowler hats were idling about. Just as she was approaching they pulled themselves up and looked up the steps towards the entrance. Barbara followed their gaze and her eyes beheld a strange sight. At the top of the steps, and just about to descend, stood her father. He was all swathed up in ulsters, and shawls, and on his head was perched an ancient top-hat. He looked enormous. On either side of him, and supporting him, were two other men, one of whom she recognised as Sir John Diehl, Secretary for Home Affairs. The cortege slowly descended, step by step. When they had reached the last step but one Barbara advanced and said timidly: "Do you think you ought to go, Daddy?" The utter banality indeed futility of her appeal struck her before the words were out of her mouth. It was like the mouse saying to the mountain:

"Do you think you ought to be here?" She felt utterly insignificant. He did not look at her. She could read the restless concentration in his eyes. Surrounded by his supporters, he seemed to exude an aura of abstract energy. It was as though she were trying to set the puny influence of her personal claims against that of vast blocks of interests. None of the politicians took the slightest notice of her. They were feverishly piloting the vehicle of their herd instincts to the place where it would operate most advantageously. Nothing else counted. One of the horses stamped impatiently. The men in the bowler hats were opening and shutting doors. She leant against the railing. The carriage vanished into the fog.

She stared after it for some minutes and said quite loudly:

'Oh, all right!"

The inanity of this remark startled her to the truth of her position. She went upstairs and talked quite rationally to the aunts about domestic arrangements. The afternoon dragged on. They had tea, and she listened to Aunt Jenny tell a long story about a series of illnesses that had occurred to a family that Barbara had never heard of. Lights flickered green in the streets below. It was just after six o'clock that Aunty Laura came into the room and said:

"Oh, those awful newsboys! They're calling out something at the back. Murder, I think."

Barbara walked quietly out and opened a window on the staircase.

"Oh, don't do that, my dear," whined Aunt Laura. "You make such a draught."

Barbara did not answer. She shut the window and came back into the room. Then she walked to the other window and looked down into the street. Suddenly she said in a perfectly rigid voice:

"Do you know what they are calling out!"

"What, my dear?"

"Daddy's dead. He dropped down dead in the House."

It was possibly a morbid craving which prompted her in after-years to reconstruct that scene in the House again and again. The enveloping grip which her father had upon her the whole of her life carried her with him into those last fateful periods. And yet, vivid as the scene appeared, the moral repercussion impressed her more, the curious shifting of values. Dignified and venerable strangers pressed her hand in profound sympathy. The world was suddenly very kind. All the venom disappeared from the newspapers. The old Shipping Bill appeared no longer a matter of controversy. Whereas before it had been the nerve-centre of conflicting passions, it now appeared an obsolete pound of parchment. A very famous Minister stood up in the House and solemnly declared:

"We may truly say of Thomas Powerscourt that he gave his life for his country."

Possibly. It certainly killed him, going down to the House that day; but little sardonic thoughts played around the fringe of her meditations. If he hadn't been so fond of game-pie, for instance, he might still be alive. If she hadn't sung "La Dome Mariee a un Puant" but why shouldn't she sing? What was this tyranny he dared to hold above her? What do these people know of the character of their gods? They are always seeking the same thing a drama, a story. They must see life in terms of heroism and action; it must be an epic of triumph or failure.

The closing episode was dramatic enough as far as that went. The House seething with excitement, the imposing factions conscious of impending crisis, but never deserted by the outward flourish of ragging schoolboyishness, uncomplimentary epithets being flung across the floor, messengers coming and going, party Whips feverishly rallying their flocks, the Government idols being knocked over like ninepins; and suddenly Cheyne-Garstin upon his feet.

Everyone knew Cheyne-Garstin, that formidable Celtic-looking Yorkshireman. He was the bitterest opponent of the Government, a brilliant dialectician, a dour fighter. He waved a sheaf of notes, and his followers roared hoarsely. In his rich deep burr he began an ironic survey of the whole Government attitude during the progress of the Bill. Then passion began to creep into his voice, and with power and closely-reasoned logic he concentrated on the pretensions of Clause 37. He carried the House with him; even the Government supporters were looking uncertain and slightly moved. It was the moment when the swallows would swing in their flight. He tore Clause 37 to pieces by moving an amendment which would leave it unrecognisable. He sat down amidst ringing cheers from his side of the House and cries of "'Vide! Vide!"

There was a restless movement of despair around the figure of Mr. Bream. What were the Government going to do! What was the Speaker whispering about? Followed a rowdy interval of nervous suspense, when suddenly from behind the Speaker's chair emerged the vast, muffled form of old Tom Powerscourt, the centre of a small supporting cortege. When the members recognised him a fierce exultant shout went up. All people love a drama, and most people love a fight here were the elements of both. The Government party roared themselves hoarse, and the Opposition were equally as excited. One schoolboy of sixty called out:

"Prop him up and let's shy at him." There was a universal cry of 'Powerscourt! Powerscourt!'"

They say he gave no evidence of any consciousness of the peculiarly dramatic mise-en-scene in which he found himself the principal actor. He stood by the table, stonily regarding the Speaker.

When he spoke his voice was cold, passionless, matter-of-fact. He spoke rather more quickly than he was accustomed to, as though anxious to gain his point within a given time. He simply said:

"The honourable member for West Bordesly has miscalculated the economic effect of his amendment to Clause 37. The figures he quotes with regard to the sliding-scale of subsidies were founded upon the original estimate made by Lord St. Gyste, and not upon those in the White Paper issued by the Board of Trade last March.... "

He stopped and fumbled with documents, adjusted his horn spectacles very slowly, then cleared his throat and went on:

"I shall endeavour to put before you the deliberate social and economic effects of these two concrete propositions. If the honourable member for West Bordesly can persuade me that the effect of his proposition will be more beneficial to the community at large, then I shall be happy to accept the amendment and the Government will accept the consequences."

He paused a long time, and then one of his colleagues whispered to him He bent down and listened intently, and then stared abstractedly at his papers, as though weighing the value of the remark. At last he continued:

"It is only too apparent that a principle which may have everything to recommend it in theory may, when passed through the mills of practice, not only not be an excellent thing, but may even be subversive of the very germ of that principle itself. Figures are facts; the friction of humanity is a fact; and in determining these issues experience must be our lodestar. The Government do not intend to lose their grip "

It was at this point that another elderly schoolboy called out:

"Limpets!"

The affect of this ridiculous interruption was startling. The big man looked at the interrupter pathetically. It was obvious that his concentration had gone. Limpets! He appeared to be turning the word over in his mind and considering it. Limpets! What is a limpet? Was he a limpet? Were the Government really limpets? Was all mankind limpets, creatures blindly clinging to the rock of their desires? He passed his hand over the back of his skull and mumbled:

"I shall endeavor to prove—"

But no; he was not destined to prove anything. Perhaps we none of us ever do. The papers shook in his hand, and he kept on turning them over helplessly. His lips moved without any sound coming. He glanced round the House, a dumb appeal and fear gleaming in his eyes. He probably knew then, but he hunched his shoulders together, as though prepared to make a last effort. He groped for his coloured handkerchief and could not find it. The incident annoyed him exceedingly. He was perspiring, and he wanted to wipe his brow. He did so with his bare hand. Then he; glanced at the mace. The object seemed to fascinate him. was obviously immersed in considering what a mace was, why it was there, what purpose it served. Very interesting thing, a mace... quite historical, almost a limpet.

Quite suddenly, without any explanation, he began to walk out of the House. His step seemed firm, as though he had a definite mission perhaps he was going to get his coloured handkerchief? He had not gone ten paces, however, when he stopped and sank upon his knees. Two members sprang forward to catch him, but he crashed heavily onto his face. They picked him up and carried him out; but he died in the lobby within ten minutes, without regaining consciousness.

XXII

On a dreary December morning Barbara found herself seated in Lawyer Bloor's office in Old Burlington Street. She was fully conscious not only of the perfection of her toilette, but of the effect it was having on the three old gentlemen in the room. When a woman is among enemies, or when she has to grope with alien difficulties, it is an enormous spur to her confidence to know that she is looking her best. While drawers were being unlocked and papers rumpled she took stock of her setting and of the other occupants of the room. It was a little difficult to do this, as the room was nearly dark, and she occupied the swivel-chair facing the light, whilst the three old men were on the other side of the table, with their backs to the light;

indeed, one of them was sitting in the angle of the fireplace. She knew who he was. He was old Sir Anthony Gyves. He had retired from the law, but Mr. Bloor, the principal lawyer for the trustees, explained that Sir Anthony had been kind enough to attend, as his presence was necessary for the business affecting the transference of certain title-deeds. He had been Thomas Powerscourt's lawyer in the old days.

The other man was Mr. Bloor 's head clerk.

"I don't mind you," thought Barbara, observing the old clerk rather feebly spreading out parchments before his chief. "I don't think Mr. Bloor 's bad, but I simply hate that old man in the chimney-corner." She knew that his eyes were fixed upon her greedily, and he seemed to be maliciously enjoying himself. He was very, very old, a little wheezy, and at the slightest excuse he broke into a shrill "He, he, he!" at the same time bending forward and massaging his kneecaps,

Mr. Bloor was studiously polite, but a little jaded and impatient. He seemed to think that the whole thing was an unnecessary waste of time, and if Barbara hadn't looked very pretty, he wouldn't have troubled to attend. He looked up at her once and remarked:

"You were indisposed and unable to attend the reading of your father's will?"

"Yes."

He obviously did not believe her answer, but he said not unkindly:

"Would you like me to read it to you now!"

"It doesn't matter."

The fact that her father had made a will did not impress her greatly. She knew that he was a very wealthy man, and that she was his only child. He would naturally leave most of his money to her. The aunts would probably get some of it, but well, she was not unmindful now of the power of money. She had seen something of the great world. One had to have money, crowds of money, to satisfy one's ambitions. She had sometimes lain awake at night and thought of all the things she meant to do. Freedom and power, running theatres, helping people, wearing lovely frocks, travelling. There would be no one now to check her activities. Oh, glorious freedom! Even at that moment little visions of the days to come were dancing before her eyes. It was the voice of old Sir Anthony which broke across these dreams.

"She doesn't want to hear all that legal stuff, Bloor. He, he he! Bead out to the girl what affects her."

Mr. Bloor cleared his throat. "I think I ought to tell you, Miss Powerscourt, that your father made a new will shortly before his death. Some of the hospitals and the Law Clerks' Orphanage benefit considerably. Um, er, the value of his estate was assessed at 421,000."

What was this all about? Hospitals and Law Clerks' Orphanage? What right had her father to give her money away like that? A cold sense of fear crept around her heart. A new will just before his death? Ah! was that because of that song? She could bear the suspense no longer. She snapped out:

"Well, what did he leave me?"

"He, he, he! That's right, Miss Powerscourt.

Wake these old lawyer-chaps up. Tell the girl what she's come to hear, Bloor, He, he, he!"

"Under the terms of your father's will, Miss Powerscourt, the trustees are empowered to pay you interest on certain specific securities. Where is that list, Mr. Green? Ah, yes; here we are. The interest from these securities will amount approximately to four hundred pounds a year, less certain legal dues. We shall require your signature on several of these papers."

Four hundred a year! And her father left 421,000. What did it mean? Why had he treated her like this? It couldn't be only just because of that song. There was something else, something deeper, more vicious at the back of it all. She felt the tears swelling in her eyes. She couldn't get her voice. Suddenly the old man in the corner lashed the air with another "He, he, he!" The sound steadied her like the whip of conflict. She was alone against these old men. She drew within herself and the lines around her mouth hardened. She stared at Mr. Bloor and said deliberately:

"Can you tell me how this is? "

"Er—I beg your pardon? How what is, Miss—er?"

"How it is that my father, who was such a very rich man, should leave me, his only child, so little? "

Lawyer Bloor sniffed and looked a little uncomfortable. It was his business to interpret and administer the law, not to indulge in emotional speculations. There was always a danger of losing one's dignity, of committing oneself. He was not prepared for such a leading question; neither was he prepared for the incident which followed. Barbara was suddenly upon her feet, her eyes blazing with anger. She shook her fist at the room. Her voice was shrill and menacing.

"If anyone knows, you old men do. Come now, I want to know what it was about my mother?"

Lawyer Bloor looked supplicatingly at Sir Anthony. The clerk lowered his eyes and coughed nervously. Sir Anthony looked at them all, and then hissed an almost inaudible "He, he, he!" up the chimney. Barbara held the floor.

"Why did he never speak to me of Mother? Why did my aunts freeze up when I mentioned her? Why was there no portrait or memento of her in the house? Why did he forbid me to learn music or acting or dancing? Mother was an actress, I know. What was wrong with that? What did she do to him!"

At last Mr. Bloor found the power of reply. He was inwardly ruffled, but the dignity of the law must be upheld.

"If you must know, Miss Powerscourt, your father did not consider that your Mother acted well by him. He treated her with every kindness and consideration, and she did not reward his generosity "

"What's that? Generosity! Isn't a man usually supposed to treat his wife with kindness and consideration? What do you mean by reward? What reward?"

In the dead stillness which followed, Barbara's mind was occupied with desperate imaginings of the past. The figure in the chimney-corner was watching her closely. Mr. Bloor suddenly snapped the table-drawer to; then, leaning forward, he said:

"In order to elucidate what must appear to you certain dubious aspects of the case, I may as well be perfectly candid, Miss Powerscourt. Your father and mother were never married."

She had felt this coming, but the shock was none the less unnerving. Nevertheless she would not be unnerved. She had got to cope with these old men. Her father and mother were never married! In other words, her father had probably refused to marry her mother. He came of the governing class; her mother was only a low-grade actress. Of course he wouldn't marry her. But he had been very kind, very generous. They meant that he had paid her well; given her everything except his good name, and she had treated him badly; she had not "rewarded his generosity." God! it was horrible. She struck the table with her left hand and hissed at him:

"She couldn't have treated him badly if he didn't marry her."

No one replied to this. Man's actions are controlled by codes, some acknowledged, some only silently implied. Barbara was stung by a sullen sense of injustice. "I was part of the price," she thought. "He looked after me, fed and clothed me, tried to make me a lady. Oh, the generous gentleman!"

There crept into her face an expression of ugly hatred, into her voice that hard quality which the world calls "common." She raged at them:

"How could she have wronged him, you damned old men? You make the laws. You look after each other. A girl has to look after herself. My father was a cad!"

There followed a dreary "He, he, he!" from the chimney corner; then the icy percussion of Mr. Bloor's voice:

"We are not here to argue about these things, Miss er Powerscourt. Your father was a great and distinguished man."

"Great and distinguished, eh? Yes, but you can't undo the evil a man does by burying him in Westminister Abbey."

She picked up her muff and tugged savagely at her furs.

"I'm going. You can keep your filthy money. Give it to the legal orphans—"

"Where are you going?"

"I'm going on the road, like my Mother did before me. I know I can get work. Maybe I'll do well and justify my Mother, after the vile way you all treated her."

Lawyer Bloor looked perturbed. Any scene of human passion disgusted him. He tapped with a pencil upon the table. He fidgeted and began to talk, but he could not marshal his phrases into any definite coherence.

"You must understand you wished us to be candid we are naturally distressed that you these er unpleasant revelations. You are, of course, entitled to act as you like in the matter. Our business is merely to administer the law. I would advise you you are overwrought—"

Barbara had reached the door, and her hand was on the handle. In another moment she would have gone, but just as she was about to open it, the shrill, cruel laughter of old Sir Anthony again broke out. The sound made her pause and look round. It was as though in that instant she saw the face of that heartless world she was about to throw herself into. It wasn't always easy for a girl to look after herself. She looked furtively out of the window and saw the dreary, grey street below. Suddenly she pulled off her glove and went back to the table.

"I've changed my mind," she said. "I might as well have that money. After all, why shouldn't he pay?"

When she had gone the hilarious screams of old Sir Anthony followed her to the pavement. The old boy was immensely ticked. He kept pinching his knees and nodding his hairless skull.

"By God! Bloor, did you ever see such a little spitfire? He, he, he! The very spit and image of her mother. "

"I only remember her mother vaguely, Sir Anthony. What was she like?"

"A damn fine woman, Bloor, a damn fine woman; the spit and image of this girl. He, he, he!"

"You knew her very well, I suppose?"

"I ought to. He, he, he! She was my mistress for some time after Tom Powerscourt threw her over. A damn fine mistress, too. He, he, he!"

"Really! You surprise me."

"Ay, and this girl will be just the same the spit and image of her mother. The way she flew out! Did you notice it? Gad! If I was a young man again! He, he, he!"

BOOK II

SYSTOLE

Barbara let herself into the flat at Ashley Gardens and, with a theatrical flourish, threw her latchkey down on to the hall table. The black fur stole emphasised the square set of her little chin. She held herself erect, and her eyes were bright with the light of battle.

Without removing her hat or furs she walked into the drawing-room. The two aunts were busily engaged looking through some papers. Without looking up Aunt Laura murmured:

"Well, dear?"

Aunt Jenny, the tip of her small tongue moving up and down mechanically between her lips, was adding up a column of figures. Both the old ladies were in deepest morning.

"I've put the latch-key down on the hall table," Barbara said abruptly. "I shan't be requiring it any more."

Aunt Laura looked over the top of her spectacles uncomprehendingly. Why wouldn't Laura want a latch-key? Aunt Jenny exploded feebly:

"There! If I start adding up from the top it comes to one thing. If I start adding up from the bottom it comes to another. What's that, dear?"

"I shan't be wanting the latch-key any longer. I'm leaving you. I'm going to live with Isabel Weare."

It took some moments for the significance of this announcement to sink in, and when it did, Barbara was vaguely amused by the quality of its reception. Both of the old ladies protested weakly. Barbara mustn't do that. She was too young, too inexperienced. Was she unhappy? Had she thought of her dear father's wishes? Was there anything they could do? Would she prefer a different bedroom?

"They 're enormously relieved," thought Barbara. "It's just what they wanted."

"I've got a cab coming at four o'clock," she said. "Isabel Weare's flat is in Northumberland Street, Baker Street Saracen Mansions, number twenty-three in case you want me for anything."

She pronounced the latter sentence in a patronising way. These two old women were nothing to her, and she was nothing to them. Both sides knew it, and so why pretend? She understood now why they had never been intimate with her, why she had never felt towards them any blood attraction. They had always deplored their dear and brilliant brother's one great lack of judgment. They had tolerated her for his sake. But now well, they would, if anything, be more Powerscourty than ever. They would be much richer. They would be able to what could they do with their money, after all? subscribe to more Bible Societies, patronise, pose, rustle about in rigid silks, and try to sustain the solemnity of the Powerscourt tradition. And she—she would take up the story from the point where her mother had dropped it. In any case she did not feel towards them any sense of gratitude or pity. The smouldering sense of outrage had reached a crisis. She rejoiced that the issue had come out into the open.

Old fools! She didn't want to be rude to them, they were too old and pitiable. To their protestations she made no reply. She walked briskly into her own room and packed her belongings. At four o'clock the cab came. A man and one of the maids helped her down with her things. When all was ready, she pecked the two aunts lightly on the cheek and said "Good-bye."

"You must come and see us as often as you can, Barbara," said Jenny.

She said yes in a voice that meant no, looked in the mirror to arrange her hat, jerkily repeated, "Good-bye," and then walked out.

When she had gone, Aunt Laura removed her spectacles and wiped them on a faded coloured handkerchief.

"She's the spit and image of her mother," she said dispassionately.

"Let's hope she doesn't go the same way," answered Jenny.

"Poor Tom. Ring the bell, dear; we'll have tea.'"

II

Isabel Weake was a girl Barbara had met at George Champneys studio, and with whom she had formed that kind of adoring friendship which one finds only amongst women of the professional classes. She was eight years older than Barbara, a fairly accomplished singer and actress, with one of those pliable, sympathetic natures of which all the world takes advantage. She was tall and rather over-developed, with a dreamy oval face also inclined to puffiness, masses of light-brown hair, which was always breaking free. She had those appealing, slightly persecuted eyes which a woman of that kind often has when experience has made her realise that sex is an ever-present source of danger.

She had been made love to so persistently, so dangerously, so cunningly, that she had come to live in a buffer state of suspicion. The eyes seemed to say: "I can't help being like this. I love everyone. What is it you really want with me?"

Men instinctively made love to her, and she had no faculty for being rude, or cruel, or unkind. With women, too, she was extremely popular. Her simplicity, good-nature and kindness of heart were irresistible. She was also absentminded and always getting into scrapes. They called her "Old Is." She was always losing her purse, or her umbrella, forgetting to turn up for appointments, being late at rehearsals, completely misinterpreting meanings; and yet everybody forgave her. Dear "Old Is" could do no wrong. It was only when she was actually performing that she appeared to be entirely compos mentis, and then she displayed a quite surprising vivacity, and her light mezzo-soprano voice had a rich, moving quality. It is probable that, had it not been for her absent-mindedness and her perfunctory treatment of managers and producers, she would have climbed higher, instead of interminably walking on or touring with musical comedy parties and pierrot troupes.

The first time Barbara met her, and heard her speak, and saw her move, she was consumed with a great desire to hug and kiss her. She gradually came to adore her like a lover. She listened for her footsteps, hung upon her words, devoured her with her eyes. Every little thing about Isabel was wonderful her clothes, her shoes, even the scent she used rather lavishly. Barbara copied her as unobtrusively as possible. She dreamed of being like Isabel. She dreamed of living with Isabel having her as her dearest friend for ever, and ever, and ever. All the other friendships of her life paled into insignificance. Cicely and Jean appeared like dimly-remembered dolls, Billy Hamaton a disturbing image, a puppet recalling an experience of which she was a little ashamed poor Billy! Her father was a forbidding nightmare; all the rest were marionettes, no one mattered, nothing counted at all except Isabel Weare and herself. She stood out like a statute of Liberty welcoming Barbara to a new world. All its delights, achievements, romance, and mysteries were embodied in Isabel Weare. She did not talk of her love-affairs, but Barbara knew that they had been many, profound and bitter. She had tasted of the cup of life, and it had not poisoned the simplicity of her outlook. She was only a little more bewildered, more alert to danger, and more tolerant of the faults of others. It took Barbara a long time to establish any special possessive claims over Isabel. She was so kind and affectionate to everyone. At these manifestations to others Barbara would be wildly jealous. She hated these other girls who kissed "Old Is" and called her darling. She hated the men who flirted with her, held her hand an unnecessarily long time and called her "my dear." At such times she would sulk, drive her nails into her palms, and crave for violence and tears.

Her insistence and her passion eventually carried the day. She hung round Isabel like a faithful little dog. She followed her about, waited on her, flattered her, gave her little presents. But her position was not finally established till one evening when she followed Isabel to her flat and wept. She wept and wept and hugged her large mothering friend. Isabel was bewildered, and kept whispering:

"What is it? What's the trouble, my darling?"

This occurred before her father's death, before she knew the truth of her own position. She had, indeed, no especial reason to weep. She just felt lonely, desperate, very much in love with Isabel, jealous, neglected, wanting sympathy, wanting to know things, shut off from life. The older woman comforted her in the best way she could. She understood women better than men, and perhaps at some time she had passed through similar experiences.

"There's nothing the matter I'm only just silly," was Barbara's constant explanation. So Isabel made some tea, and talked about Mr. Champneys, and Irene Frewin, and Lettice Strangeways, and religion, and love, and frocks. In half-an-hour's time Barbara was laughing and chatting volubly.

It was a different Barbara who came to her and told her about her father's death and the truth about herself. There were no tears this time; only a kind of ice-cold pugnacity, almost a sense of relief and freedom.

"I want to get on," was the outcome of her complex confession.

"I'm going to cut myself off from all these associations. The principal feeling I have, Isabel darling, is that I just feel sick. It's funny how any great emotion always affects my tummy first. I'm sure I should be sick on a honeymoon.'"

Isabel thought the matter over for some moments; then she said:

"Would you like to come and share my flat? if you'll promise not to be sick."

Barbara stared at her friend with eyes that could not control their amazement and delight. Then she gurgled, "Oo ooh! you don't mean it, do you, Isabel?"

Of course Isabel meant it.

"Can I live on four hundred a year if I don't get any work to do?"

Of course she could live on four hundred a year, and of course she would get work. Mr. Champneys thought a lot of her, and so did all the others. There would be no difficulty at all. They would keep a little maid, so that when one was on tour there would always be someone in the flat. Barbara could not believe her good fortune. She hugged and kissed her new friend with such an excess of frenzy that she began to feel sick once more.

"I must go for a long walk to calm down. I will come in on Thursday, darling."

And so on that Thursday she gave up her latchkey to the aunts, and drove with all her property to Northumberland Street.

III

Isabel at that time had a small part in a musical comedy at Daly's. She was getting a fairly good salary, and the play had been running for six months and promised to run for years; consequently, with Barbara's four hundred a year the two girls were comparatively well off.

"You're a lucky child," Isabel said. "There aren't many girls in our profession with four hundred a year to fall back on. There aren't many with anything at all. But you take my advice, dear, and keep it dark. They don't like it if they think you've got money. They look on you as an amateur, taking the bread out of working-girls "mouths."

"If I had four thousand a year which I ought to I should still go on the stage, darling."

"Well, you keep it dark, darling."

The first person Barbara visited was naturally George Champneys, who was very interested and amused at the earnestness of her resolution. Most certainly he would do what he could. He had promised, and he would stick to his promise. He would try to get her on in London as soon as possible. In the mean-time she must get some hard, practical experience. In a month's time he was sending a pierrot troupe out on short runs, a week here and there, and then back, another week later on, and so on. would she care to be in it? The pay was negligible, but the experience would be good.

Would she care to be in it! Barbara glowed with excitement. At the very first bound she was to become a professional actress, with a name and a salary, perhaps Press notices, and bouquets from unknown admirers.

"What are you going to call yourself?" George remarked. "I don't think Barbara Powerscourt's very good too long. Besides—"

"Exactly besides," quoth Barbara, "I want to drop the Powerscourt altogether."

"Fancy that!"

"Fancy what? Oh, Mr. Champneys, Fancy's a nice name."

"Fancy's a very nice name. Now, what shall it be? Fancy what?"

"No, not Fancy Watt."

"I know."

"What?"

"Fancy Telling."

"Oo oooh! Yes, that would be rather quaint, wouldn't it? Fancy Telling. I like it."

"Fancy Telling tops the bill this week at The Grand, Croydon. Yes, that's very good. George, my boy, I congratulate you. Don't forget, Miss Telling, on the day of judgment, to let them know that it was I who invented your name."

"Fancy telling!"

"Come in on Monday, and I'll get you to sign a piece of paper, old girl. Carter is handling this company. I expect they'll pay you two pounds or two pounds ten a week. We'll push you on as fast as we can."

He pressed her hand and patted her shoulders as he showed her out.

And so Fancy returned to Northumberland Street in a wild state of excitement. The metamorphosis was complete. She had new friends, a new interest in life, a new job, and a new name."

"You're a lucky little devil," Isabel remarked when she emerged from her friend's embrace. "I never had anyone to help me when I started not a friend or a bean. I used to traipse round calling on dirty, fat little agents, who used to insist on holding my hand all the time I talked. Some of them used to oh, they were swine!"

"Oh, Isabel, how rotten! People don't do that sort of thing now, do they, darling?"

"Oh no, my dear, only pretty frequently. It's lucky you've got me to look after you, and that you struck George C. straight away.

"He's a dear. I love him."

"You've got a very passionate nature, Barbara. You must watch out that it doesn't get you into trouble. When you've had men try to maul you about as long as I have you'll quiet down. Let's have lunch; I'm hungry."

Oh, those glorious days! all too short for the wonders and portents which crowded upon her. Everything was coloured by the glamour of discovery and anticipation. She thrilled at the vision of Isabel sitting up in bed, in a dressing-gown, drinking tea. Washing up the breakfast things, because the maid had failed to turn up, was a positive ecstasy. Making toast, cleaning Isabel's shoes, ordering groceries, rearranging the sitting-room, mending some under-linen of Isabel's, darning her own stockings all these things were pleasures, of which she sometimes felt quite unworthy. And then the adventurous world outside. The busy streets brimming with life, the shops full of things she meant to buy one day lovely frocks and hats, old furniture, precious stones, jewels, vanity bags all for Isabel and herself. If only her father...

Then, most important and thrilling of all, meeting with Mr. Carter, the producer. Rehearsing, really rehearsing a proper professional performance, glancing at the other girls and men; trying to appear as though used to it, every day picking up a little more of the slang of the profession, getting familiar with the terms which governed this delightful world afterwards the streets again, rich women in furs and motor-cars, jolly men walking furtively, looking at her inquiringly, poor old men playing hurdy-gurdies, giving them sixpences and shillings, the tears swelling to her eyes. Tea with Isabel, Isabel looking scrumptious, rather languid and cosy, in a bright jade-green kimono. Talk, delightful talk, all about people, and the profession, and the things that may happen to two girls with the world before them. The glow of sunset on the wet pavement below. Isabel's chop at six-thirty and a raw egg for Barbara. Then going down to the theatre with Isabel on a motor-bus, getting off at Piccadilly Circus and walking along to the stage-door at Daly's sometimes being smuggled in. Oh, that was joy indeed! The narrow stone staircase and passages, curious people in various stages of make-up. Small boys calling out;

"Beginners, please!"

Isabel's dressing-room, with two other real actresses in it, the smell of grease-paint and powder, the bright glow of the mirrors.

Then out in the street once more, the myriad coloured lights and signs of Leicester Square, the enveloping mystery of early darkness, with its provocative, mysterious appeal. She would hurry back to the little flat then, rather scared, and eager for escape. The flat seemed melancholy without Isabel, so she would rush to the upright piano, and with puckered brows and intense concentration, practise the songs Mr. Carter had given her to sing for the tour. Then she would curl up in front of the fire and read, or stare at the embers and dream of the great and wonderful world awaiting her. It would be nearly twelve before Isabel came in. At the click of the door she would jump up, rush out and kiss her friend, take off her cloak, fetch her slippers and the tray of stout and sandwiches, ensconce her comfortably in the easy chair. Then she would brew herself some cocoa, kneel on the tuffet, ask for news, and hungrily worship her goddess.

"The young man who marries you will have a hot time," said Isabel on one of these occasions.

"I don't like men. I'm never going to marry," answered Barbara.

"That's right, darling, don't you do it. Will you be an angel and go and fetch me a hanky from my room?"

IV

Just before the tour started there was a disquieting irruption in the flat. Isabel developed a persistent lover. He was a dark, heavily-built man, about forty years of age, and the owner of a successful business in Bloomsbury, concerned with trimmings, gimp, buttons and embroidery. He called at all kinds of inconvenient hours of the day, and began to see Isabel home at night. He spoke very little, and then in a soft mellow voice. Barbara suspected that he was less silent when she was not present. He had a way of staring at her with an expression of amused contempt thoughtfully tugging at his black moustache. His eyes seemed to say:

"Can't you see, you little nuisance, that two is company, three's none?"

It is needless to say that Mr. Basil Cleethorpe for such was his name roused in Barbara's bosom feelings of violent jealousy. Before a week had passed she could have killed this man who had come between her and Isabel. At first she was polite to him, then curt, and then definitely rude. But she recognised in him one of the strong, silent species, or perhaps not strong and silent so much as thick-skinned and dull. He withstood her attacks with amused indifference. She did not interest him. His quarry was Isabel, and he would take infinite trouble to secure her company, and that alone.

The alarming aspect of the case was that Isabel seemed not only to tolerate him but positively to like him. She went out to lunches and dinners with him, and left Barbara to shift for herself. And jealousy and suspicion gnawed at her vitals. Isabel didn't love her. Isabel had deceived her. What did she mean that time when she talked about being "mauled about by men?" How loathsome the whole thing was!

She would return from rehearsal and find Isabel and Basil awful name! sitting side by side on the Chesterfield in the firelight. Isabel would be just as affectionate to her, but she was tortured by the suspicion that her presence was unwelcome. Isabel took to being out more, and sometimes returning at an unearthly hour in the morning. This couldn't last; something would have to be done.

She waited till three nights before the tour started, and then she determined to have it out. She waited up for Isabel, who arrived home at a quarter past one. Then she followed her into the sitting-room and pulled her down on to the Chesterfield.

"Where have you been, Isabel darling?"

Isabel yawned sleepily.

"Been, my dear? Oh, I've been having supper with Basil."

Barbara's breath came in little gasps.

"Are you very fond of him, Isabel?"

"B? Oh, yes, he's a nice boy."

"Do you love him? Are you going to marry him? Are you going to leave me, Isabel?"

The older woman held her away, and looked slightly bewildered.

"Love him! Marry him! Oh, dear! what a queer child you are! Haven't you ever had a boy?"

"No."

"Well, you get one, my dear. They help to pass the time. You've only got to look after yourself, not lose your head, if you know what I mean."

That phrase again "A girl has got to look after herself!" Isabel was still speaking in her cosy enveloping voice.

"I'm very, very fond of you, Fancy darling. Don't be silly all this talk about leaving you. There's one thing we must have clear, though. Living like this together, we must each be free to do what we like. I wouldn't be jealous of you, if you had a boy. It's natural."

"You're really only playing with him, then?"

"We each know what we're doing, darling. How did the rehearsal go to-day?"

So that was it. On her pillow that night little Fancy Telling wept, almost wishing, for the first time since her new departure, that she was once more Barbara Powerscourt.

The tour, which opened at Harrogate, was also rather in the nature of a disillusionment. In some respects it was almost a triumph. They played to good houses. The programme was a clever production, the joint work of George Champneys and Mr. Birtles. Her own part in it was by no means negligible, and she carried it through with considerable success indeed, she was surprised how easily the whole thing came to her, and how the people applauded her. But the company she found anything but companionable. The men were always making vulgar jokes and suggestive remarks, and she resented their over-familiarity. Between the shows their principal interests appeared to be horse racing, cards and beer. The women erred by applauding and approving the men's behaviour, and by being jealous and catty to each other, and to Barbara. Mr. Carter, the principal, was far less vulgar than the other men, but he was inordinately vain, jealous, and self-centred. On the stage he was an excellent comedian, off it he was self-conscious and awkward.

The only member of the company with whom Barbara struck up any kind of friendship was Angela Lupin, the accompanist, a solemn, sallow-faced girl, with short black hair, and no sense of humor. She had been a student at the Royal Academy of Music. She confessed to Barbara that the whole pierrot performance bored her to tears. She played the accompaniments because she had to earn money. Her career at the Academy had been cut short by the death of her father, a clever and thriftless journalist, who had left her mother and herself penniless. She was being paid two pounds a week, a goodly portion of which was regularly despatched to her mother. Barbara discovered that Angela 's meals consisted almost exclusively of tea and bread-and-butter. It was the first time in her life she had come up against real want, and the spectacle sickened and shook her. Poor sallow-faced child! How unfair it all was! With her four hundred a year and her own small salary, and no one else to spend it on, Barbara realised that she was an enormously wealthy woman. Henceforth she insisted on standing Angela lunches and teas and dinners. She bought her fruit and eggs and bottles of stout. At the same time she followed Isabel's advice and kept quiet about her own private income. Sometimes she imagined that Angela regarded her suspiciously, but the child was too hungry to care.

The party went on to Leeds, Huddersfield, Hull, and "Whitby. Added to the nervous discomforts of this first tour was the constant worry as to what was happening to Isabel. Barbara was always dreaming of the awful black Basil, grinning at her superciliously. He would be taking advantage of her absence. He would spend half the day in the flat, sitting on her chairs, using her things, perhaps resting on her bed! Oh, what could Isabel see in him? A boy, indeed! Perhaps at that very moment he was "mauling Isabel about!"

Was it natural to have "boys" to be mauled about indiscriminately? A fierce resentment at the idea stirred within her. Was she different from those other girls? Certainly all the girls in this company seemed to be boy-mad. They chopped and changed about, squabbled and flirted and made it up quite amicably over tankards of beer. She would never be able to do that. She didn't care for "boys" not in that sense. Of course there was that one wonderful person somewhere in the world; that would be quite different. A sudden fear seized her. Her mother? Was she a woman who was boy-mad? Was her father one of her mother's "boys," and that was why he treated her like that? Oh, no, no she thought of those letters. They were not the letters of these fly-by-nights. Whatever the true circumstances of the story were, one fact stood out poignantly her mother had suffered. The capacity for suffering is one of the acid tests of character. It is only profound people who can suffer. Girls like Maisie Jewel, the leading comedienne, were capable of fits of the blues, of peevishness, jealousy, bad temper, but a little flattery or a pint of beer would wash it all away. They could not suffer.

When the five-weeks" tour was over the company were to return to London, and they were not to go out again for another three weeks. Reacting from the disappointments of her first experience, Barbara determined to make the best of things.

"I'm Fancy Telling, not Barbara Powerscourt, "she repeated to herself. "I'm going to get on. Mr. Champneys said it wouldn't be much of a show, but that it would be a good experience. I must work and study and find out things."

At Leeds she had quite a personal success, one of her songs, "The Garden of Regrets," seeming to.be the most popular item on the programme. It was very much to her surprise, therefore, that on the last night Mr. Carter took her on one side, and said:

"Oh, we're making a few changes at Huddersfield, Miss Telling. We've got some more comic stuff to work in. I'm afraid we shall have to cut out 'The Garden of Regrets'."

For an instant she was about to protest violently. Then she reflected: "What does it matter? Carter's no one. I'm out for bigger game."

She contented herself by remarking bitterly:

"I suppose it did go rather well."

And then she turned away and left him to ponder the insinuation at his leisure. The result made him her enemy, for the rest of the tour.

VI

At the end of five weeks the company returned to town, and Barbara to Northumberland Street. There she found that her worst suspicions were to be confirmed. The black Basil was still much in evidence. On the other hand, she could not but be moved by the warmth of Isabel's reception. Isabel was genuinely pleased to see her. She hugged her and cross-examined her about every little detail of the tour. She was a dear old darling Isabel, too easy-going, almost incomprehensible. Barbara, like many young people with definite ambitions and indefinite ideals, was beginning to learn that one cannot interpret anyone else's visions through the light of one's own eyes. She had lain awake at night, pitying Isabel, dreaming all kinds of disturbing dreams about her, but when she once more was in her society she found her quite happy and unchanged. She was certainly not being worried by anything. It comforted Barbara, therefore, to conclude that Basil was only an interlude, in spite of his prehensile grip upon her friend's affections.

The crust was already hardening. So long as Isabel loved her it was not her business to interfere with her sex adventures. She knew from what Isabel had told her that men were transitory experiences. She busied herself in the flat, revelling in the crumbs of Isabel's society which fell from the rich button-and-gimp man's table. After all, he was not there all day she had breakfast with Isabel, and all morning, and very often a good part of the afternoon; and she could still sew and mend for Isabel, and write her letters and run her errands; she could still hug her, and listen to her deep lazy voice talking familiarly about "May" May being no less a person than May Mendelssohn, the leading lady at Daly's. Isabel knew all these people, and always referred to them by their Christian names. It added a piquant thrill to their friendship. To think that she, Barbara no, Fancy Telling an ingenue of five weeks" experience, lived with a girl who referred to May Mandelssohn as "May"! May, an almost inaccessible goddess, who drove to the theatre in a motor-car was always having her photograph in the illustrated papers, supped at the Savoy with the scions of the aristocracy, lived in a large house near the park, kept several servants of her own, had been married once, and had divorced her husband when she was twenty-two, and, above all, sang and danced and acted divinely. Would such a destiny ever be the lot of Fancy Telling? She tried to analyse this fate. She, too, passionately desired to see her photographs in the illustrated papers, to drive to the theatre in a motorcar, to sup at the Savoy, to have, a house and servants of her own; more especially did she passionately desire to sing, and dance, and act divinely. But she had no desire to marry and divorce; she had no desire to be "mauled about by men." Her erotic impulses were at that time entirely unawakened.

The day after her return she repaired to George Champneys', and gave him a voluble account of the tour, not excluding the incident about "The Garden of Regrets."

The large man regarded her quizzically, and nodded his head.

"I'm afraid Carter is like that, my dear. I'm sorry. I'll speak to him about it, but I can't insist. It's in our contract that he has complete control of the programme. Don't you worry. I'll soon have you in something better. How have you been?"

"I wish he would take me seriously," thought Barbara. "He likes me, but he treats me like a kid."

Champneys was certainly very paternal and kind, but he was a little preoccupied concerning a big new London production. He did treat her like a kid. But how else can one treat twenty-one? He himself was forty-five, at the very zenith of his fame, his palate a little jaded by the flavour of every human experience. He had met many young girls like Barbara, and he liked them and treated them all kindly. Bless their hearts! He would like to give them all leads and big salaries, but even kindness of heart has its physical limitations. A secretary was fidgeting with papers; a telephone bell went.

"Come and see me again soon, La pauvre innocente," he said genially. Barbara thanked him and went. When she got to the street a little lump came in her throat.

"It's not going to be so darned easy," she thought. "I can't keep on worrying him."

This intermittent tour of the Pierrot troupe continued for eight months. It was a mixed experience. Mr. Carter had his knife in her, and reduced her part in the performance till it became almost negligible. The other men tried the "mauling" process, but finding that she did not respond, they treated her with contempt. The other girls were jealous of her because they knew she had real ability, and also because it was known that she was a personal friend of the great George Champneys, and was not to be "given the bird." Angela Lupin left. She had been given the bird, because she had not a friend at court, and Mr. Carter wanted to work in a fat girl named Ruby Isaacs for some reason of his own. The tour was a series of disillusionments; nevertheless Fancy Telling managed to survive it. Moreover, she did gain experience. She learnt to broaden her methods, to act with assurance, to come down slick on her cues, to force an encore if she wished to. She learnt to make points by giving just the right pause, to play to the back of the hall, to judge its acoustics and adapt her voice to its possibilities. She learnt to make up to the best advantage, to judge her distances accurately in dancing. She learnt to drink stout and to eat tripe. She gradually learnt how to manage "maulers" without eternally offending them. She gradually learnt how to flatter, and cajole, and humour her fellow-artists as well as the managers and people connected with the hall.

During the last week of the tour she was more popular than she had been all through. Several members of the company were coming to the conclusion that little Fancy Telling was not such a rotter after all. She did not mind this one way or another. She stuffed all this experience away into odd corners of her brain for future use. She had her eye on a larger canvas.

The third time she returned to London, she found that the black Basil had been superseded by a youth named Walter Podmore, a rather vacuous fair young man who was forever chuckling over Isabel's irresistible charms. Her experience had fortified her against the shock of this development. So this was Isabel darling old Isabel, still loyal, affectionate, and adorable, still talking about "May," still having love-affairs and managing them adroitly. These were the people, and this was the life from which her mother sprang. She envisaged her father's ponderous, judicial figure glowering above her, and her resentment quickened at the thought that he should have sat in judgment on it.

VII

During the intervals of this tour she called on George Champneys three times, and on no occasion did she feel that she made much progress in his good graces. He was always the same, paternal, kindly, and mildly encouraging. At the end of her third visit she became haunted by a disturbing suspicion. Of his sympathy and kindness of heart she had no doubt, but was it quite the same thing flattering and encouraging the daughter of a famous and wealthy Chancellor as flattering and fulfilling promises to an impecunious and unknown actress? She tried to persuade herself that there was nothing in it, that George was quite sincere, that it was only natural that he should send her out on these miserable little tours to gain experience, but the canker of suspicion once being there developed and grew, and moreover bred other suspicions. Was it possible, for instance, that darling Isabel found her well, rather useful in the flat, with her assured income, and her ingenuity and anxiety to help her? Why was it that she had never had a line from Cicely or Jean since her father 's death, or even from the aunts? Did Billy Hamaton still love her? Should she sacrifice everything throw up the stage, seek him out, marry him, and nurse him to the end of her days?

Her impulses swung hither and thither, but at the end of the tour they had solidified to the extent of a determination not to give in so soon.

She became obsessed by another determination to break free from George Champneys. She would show him that she could get on by herself. Whether she expected that he would give her a leading part in town right off she could not say. She only felt that he was not treating her in quite the way he had led her to expect on that afternoon in the Stradlings' drawing-room when she had sung "La Pauvre Innocente." Perhaps that day was charged with an indescribable glamour the kind of day that blinds one to the stern realities. On that day she had caused the destruction of her lover, and even that event did not really destroy the enchantment.

Life was like that, a lot of drab monotony and disillusion, and then moments almost too wonderful to bear. Moments when one was up in the tree-tops and the earth did not exist. One lives on through the dreary business because something in one's heart tells one that such moments will occur again. Perhaps that is how the utterly destitute, the downtrodden, the unhealthy go on living they have that secret buried well away, a treasure that cannot be shared. Having once beheld "those trailing clouds of glory," the vision sustains us through eternity, and neither adversity, disilluson, nor even our own vicious habits can ever utterly abolish or destroy.

She told Isabel of her determination, and that lady said:

"Oh, my dear, don't you be a ninny. You'll never do better than George. You stick to him. He's becoming 'the big noise,' as the Yanks say. You don't expect him to put you on in town with only eight months experience, do you?"

Barbara didn't know what she expected. She was hungry for success, and impatient at its uncertain delays. The next morning she set off in her smartest coat and skirt, and a hat of black velour with an emerald paste buckle, and called on agents.

She spent a fortnight calling on agents and trying to see managers, and the result made her weep. She waited for hours in stuffy rooms with crowds of other girls and men. When she eventually saw the agent the interview invariably followed identical lines.

"Well, what experience have you had? What is your line? All right. I'll let you know if I hear of anything. Good morning."

She did not have quite such sultry experiences as Isabel had described, but they were sultry enough. Only two of the agents actually tried to hold her hands, and only one tried to kiss her, and then in a rather fearsome, tentative manner. He wanted her to go into an inner office and "see some pictures," but she declined. The general attitude was that the agents were conferring an enormous benefit in seeing her at all, and she ought to appreciate the fact and recognise it suitably. They looked her up and down like a farmer judging cattle at a cattle show. Into the sanctum of a theatrical manager she never managed to penetrate. Mr. So-and-So only saw people by appointment. Would she kindly write about her business? She wrote to seventeen managers. Three of them replied in each case a typewritten slip to say that the manager regretted to say that he had nothing to offer Miss F. Telling at the moment.

At the end of three weeks she put her pride in her pocket and went back to George.

VIII

It took her just two years to reach that little niche in George Champneys' autocratic temple which she regarded as the resting place worthy of a certain glamorous summer day; and the end was attained in the most surprising way.

Two years of delight and bitterness, hard work, vivid experience, disappointment, moral questioning, spiritual unrest. The lamp flickered, but at every flicker the light became stronger. She learnt to take care of herself, to adapt every experience to serve her ends. She learnt how to make herself popular, to flirt a little, to overlook the delinquencies of her fellow artists. She quickly realised that they were far better than she had thought at first, far better than they appeared on the surface. Her own hothouse training had prejudiced her against them, but she discovered that beneath their little vanities and childish jealousies there was a rich streak of real humanity and kindness. They would behave outrageously, and five minutes later they would give their last shilling to help a colleague. They were just children, these people, egotistic, impetuous, wilful, but quick in sympathy, sentimental and strangely loyal. She began to love them and to fall into their ways. Physically the life agreed with her. She found herself getting plump. All the boyishness, with its quick and jerky movements, vanished. The lines became rounder and softer, the gestures more deliberate and significant. She had a genius for dressing, for making the most of her materials, putting a touch of colour in the right place, catching up her rich dark hair in cunning sweeps under her hats. Her rather square pale face was dominated by—

Those deep dark eyes where pride demurs.

She was a creature ever adjusting her outlook to a shifting panorama. She desired passionately to be a part of this corporate existence which went on round her, but her attitude was always being controlled by some obscure, submerged sense of protest. She had strange moods when she was both buoyant and desperate. The joy of life was in her veins, but not in her mind. She distrusted herself, and therefore humanity. She had read too little and imagined too much. Between her and a frank interpretation of living were little frozen reticences governed by a subconscious voice which was already pleading for delay. She felt that in some way her very soul had been outraged, and the outrage was so colossal she had not the wit to understand it as yet. "You are an instrument of readjustment," the voice would whisper.

Then she would tremble, and wish it were not so. It was so easy to drift and be jolly.

George Champneys had an excellent library, and during the intervals of the various tours she would often call and borrow a book. Even then she didn't know what to read, and how to read it. When she consulted him he said:

"My dear, I haven't read a book for years. I never get a minute. What do you want? When I was young like you I read Emerson^ and Stuart Mill, and Schopenhauer, and Kant, and all those people. I don't remember a word that any of them said. Why not read some fiction? You get profit and pleasure at the same time. Now, what about Pickwick?"

That was the worst of her world. No one had a minute for reading. Some of them would play cards for four or five hours a day, or spend the morning cutting out a skirt or the afternoon at a race meeting, but beyond glancing at a daily paper no one had a minute for reading. So she set out on her lonely pilgrimage of mental improvement, and she struggled through Herbert Spencer and tried to read Darwin's Origin of Species. She was so frankly bored that she decided to take George's advice and read fiction not the kind of thing that Isabel kept under her pillow, lurid novels about high life but real, elevating fiction: Meredith, Hardy, perhaps Hall Caine. Or wasn't Hall Caine a great writer? She didn't know. She had heard some of the girls on tour rave about him. She must ask George. And George said, "No; Mr. Caine was all right, but he wasn't ranked as a classic. Why not read 'Diana of the Crossways'?" He had not read it, never had time but the high-brows spoke well of it. So she read "Diana of the Crossways," and was bewildered. Were there rich and clever people who really talked like that f Her father had known many rich and clever people, and they had visited at High Barrow, but she had never heard them talk like that. They used to mumble and talk in little jerky sentences about hunting or eating or politics. They were always fairly intelligible, but Diana!

Hardy she found more companionable he, in any case, dealt with humble people and the tragedy of Tess moved her more profoundly than any experience in her life. She wanted to get in between the pages of this book and take a part in the unfair struggle. Tess epitomised to her the tragedy of her mother, the tragedy of herself, the tragedy of woman. The whole scheme of life was unfair to woman. But through the tears which blinded her when she put the great novelist's book down she saw a star of hope. Her senses quickened. Fortitude springs from trial and adversity. She already beheld in herself qualities of heart and brain which she had not possessed and would probably never have possessed in the shelter of her father's house. Of course, men were like that. It was part of the regime to keep women sheltered and safe, to divorce them from intellectual realities, to hang them up on a peg behind the door, to be taken down when required. Her father had wanted her to "paint flowers"! People had painted flowers, and painted them very well; there was nothing wrong about it, except that it typified her father's attitude towards women. While she was painting flowers she was quite, out of the way; she couldn't get into mischief, and he knew exactly where she was, so that if he wanted her he could send for her. Flowers were pretty, and women were pretty and soft and clinging, and almost as perishable admirably adapted to each other.

In a defensive mood she sought out Billy Hamaton. He was living at his father's house at Epsom. She found him lying on a portable bed by the window of a sunny room overlooking a garden. His face appeared to have lengthened, and the freckles stood out pronouncedly on his hollow cheeks. The eyes were sunken and weary looking. He was almost unrecognisable until he smiled in his old way. At the very first glance she knew that her half-formed resolution to marry him and nurse him all her days was an ideal impossible to fulfil. She pitied him intensely, and his face would haunt her all her life, but she knew that not only did she not love him, she never had loved him. He was a complete stranger to her, and a stranger who produced in her little tremors of a queer physical revulsion.

He seized her hand and whispered:

"Barbara dear Barbara."

"He's going to be sentimental," she thought. "I mustn't give way to him. If I do I shall be sick."

She pressed his hands warmly and said:

"Hullo, Billy. I've been meaning to come so often. How are you, old boy!"

The "old boy" was a comforting term from her new world. She never used to call him "old boy." She rattled on inconsequently:

"I do hope you'll soon get right, Billy. I feel sure you will. I had an awful journey down; train got held up at Surbiton for some reason or other. What are you reading? Do you ever hear from Jean or Cicely? What a glorious day, isn't it!"

She hemmed him in with a stream of banalities. He never got a chance to be sentimental, or to say all the things he had been saving up to say. She told him about her tours and her work, and about George Champneys and Isabel, and a score of people in whom Billy could not possibly have been interested. They had hardly had tea together before she found that she must rush to catch her train back. She patted his hands perfunctorily and exclaimed:

"Well, good luck, old boy! I'll come and see you again soon."

On the way to the station she muttered:

"Oh, Barbara, you're a brute a horrid, selfish little brute!"

Well, doesn't one have to be selfish? she argued. Wasn't her father selfish, and even Isabel, and probably Shakespeare and Thomas Hardy? One has to be selfish to protect oneself. A person who doesn't protect oneself is a sentimental fool.

She dined that night with Isabel in Soho, and they drank red wine with their dinner. She was flushed and excited. George had sent word that he wished to see her at "The Frivolity" between the acts.

She was shown into the Master Pierrot's dressing room, and she found him talking to a gentleman in his shirt sleeves, with a bowler hat tilted at a dangerous angle over his left ear. They were drinking whisky-and-soda. He nodded to her casually and said:

"Hullo, Fancy. Wait two minutes. I want to see you."

He went on talking to the man in the bowler hat about floats for some minutes, and then dismissed him. When he had gone, George said in his thick comfortable voice:

"Now, look here, my dear, it's like this. Miss Roland, who has been understudying Rosie, is ill. She has got to go to a hospital and have an operation. How would you like to take her place?"

Made! She was made! In that wild moment Barbara^ saw her whole career in a tumultuous flash. Miss Roland would go to the hospital (and probably die). Next week Rosie Ventnor, the leading comedienne in the London Frivolity company, would also be taken ill. (She might also die.) She, Barbara, would step into her place. She would make an instantaneous hit. There would be headlines in the newspaper: "Brilliant Debut of Young Actress." There would be her portrait in all the illustrated papers. There would, be cheers, and bouquets, fame and a house with servants in the park. London would kneel at her feet.

She blushed, smiled at George demurely, and in a timid voice said:

"Thank you, Mr. Champneys, I should like it very much."

"All right then; there's a call at eleven in the morning. You'll have to work hard, because she may have to go off at any time. Go round to the front and find Mr. Stiles' office. He'll give you the script and the songs. Have a drink? No, of course not; you're too young. So long, old girl, I've got to get ready."

Oh, George, George, what a splendid person you are! As she walked dazedly through the streets on the way back to the flat, he seemed to hover above her like some vast benignant destiny. In a shifting and unstable world he, and he alone, appeared a creature charged with kindliness and real affection. The mere thought of him made her quiver with gratitude. From that day when he had first heard her sing "La Pauvre Innocente" a new joy and sense of freedom had enveloped her. He was so vast, competent, reliable and successful. She hated herself for having once doubted him. She was a wretch to have thought of deserting him. Didn't he say that he would push her on as quickly as possible? Didn't he promise solemnly? And everyone affirmed that George was a man of his word. How clear it all was now, this careful planning of her three years' experience? She adored him: he was like a father, a brother, a protector. She knew that during all that time if she had been in any kind of trouble he would have helped her. No, it wasn't necessary to be selfish to protect oneself; it was necessary to be unselfish. Isabel might be selfish and even Shakespeare or Hardy but in this glowing, thrilling world, one man stood out as a supreme example of the opposite George Champneys.

IX

The position of an understudy is somewhat similar to that of a poor man at a rich uncle's bedside. His solicitude for the other's welfare is apt to be double-faced.

Barbara's interest in Rosie Ventnor's health was an enveloping obsession. She hung about the stage door all on edge for her arrival. When Rosie did arrive she glanced eagerly at her face to detect any signs of indisposition. She watched her from the wings; she watched her at the back. She listened to find evidence of a cold or crack in the voice. She tried so hard not to want Rosie to catch cold or fall down and sprain her ankle, but it was impossible. She even endured nightmarish temptations to do her some hurt surreptitiously, trip her up, or put something into the water in her dressing room which would make her just a little ill for a few days. Her malicious impulses were the more to be condemned in that Rosie was a very nice girl, and was perfectly charming to her. If only she weren't so disgustingly healthy! The nights passed, and the weeks, and even the months, and still Rosie Ventnor came bouncing through the stage door, smiling and showing her splendid teeth, which had already served a sound commercial purpose in advertising a well-known dentifrice. Even this advertisement embittered Barbara. With a little luck, she might have appeared on the back page of the Star above the statement: "Miss Fancy Telling, the famous actress, says, 'I always use Blogg's Dentifrice. I find it admirable in every way. It keeps the teeth splendidly white, and is refreshing and pleasant to the palate'." Apart from her resentment at Rosie's splendid health and teeth, she was very happy.

In the first place she felt that she was on the eve of recognition. She had an engagement in town, and at one of its most successful productions. George would not run the risk of allowing her the possibility of playing a leading part unless he thought highly of her. She thought she had done well at the rehearsals, and Mr. Lamb, who was himself an understudy of the great producer, Julius Banstead, had openly praised her performance. In the second place, the company were far more companionable than any of the companies she had been with on tour. George's genial spirit seemed to permeate them all. There were all kinds of little social gatherings in various dressing rooms, all kinds of jokes, discussions and stories. Even the stage hands were pleasant, uncommon people, with queer characteristics and friendly manners. There was Sydney Ebbway, a rather ugly, lantern-faced man, very thin; he acted as a foil to George on the stage. He had a deep, lugubrious voice, and a massive sense of humour. He would sometimes take her on one side, and tell her about his three children, or his garden at Chiswick. From that he would get on to social questions, and then religion and God. He talked above her head, and she was never quite certain how serious he was, but the steady grey twinkly eyes were irresistible, and after a time she had to shake her head and laugh. Then he would seize her by the shoulder and say:

"Why do I waste my eloquence on a baby like you?"

And she would answer:

"I'm awfully sorry, Mr. Ebbway."

On one of these occasion he looked at her eyes thoughtfully for a long time; then he said:

"I know why it is you 've got it all."

He turned away and left her to ponder his meaning.

For some reason or other the phrase excited her tremendously, and in an obscure way she felt that it was true. She had got it all! What? she didn't know, but she knew she had got something. It must be something enormously important, because the sentence implied that it was almost unique to "have it all." Some of these other girls.... Oh, yes, it was a glorious life. It made Mr. Ebbway melancholy to reflect that she had it all. He had sighed dismally. It was evident that she had something which he had not, and she was only an understudy.

Days and nights and weeks passed in varying moods of delight and misgiving. If only Rosie would get ill! The production was still playing to packed houses, but it couldn't go on forever. She was kept very busy, because George was always introducing new skits, and gags, and songs, and she had to keep up to date with everything.

One night she arrived home very late and found Isabel lying on the Chesterfield, sobbing. She rushed and threw her arms around her.

"What is it, darling? What's the matter?" Isabel cried and cried, and could not get her voice. At last she said:

"Oh, God! the fool, the fool!"

"What is it, darling?"

Isabel seemed angry and a little unresponsive.

"Oh, you can't help me, Kiddy. I'm all right. I didn't mean you to see me."

"There must be something. Oh, tell me, what is it, darling Isabel? I must help you."

"No, no go away. I shall be all right.

She could get nothing further out of her friend, and retired to bed in a state of dubious anxiety.

Two days later Isabel came to her. There were dark rings round her eyes, and her lips were pale. Without looking at Barbara she said:

"I want you to do me a favour, darling."

"Of course, Isabel."

"I want you to go away and stay somewhere else for a week."

Barbara was aghast. Something awful and tragic was afoot, and an inner voice told her that she had better not inquire. She was not to be in this at all. She replied in a whisper:

"All right, darling."

She was frankly scared. Somehow the chilling fears which crept around her heart were less fears for Isabel than the uncomfortable sense that she was dealing with the unknown. It was also obvious that Isabel was frightened and desperate. It was also obvious that she was terribly anxious not to impart her trouble to Barbara, but to get rid of her as quickly as possible. She immediately went over to a private hotel at Paddington, where she knew that one of the girls from the Frivolity stayed, and booked a room. Then she went back and packed her trunk.

Isabel hovered like a spectre in the background.

"Take everything you may want, Kiddy. I want you to promise me you won't come back, or call, for a week. "

"All right, Isabel I promise." More mysteries! She was frightened of her own emotion when she kissed her friend good-bye. She pecked her cheek perfunctorily, and steadied her voice to say:

"So long, darling." In the cab her heart beat violently. "I shall never see her again," was the purport of its beat.

Everything was slipping away from her. Her friends? If Isabel died and of course she would who else was there to cling to? Only her career, her career and the dole flung to her by her father. George? Yes, George was a dear good friend, but she did not regard him in that way. She felt no desire to cling to George. And that is the trouble. It isn't sufficient to have friends, and fame, and money; when we get down to the raw stuff of our being, we demand someone to cling to both physically and spiritually. Upon this impulse rests the survival of God and humanity.

That night she hovered in the wings like a little scared ghost. For the first time she dreaded that Rosie might fall ill. If she had done so, Barbara felt certain that she could not have gone on to take her place. Her nerves were all unstrung. In one of the waits George came across her. He regarded her critically under the light of the floats, and said:

"What 's the matter, Fancy? You look ill."

Tears sprang to her eyes. If anyone started being sympathetic she would break down. She shook her head and looked away.

"It's nothing, Mr. Champneys. I'm a little worried about something."

For a moment he appeared to be about to turn away. Then he stopped and looked at her again, and a most queer expression came over his face. It was as though, after looking at her for three years, he had suddenly seen her for the first time; or as though some entirely novel aspect regarding her had presented itself abruptly. He spoke kindly.

"Come round to my room after the show. I want to speak to you."

She wished he had not asked her. She was tired, jaded, and in no mood for any emotional experience. She went to one of the dressing rooms and tried to read a book till the final curtain, but the words danced before her eyes meaninglessly. Would the performance, with its interminable encores, never end I "When at last it really did come to a stop, she followed the chief to his door. She waited till he had gone in, and then tapped timidly. The dresser opened it, and admitted her.

George I was already smearing cocoa-butter on his face. He said:

"Come in, Fancy. Sit down. I won't be a minute."

He cleaned up his face and dismissed the dresser. Then he turned to her.

"Now, you've got to tell me what's the matter, Fancy."

She had determined not to give way. She tried to speak brightly and cheerfully.

"It's really nothing, Mr. Champneys; nothing at all. I'm only a little out of sorts."

"You said you were worried about something."

"Yes. No, it's nothing, nothing of any importance really."

He searched her face and did not speak for some moments, and when he did his voice had a strange, appealing ring:

"You haven't been getting into trouble?"

"Getting into trouble?"

Oh, la plauvre innocente! It was difficult to know how to talk to the child. He mixed himself a whisky and soda a stiff one. Then he sat back in a paternally judicial attitude.

"You don't you're not one of those people who go about much with boys, are you?"

She was offended, offended and yet at the same time fiercely grateful. He was hurting her in the way she desired to be hurt. She would rather quarrel than anything. She replied brusquely:

"No, I'm not"

"Did you know why Miss Roland had to leave the theatre?"

"No not exactly, except that she was ill."

She cowered against the wall, a ruffled kitten. Yes, yes it was perfectly true. She was an extremely pretty girl and completely innocent. He looked away, slightly confused, and said rapidly:

"I'm sorry, Fancy. I didn't want to offend you, my dear. I only wanted to say that you must always tell me. If ever you are in trouble of any sort, come and tell me at once."

"Thank you very much, Mr. Champneys."

"That 's all. Good-night, Fancy."

"Good-night, Mr. Champneys."

In the days that followed she found it impossible to evade the realisation of the metamorphosis taking place in George Champneys, or to gauge rightly the effect reacting upon herself. It was as though through the glance of an eye she had jumped several years' experience. The need for considering and understanding these readjustments was urgent. Even the affair of Isabel became of secondary importance.

It was not that he spoke much to her, or acted towards her with any manifest difference. It was just the way his eye dwelt upon her with a faraway, hang-dog appeal, and when he did speak to her she noticed that the timbre of his voice warmed perceptibly. Her intuitions told her that he desired her intensely.

The immediate outcome of this realization was a consuming sense of pride. She examined herself in the mirror at various angles. She subjected her natural charms to a searching analysis, and came out of the ordeal with flying colours. She was, indeed, a pretty woman, a woman of the world, a woman sought after, a person of considerable importance, and only the previous week the mirror had told her nothing about all this. She was all aglow and aquiver with a novel sense of assurance and delight. She read the yearning and the pathos in his eyes, and her heart went out to him. How tragic it seemed that a man like he, a darling of the people, a man whom everyone regarded as the personification of success and fun, should carry this secret sorrow in his heart. She visualised the wild nights of triumph, the shouts and cheers: "George! George! Bravo, George!" and then the utter loneliness and melancholy of his home. Poor George! Why hadn't he married years ago? He must be forty-six? forty-seven? and she was twenty-two. Of course, the whole idea was ridiculous. She could never marry him, but oh! there was something very wonderful in being loved. There was something very wonderful in realising the power of love. Love. Power! The connection could not be idly disregarded. The Billy Hamaton affair was an episode, an incident. If George loved her she would have to face the potentialities of dynamic action. George was not a person to be dismissed or passed over lightly. The day would come rapidly when she would have to show her hand.

Of course, he was not the knight of her dreams, but does a girl ever meet the knight of her dreams? Besides is she always certain to recognise him? Does anything ever happen as we expect it? He was so good, so kind, the dearest friend she had in the world. When the test came she would have not only to have the measure of her own emotions and desires, but to face the cleavage of two very definite material positions. On the one hand dismissal, drifting away into obscurity, possibly touring with third-rate companies, being out of work for months on end, calling on those objectionable agents, being insulted and "mauled about." On the other hand, the certainty of a "lead" in one of the most popular theatres in London, fame, considerable wealth Power. Oh, yes, there was certainly something very wonderful in the power of love!

One morning, whilst dwelling on these disturbing reflections, there came a telegram from Isabel:

"Come and see me. Am all right. Isabel"

She was at the flat within half an hour. She found Isabel in bed. in charge of a queer middle-aged woman, who said:

"You must keep quiet and not mug her about. Don't shake the bed. She's all right, but she's got to stay there weeks yet."

Isabel looked very ill, and she wept a little when Barbara kissed her. Of the nature of her illness she would say nothing except:

"Thank God that's over, kiddy."

Barbara felt embarrassed. Such a lot had happened that week, and she and Isabel each had secrets they could not share. Never mind. Dear old Isabel! She would soon be her dear, sloppy, kind-hearted self again.

"Can I come back?" Barbara asked.

"Yes. Do come back, dear. I'm lonely. That hateful old woman.... You must be very quiet, though, and not make me cry."

Barbara promised, and that same afternoon found her re-established in the flat. Before she left for the theatre she went in to see Isabel again. She seemed feverish and worried. Barbara remembered her promise not to make her cry, so she said in a matter-of-fact voice:

"Is there anything else I can do, darling?"

She did not know why that innocent question should make Isabel cry again, but it did. At last, with their cheeks pressed together, Isabel whispered:

"Do you still love me, Fancy?"

"Of course I do, darling!"

"There's no one else, is there? You look different, kiddy brighter and prettier."

Barbara did not know how to reply, and Isabel suddenly added:

"It's like this, dear: I've no money, and that awful old woman wants ten quid by to-morrow morning."

"I'll pay it," said Barbara eagerly. "And any more that you want."

She left Isabel weeping with relief.

XI

At the theatre that night her sense of importance increased. She glanced at the other artistes and the stage hands to see if she could detect any signs of knowledge of the situation on their part. She peeped through the curtain and surveyed the packed house. What a lot of money it must hold! Rows and rows of people who had paid ten-and-sixpence for a seat. She had never thought about it that way before. Her mind was subtly intrigued by the image of proprietorship. And all these other people the "lights," the scene shifters, the assistant stage manager how different their attitude would be if they knew, or even suspected. She mustn't let them know or suspect, because, of course, the whole idea was ridiculous. One of the girls was short with her because she got in her way at an exit.

"I could put you in your place, my dear," she thought.

George was there early, watching out for her. She could tell that by the expression of his face, a little preoccupied, and then lighting up with pleasure, almost with relief, at sight of her. He smiled and regarded her wistfully across a group of people, but there was no opportunity to speak. Between the acts she avoided him intentionally, and before the show was over she left. This silent communion went on for several weeks, and the commitment was no less definite for not being outwardly expressed. She observed the struggle going on in him, the lines of. desire deepen about his eyes and mouth. Occasionally he would make excuses for touching her when they were waiting in the wings. On these occasions she would feel the deliberate message of the contact. He would look at her hungrily, and whisper, so that the others could not hear:

"Barbara, Barbara."

She knew that the position could not remain long so, and when one night he said: "Barbara I want you to come out to my place and lunch with me tomorrow," she felt relieved, although still utterly unprepared for action.

The lunch was a curiously constrained entertainment. They were waited on by an elderly housekeeper who did most of the talking. The great comedian for once had lost his touch. He was sombre and ill at ease. She felt that the positions had been reversed. She was no longer a child. He was the child, and she a grown woman. She mothered him into a state of subjection, and when the old woman had retired it was she who suggested that they should adjourn to the studio. Once there, she managed to get him ensconced in the big easy chair by the fireplace, while she sat some way off, and chatted indifferently about the affairs of the theatre. She tried manfully to plug up the gaps and reticences with gossip and mirth, till she became painfully aware that her measures were but a temporary shift. Her defensive chatter was like attacking an elephant with a pea-shooter. He was occupied avidly with his eyes, and with his ears not at all.

At last he rose, and stood with his legs wide apart and his back to the fire. Steadying his voice he said with quiet emphasis:

"Do you know that Rosie Ventnor's contract expires next month?"

What was the significance of that? What was he implying? Surely not that she.... She snapped out breezily:

"Really? Well, you'll renew it, of course. She surely won't be leaving?"

He held her in an inquisitorial glance as he murmured:

"It all depends."

She knew then that the issue was joined. George was coming out into the open. She must gather together her scattered, unprepared forces. She repeated mechanically:

"It all depends?"

"Yes. On you."

Having delivered his message, he advanced slowly upon her, before the flavour of this glittering implication had had time to dissipate. She was indeed held by it, his own propinquity for the moment disregarded. She... the star of the Frivolities! As in a dream she was aware of being picked out of her chair and crushed in his arms. From a long way off she seemed to hear the low, vibrant notes of his voice.

"Oh, Barbara, Barbara. You know I love you, don't you? Give me your lips. I want you. Barbara, Barbara."

The effort appeared to wind him. His breath came in short stabs.

She hung rigid in his arms, her eyes closed. He kissed her lips, but she did not respond. Somewhere in the house someone was practicing a scale. The sound took hold of her. All her physical, mental and moral being was in a state of suspense. She could neither think nor focus. He was hurting her as he puffily sought to make her respond to his embraces.

She cried out limply:

"Oh oh, Mr. Champneys no, please!"

"Barbara, I love you. Can't you? can't you?"

At last he withdrew his arms and lips, stung to reaction by her lack of reciprocity. He had found out the answer to the query which had been torturing him for weeks. She did not respond. She did not love him. He held no physical attraction for her. Fool! what could he expect? The position was not without hope, though. He had failed to carry the ramparts by storm, but other methods could be tried. He meandered helplessly to the fireplace, and buried his face in his hands. He looked a pathetic figure standing there, a large, unhappy child. She pitied him, and desired intensely to envelop him with maternal tenderness.

"I'm so sorry, Mr. Champneys. Oh, you have been so kind to me. You are one of the few dear friends I have. My dear, I'm so sorry. It's only that somehow I..."

She could not express herself. He shrugged his shoulders and spoke in a low, husky tone:

"I know, I know, old girl. I know I had no right to ask you. I wanted to ask you to marry me, but I know it's all utterly absurd. I'm twenty-three years older than you, Barbara. I'm battered, shop-worn. I've played ducks and drakes with all the ten commandments. You're only a kid."

"I wouldn't care about all that side of it," she flashed out, trying to relieve him.

He regarded her thoughtfully.

"No, you wouldn't care about that side of it, only that you feel it. Your intuitions, eh? I revolt you—"

"No, no, no."

Suddenly he turned away, and cried out desperately:

"There's one thing I won't have your pity. If you can't love me we must cut it out. But I can't stand you pitying me, Barbara. See! You can't think how that would torture me. When a man asks for love and only gets pity, my God! it's apt to drive him mad. I should think of you almost laughing at me—"

"Oh, my dear, I'm too fond of you for that."

"No, no, but it might come. There would always be the ugly dread. I believe I could make you love me, Barbara. To a girl like you—you don't understand love would come afterwards. It's better for you to be loved than to love. God! I would be good and loyal to you. I would surround you with everything you wish. I would be tender. I would never do anything you did not approve of. I would make you famous, if you desire it rich."

Yes, the material issues were clear enough. She had no illusions on that score. Their very definiteness augmented her sense of an outrage on her liberty her freedom to decide, her freedom to develop on her own lines. She spoke in a voice under complete control for the first time during the interview.

"What did you mean, George, when you said it all depends!"

He looked puzzled.

"What did I mean! What do you mean, Barbara?"

"I was thinking of the alternative."

He snatched at her meaning, and shook his large head almost angrily.

"Oh, I wasn't meaning to blackmail you, Barbara. I don't want to tempt you like that. It's only that well, if you won't have me, I simply couldn't have you in the theatre. I couldn't stand it, you see. I wouldn't let you down. I would get you a good tour, or a part somewhere else. I'd pay you. I'd do anything you like, only I couldn't bear having you so near me, torturing me to distraction. If you'd have me, well, it's natural for a man to do everything for his wife's career, if she wants to have a career. And it isn't as though I should be foisting inferior goods on the public for personal reasons. I should be proud of you. You'd soon be as clever and popular as Rosie Ventnor."

George made this statement quite simply and sincerely, little suspecting what a big influence it would have upon his case. He saw her face flush with eagerness, her troubled brow clear with relief. Not so hopeless, after all. She's a little unstrung. Leave her alone. Give her time to reflect.

He smiled at her in his old friendly way and held out his hand.

"I'm worrying you, old girl. I didn't mean to do that. Now, you trot along home and think about it. Only don't keep me in this state of torment long."

At the door she kissed him rather primly on the cheek, and said:

"You're a dear nice person."

XII

She did not tell Isabel about her affair till two days later. She was impatient with her friend's illness. She would have liked to have dined out with her at some gay restaurant, and over a bottle of red wine lain bare her soul. Isabel was still flaccid and entirely concentrated on her own troubles. She had irretrievably lost her place at Daly's and she would probably be unable to work for months. She had no money, and appeared to have contracted various inexplicable debts. Poor old Isabel! Barbara did not mind that. Her money was Isabel's money, so far as it went. But it was beginning to dawn upon her that in a short while it would hardly go far enough. Bills came in for all kinds of luxuries the girls had indulged in before Isabel's illness. Isabel had been hopelessly vague in money matters, and Barbara had been careless. Now she realized that all her available capital was gone, and that they were depending entirely on her own small salary and the cheque for 33 10s. which the lawyers sent her every month. This was a sheet anchor, and she felt that whilst there was that to rely on she could go on borrowing and running up bills indefinitely. These were trivial considerations, if only Isabel would be her old self. She was bursting to discuss George's proposal with someone, and so on the second day she went out and bought a bottle of port. After lunch she poured out two glasses, one for Isabel and one for herself, then, to her annoyance, found that Isabel had been forbidden to drink anything alcoholic for some weeks. So she drank her own glass, and, still lacking the encouragement of her friend's response, she began on the other. Then she talked.

"You know I lunched with George Champneys the day before yesterday, darling? Well, I haven't told you he proposed to me."

Isabel sat up in bed, her eyes vividly awake at last.

"He proposed to you! What marriage!"

"Yes, of course."

"My God!"

"What do you think, Isabel?"

"You lucky little devil!"

"Would you marry him?"

"Marry him! Of course you'll marry him. You are the luckiest little devil I've ever struck."

"But, listen, darling. That's what I want to talk to you about. You see, I'm very fond of him, very fond of him indeed he's a perfect dear but I don't love him, you know not really. I don't feel I want him. I don't love him as much as I do you darling."

"My Lord! do you realise what this means? It means "lead" for you forever, and you can wangle all your pals into fat parts. It means you're made. George is rich. You'll have a big house, and a car, and dine at the Savoy and the Carlton. You'll get into all the papers. You'll be another May Mendelssohn without having to push for it like she's had to. Oh, you lucky little wretch!"

"Yes, but, darling, I know all that but do you think you could be happy with a man you don't really love?"

"Love! You'd soon get to love him. He's a white man, George, a good chap. He'll play the game by you."

"That's what I want to know. He said it was almost a promise that love would come after. Is it possible? Does it ever come after?"

"Of course it does. It would with you. You can be taught to love in the same way that you can be taught to sing and dance, if you have a natural talent for it. And if anybody has, you have. You're a passionate little devil. A man would have a good time with you. Excuse my crudeness, but you know what I mean."

The port-wine had gone to Barbara's head. She regarded Isabel's statement without disgust. She wanted to know the truth of things. She ruminated.

"When he kissed me, I didn't mind it. I wasn't revolted, as he suggested. I only felt that I didn't want to kiss him in reply."

"You wait till you've been kissed properly a few times; you'll soon want to reply."

"Isabel darling, all this 'mauling about' you speak of, what does it mean?"

"It means that when you've been kissed properly it gets into your blood. You can't do without it. That's why I'm no, I can't tell you anything. You're an innocent lamb. But I'll tell you this. You could soon get to love George in that particular way if you like him very much in the other way."

"Isn't there a kind of combination, where you love a man in every way?"

"Yes, in novels and plays, not in real life, except perhaps one in ten thousand. Don't you be a fool. You're on a good thing. If George was rich and influential, and a blackguard. I'd say no, cut it out. But he isn't; everybody in the profession knows that George is all right."

Barbara finished up her second glass of port and kissed Isabel more passionately than the occasion seemed to demand.

"You're a darling old thing," she said. "I suppose it means I shall do it."

Her decision, however, swung backwards and forwards like the pendulum of a clock. When the effects of the port had worked off she decided not to do it. On a walk just after tea she decided to do it. On her way to the theatre she said "No." "While the orchestra was tuning up she thought "Yes." When she went to bed at night she murmured, "No, no, no; a thousand times no."

The following evening, just after dinner, she promised George Champneys to marry him.

XIII

The announcement of her engagement to George created a thrill beyond her wildest expectations. As she anticipated, the, attitude of everyone at the theatre changed electrically., Rosie Ventnor and the other girls embraced her as though she was, and always had been, their dearest friend. Sydney Ebbway and his male colleagues treated her- as a person of consequence, and not an insignificant little understudy. Stage-hands who had hitherto ignored her touched their hats and said: "Good evening, miss." The assistant stage-manager, who had been rude and abrupt with her, cringed with civility. Moreover, her name appeared instantaneously in nearly every daily paper. "Hearty congratulations to George Champneys! We have the pleasure to announce that the famous comedian is engaged to Miss Fancy Telling, a promising young actress at present understudying at the Frivolity. The wedding is to take place shortly."

"At present" had a thrill of its own. Three weekly illustrated papers published her portrait. Seven photographers wrote begging to be allowed to take her photograph free of charge. The leaves were already whispering in the winds of triumph. The decision being taken, she was determined to give no hostages to fortune, to indulge in no regrets or fears. George was a person worthy of her love, and she would love him to the very best of her ability. She had no standard by which to judge the nature of her affection. That she was fond of him she knew. She admired his genius, his strength, his simplicity. She felt happy and proud in his society. She desired to have charge of him, to minister to his wants, to mother his weaknesses. And of that other love, had not Isabel said it could be learnt? Had not George said nay, promised that it would come afterwards? In the meantime the days and nights were crowded with a thousand anticipations and delights. Amidst their welter one thought stood out. Once married to George, she would reject the dole her father had flung her. She would free herself of the Powerscourt taint. The price had been paid. In marrying George she would perhaps reconnect the chain which her mother's misjudgment had snapped. Where her mother had failed she would succeed. She would justify her mother. She would carry on her story to a happier and worthier climax.

George's days were very occupied, and there was little time for dalliance. He gave her a wonderful diamond and emerald engagement ring, and having placed it on her finger he patted her hand, smiling in an expansive and possessive manner, as much as to say:

"There, my dear, that's that."

When they were alone he was tenderness itself, a little humble and sentimental. She observed that, although he kissed her, he very seldom "kissed her properly," to quote Isabel's phrase. He seemed terrified of shocking or frightening her. She had never realised before how pliable a strong man may become. She could do anything with him she liked: he was her slave. This sense of power, although it intoxicated her, fortified some of her saner resolutions. In the first place, she decreed that Rosie Ventnor was not to be dismissed so summarily. The action would appear, and be, crude and venomous. She suggested that at first she should play a minor part in the revue, and then, if she made good and the London public liked her, she should eventually take a lead in a later production. George readily acquiesced, and he was pleased with her for suggesting this. In the first place, Rosie Ventnor was a popular favorite, a draw, and Fancy Telling was quite unknown. In the second place, he was not fully persuaded that she was endowed with sufficient sense of comedy to fill a niche evacuated by the popular Rosie. Barbara was a better singer and a better dancer, but she lacked the gift of burlesque. She was always herself; she had no power of imitation. She had the joy of life, and she was not without humour, but it was the humour of high spirits and good health. Her humour was never acid, or mordant, or particularly subtle.

In his present mood he would have sacked Rosie at a moment's notice to please Barbara, but his managerial acumen applauded her decision. Not only was she a dear, warm-hearted, passionate, entirely innocent little thing, but she was sensible. During his life George had found that beauty and sense were seldom bed-fellows.

He bestirred himself to please her in other ways. His bachelor house at South Kensington would have to be renovated and brought up to date. The thought of it made him shudder. He had an excellent housekeeper, an excellent cook, a reliable valet, who also acted as a dresser, and several other servants who had been with him for years. How would they welcome the invasion of a mistress? The establishment had got into a bit of a groove, perhaps, but how smoothly and perfectly it worked! George was of opinion that anyone doing his kind of work must have all his creature comforts liberally catered to. At home he wore a shabby old suit and carpet slippers, but everything in the household was ideally arranged. In the morning when he awoke he pressed a bell which set the domestic machinery in motion. Tea was brought him on a tray; his bath was turned on with the water regulated to exactly the right temperature; clean linen and clothes were put out for him; when he arrived in the breakfast-room the silver entree-dish was awaiting him and the tea made, his letters in a neat pile, with a silver cutter by their side, and the daily papers in an orderly array on the other side of the table; after breakfast the fire would be glowing in the library, some two dozen beloved pipes in a rack by the sideboard, probably his secretary awaiting him with a report of last night's returns. He was a chubby-faced young man, and he would call out: "Good morning, guv'nor."

Then the day's work would begin. And the domestic arrangements dovetailed themselves with silent perfection into the demands of the day's work. He did not even say whether he would be in to meals. A man in his position can't commit himself to such trivialities. Anything might happen. He might say yes, and then the telephone would go, and he would have to rush down to the theatre, or to lunch with a syndicate or a colleague. And so these perfectly cooked meals were always there if he required them, and if he brought three or four people in unexpectedly it seemed to make no difference. Furniture was polished, curtains cleaned, clothes repaired, breakages replaced, coal stored for the winter, rooms vacuum-cleaned, the garden kept in order, enormous quantities of food and drink stowed away in cellars, and then either cooked, eaten, drunk, wasted or destroyed.

And from all these details George kept carefully aloof. He did not even pay the bills. Every week this competent and masterful housekeeper, whose name was Mrs. Piddinghoe, had an interview with the competent and masterly secretary, Mr. Toller, in the library. She presented all the bills, and he gave her cheques for some and cash for others. If you had asked George whether cheese was as expensive as York ham, or whether thirty shillings a week for a bachelor's laundry was rather a lot, he would not have known the answer. The theatre was playing to capacity, and whether his household expenses came to forty pounds a month or one hundred and forty did not seem of much importance.

Neither had he ever known the shifts and struggles of most successful actors. He had always been rich. His father made a large fortune with a dyeworks in Lancashire, and it had all been divided between George and his brother, who was a shipbroker in Liverpool. After going to Rugby he had spent two years at Owen's College, Manchester, and from there had entered his father's dye-works with a view to taking an active part in the business. He showed, however, little aptitude for it, and office life cramped him. His fine baritone voice and droll sense of fun delighted his friends but annoyed his father, who was a hard-headed Primitive Methodist. At the end of three years they quarrelled, and George was threatened with the risk of learning by experience the relative values of ham and cheese, when his father died suddenly from blood-poisoning as the result of a trivial accident in his own works. No will was found, and so the estate which was assessed at one hundred and forty-five thousand pounds was divided between the two brothers. The mother had died when they were at school.

George then packed up his traps and came to London. He had not at first any idea of the stage or of the theatrical enterprise. He was young and rich, and he desired to see the world. He stayed at a club in Jermyn Street, and there he made friends, entertained, and went to concerts and theatres. The only thing in the nature of work which he indulged in was to have singing lessons from a well-known professor. After a dozen or so lessons the professor became irritated with him. He said:

"I can't make you out, Champneys. You've got a good voice, but I can't make you do anything with it. It's just as though you're laughing at yourself all the time."

George sighed, and reflected deeply upon this criticism. He began to realise that it was true. He could sing a parody of an Italian opera, or a German opera, with a richness and fullness of voice that would have done credit to some of the leading opera singers themselves, but when he attempted to sing seriously it never came off. Well, perhaps the professor was right. He didn't take himself seriously. "Why should he, after all? He would see what experience the Continent had to offer him.

He went to Paris, Vienna, and Buda-Pest, and indulged in the normal dissipations of those cities. Then he went on to Milan, Venice, and Florence, and at Fiesole he experienced the first great love affair of his life. She was a pretty woman, the wife of an American who was comfortably ensconced in his own country. The intrigue was unquestionably sordid, but wrapped up in the romantic glamour of ilex groves, Renaissance temples, and the perfume of white flowers by moonlight. She was staying alone at the hotel, but was known by many people. They had to be circumspect, and therefore sordid. So great, however, became the call of their mutual passion that they sneaked away, and lived together for six weeks at Rapallo. That was the golden era of George's life. When afterwards he dreamed of love, when afterwards he had other experiences, that pervading vision would haunt him the yellow sands of the little bay, the villa entangled with flowers against the dark trees, Maisie leaning over the balcony, holding out her arms. In that vision dwelt the flavour of perpetuity.

She got frightened at last frightened of her friends, of her fate, of her husband. He tried to persuade her to stay with him for ever, but her nerves were all unstrung. She must go away. Oh yes, at once to-day. Maisie was like that impetuous darling!

XIV

He never saw her again. He wrote innumerable letters, but they were never answered. He wandered disconsolately back to Paris. He had a vague idea of continuing singing and perfecting his French. To this end he stayed at a quiet hotel in Etoile and sought a new professor. For a time he worked stolidly, avoiding the, normal distractions of the Gay City. He went to theatres, but more with the idea of studying French and French acting than of enjoying himself. The attic spirit of French comedy and satire intrigued him. He got introduced to a famous comedian, with whom he made friends, and it was in his house that he met Licette Rameau, a fair-haired, vivacious young actress, at that time playing an insignificant part at the Odeon. Mutual attraction quickly ripened into a passionate attachment. Eight months after the disappearance of Maisie he was keeping Licette in a little flat near the Quai d'Orsay. He became absorbed into Parisian theatrical life, where many distinguished men kept their mistresses and were a little proud of the achievement, and not infrequently took them about with their wives. During that time George learnt a lot about the technique of the French theatre, as well as about the technique of love and the ordering of a good dinner. It cannot be said that Licette treated him very well. At the end of a year he discovered that she was getting commissions from tradespeople for the goods he was supplying her! And when, a few weeks later, he happened to come in unexpectedly one evening, and found a fair-haired minor poet hiding in the bathroom, he decided that the time had come to part.

It was at about that time that he met Miles Ronnie. He was a theatrical manager who had gone to Paris to see whether there was anything worth adapting. In George he found the very man he was looking for. George knew everything that was on, was a shrewd judge, and spoke French fluently. The outcome of their few days' acquaintanceship was that George agreed to translate and adapt a French farce. He arrived in London a few weeks later with the farce nicely trimmed up and bowdlerised for the English stage. Miles Ronnie was very pleased with it, and decided to send it on tour; but what most impressed him was the value of George at rehearsals. He was a born comedian.

"Why in God's name don't you come into the business?" he asked one day.

George laughed. Why should he go into the business? Nevertheless he found himself restless and bored when not doing something connected with the theatre. One day he had a bright idea. He would write a revue on the pattern of the French revue. He would write the libretto and some of the lyrics, and get hold of some rising young composer to do the score. The farce had gone on tour and was being a reasonable success. Miles Bonnie was enthusiastic at the idea of the revue, so he settled down to work. And then one evening at Ronnie's house he found himself gazing into the eyes of Peggy Alcester. They were deep grey wistful eyes, with just sufficient maliciousness to keep them from being sentimental. George said to himself:

"George, old boy, it's time you settled down."

He spent an inspiriting summer, writing and producing the revue, and making love to Peggy. In July the revue was produced, and failed. In August he proposed to Peggy and was accepted. Of the revue Ronnie said:

"It's a damn good revue, Champneys, only too close to the French model. You can't expect to get our people to act it."

The failure of the revue annoyed George intensely. He felt that he had done good work, but that he had been misunderstood, and misinterpreted. Peggy went down to Cornwall with some friends, and in spite of the temptation to follow her he decided to reconsider some of the revue, rehearse it again, and play the leading comedian's part himself, just to see whether it couldn't be made a success. Ronnie had laid out a lot of money on it, and George felt that he had rather let him down. The marriage was arranged for October.

The revue was put into rehearsal again, and George was an enormous success as a fat showman. A seasoned company could hardly get through rehearsals for laughing at him. The night for the new edition was announced.

Going down to the stage for the dress rehearsal he met a telegraph-boy, who handed him a telegram. When he read it he groaned, and collapsed in the stone passage. Peggy had been drowned bathing at Trevagissy.

After that he sulked from the stage, he sulked from life. In a state of extreme depression he went to stay with his brother in Liverpool, and made a tentative survey of ship-broking, finance, and religion. Something within him hardened and crystallised. He felt that he had been badly treated by life. He wallowed in self-pity. He almost decided to become religious, to marry some decent girl, whether he liked her or not, have children, go into business, deal with the world on its own terms. But the women he met in his brother's circle bored him to a frenzy. He knew nothing of their world, and they knew nothing of his. High finance gave him a headache. In a short while he found himself sneaking away alone to theatres or music-halls, and creeping into the bars of obscure pubs in search of congenial society.

One day he met a man shortly leaving for New York. An impulsive desire came over him to visit the New World. He managed to secure a berth on the outgoing liner. On the voyage he had an affair with a French widow; it was highly distracting, but did not touch him very profoundly. At Hoboken they swore eternal fidelity, and never saw each other again. In New York George found society after his own heart in various clubs the Lambs, the Lotus and the Players. It was April, and the atmosphere of New York acted like wine. His vitality had never been so high. His previous experiences paled before this blast of American hospitality. This was indeed a new world. He was always in demand for his songs, his droll stories, his genial personality. He became tremendously excited by the warmth of his reception. He would be up half the night, and yet not be tired the next day. And then he met James Byron Eberfeld, who was taking a star company of top-notchers to tour the middle Western States, and James proposed that he should accompany them. The idea fitted in with his mood, and so he made his first professional appearance in Columbus, Ohio. He little suspected on that opening night in Columbus that he was destined to climb to the top of the tree. They were away five months, and although the tour was a great success, George was not conspicuously successful. They enjoyed his singing, but he was handicapped by his ignorance of the vernacular. His humour was a little too English in diction and French in method, and at the same time he had actually had very little experience, and his face and figure had not filled out to that expansive condition which later on invited a laugh in itself. They were a congenial, good-tempered company, and he learned to play poker, and eat clams and hashed beef and squash pie, and by the end of the tour his knowledge of cocktails was not to be despised.

Returning to New York at the beginning of September, he plunged into a wild and unaccountable mood of dissipation. He had probably arrived at the apex of his physical powers, and his moral powers offered little resistance. He was drunk with the partial success of his own theatrical experiences. The wine of glamour and publicity had gone to his head. Backed by his own considerable fortune he foresaw the possibilities of achieving a great success. In any case he had found out what he was fitted for, and the realisation gave him a sense of freedom. The stage was his destiny, and he would worry about women and domestic happiness no longer. Women? Yes, but not as co-mates or companions. - Nothing should stand between him and the flattery of the crowd, the augmentation of his individuality. He was astute enough to see that he would have to go back home. In America there were many and excellent comedians working in their own particular genre; he would not be able to compete with them, but in London or Paris he would be in his normal environment. Although the vision dazzled him, he could not make up his mind to leave New York. He had drifted into a dubious company of underworld spirits. He began to drink and carouse and eat into the capital of his conscience. He lived in a flat in Twenty-Sixth Street with Betty Saskewan, a woman with the record of a degenerate, who still retained certain opulent charms. They gave parties which could only be described as orgies. This unaccountable wave of depravity lasted eight months. George's figure grew fat and puffy, his face flabby and lax, his eyes dull and heavily lined. And then one day he was seized with a serious illness. He was sent to a nursing-home and had to undergo a major operation. He hovered between life and death, and Betty vanished into the Ewigkeit. He was in the nursing-home two months, and then went up to the Adirondacks to recuperate. One day he looked at himself in the mirror, and he said:

"This won't do, old boy, this won't do. Cut it out, old boy, cut it out!"

He pulled himself together and obeyed the doctor. He reviewed this period of abysmal folly through a blurred mirror of introspection. He was not fundamentally a depraved and vicious man. Truly he liked good things, and he had the material means and the physical abundance to obtain and enjoy them. He was a spiritual opportunist, a little abnormal and weak. He had been spoilt by good fortune, a strong frame, and a complete lack of incentive. He was just carried along by the riches of his vitality. But now his vitality was a little broken his fortune considerably impaired, and he was lonely. That was it; he became convinced that the basic cause of his unwarranted outbreak was the condition of utter loneliness. If only Maisie or Peggy if he had only met Maisie or Peggy when he was quite a young man, how different he might be now! He had wandered over the earth seeking love, and he had found only entertainment. And soon he would be reaching that stage when he could no longer compel love the thought horrified him. Women would pity him; they would throw crumbs of pity to his hungry heart. He had never been good-looking, and now he was already getting a little passe, shop-worn.

When well enough, he went shamefacedly back to New York, and took the next boat to England. After his New York experiences the more staid atmosphere of London fitted in with his contrite mood. He went back to his old club in Jermyn Street and sought out some of his old theatrical friends. He met a man named Morgan Menges and they started a Pierrot entertainment of six, three men and three girls, at an obscure concert-hall at Netting Hill. The entertainment was a complete failure. George was unknown, and he had got rather out of touch with the topical feeling of London at that time. Moreover, people at Notting Hill don't go to Pierrot entertainments. They lost several hundred pounds, and the partnership broke up.

George was not unduly discouraged. Although he had squandered a good part of his fortune he was still a comparatively wealthy man; he could afford to start again. He was now middle-aged, but he knew that he was at the zenith of his powers. He engaged a company of his own and took the lease of a small hall in Great Portland Street. He advertised the entertainment extensively. It took London three years to recognise that in George Champneys it had a comedian quite out of the common. Then he began to come into his own. That three years hard work cost him several thousand pounds, but it made his name. He received innumerable offers from theatrical managers. Whilst hesitating about his next move an aunt in Scotland died and left him an estate consisting of a large bleak house in Fifeshire and many thousand acres of land in varying stages of cultivation. He went up and inspected it, with a vague idea of "settling down." He spent one night there, and awoke to the horror of his loneliness. It was winter-time and the place was buried in a thick white mist. Dripping cattle glared menacingly at him on the moors. The natives appeared frigid and unresponsive.

"Oh, no, old boy," he said, as he drove back to the station; "you've still got a sense of humour Don't kill it."

He eventually sold the whole estate for twenty thousand pounds. On his return to London the great opportunity arose. By a great deal of wrangling behind the scenes he obtained a fourteen years lease of the Frivolity Theatre. He engaged some of the best artists of the day, librettists, composers, conductors and actors. He welded the ideas of a dozen people into a gigantic Pierrot entertainment, fortified by rather elaborate scenery and properties. He played the principal part himself, but he was careful to see that the rest of the company were not only good artists but that they had names. The thing began reasonably well, and, its success increased like a snowball being rolled down a hill. Within a year it was the one big attraction of the town. George worked hard and spent money lavishly. New material was constantly introduced, new ideas, songs, gags, scenes, properties purchased regardless of cost. Surprisingly ignorant on matters of business and finance, he nevertheless had the knack of picking the right man for the job. He had clever managers, and secretaries and producers men who had been in it all their lives.

The effect of this sudden leap to fame and success reacted upon him rather surprisingly. It made him swollen-headed and egotistical, but in a manner that it was easy to conceal. Generally speaking, it mellowed him. He became essentially calmer, more considerate of others, gentler and kinder. Everyone connected with the theatre adored him. Perhaps under the circumstances it was not difficult to be generous and kind; but the quality of consideration for others is always rare. It was as though the emotional experiences of his life had disillusioned him in the search for personal gratification; he had become simply the medium for the entertainment of his fellow-man. He regarded himself detachedly, but with a comfortable sense of complacency. Spiritually, perhaps, he had settled down.

As the years went on this aspect of him became more accentuated. If the loneliness were there it was warmed by the glow of service and accomplishment. Emotional dreams were destroyed by the friction of physical realities. "Put it all by, old boy, put it all by."

He was quite happy; too busy to be otherwise. Erotic desires were captive to the bow and spear of youth. Heigho! a man who ceases to desire cannot be said to resist temptation. The star of his moral abstractions was becoming fixed. His pulses beat to the steady rhythm of ordered life.

And then one day he beheld Barbara whom he had known for three years and he realised that he was seeing her for the first time. Her hair was ruffled, her eyes troubled, tears swimming in their mystic depths. She was unhappy, wanting something terribly, hungry for the thing he had missed. The desire to touch her was almost irresistible la pauvre innocente!

XV

The wedding was as quiet as it is possible for a theatrical wedding to be. That is to say, that it was understood that only intimate friends of the bride and bridegroom were to be invited, but many people got wind of it, and the little church at Kensington was fairly crowded when these two went through a service which neither of them believed in, and when Barbara promised to love, honour and obey one of the greatest comedians of his time.

It took place in August, between the run of two productions, so that they were able to get away for two weeks "honeymoon. All the company were there, and George was in very good spirits. Barbara was solemn and wide-eyed, and Isabel wept abundantly. They went to St. Mawes, the little fishing village, opposite Falmouth, and Barbara persuaded herself that she had met the idol of her dreams. She was, indeed, deliriously happy. The weather was glorious, in spite of the heat. They bathed, lolled, and basked in the sun. George seemed to revert suddenly to boyhood. He was a child, whimsical, passionate, rather sentimental. He could not bear her out of his sight. He anticipated all her desires, waited on her, smothered her with kindness, presents, flowers, surprises. He sustained the fantastic mood that he had been in on that summer's afternoon when he found the three girls in the Stradlings' drawing-room and talked about the weird animals. He treated her alternately like a child and like a mother. That which he had vaguely yearned for all through life he found in the mere contact of her presence, the mere knowledge that she was there near him, needing him, relying on him.

Oh, but he would be good and tender with her. In the darkness of the night some of the ugly memories of the past would torture him. Was it too late? Was he justified in doing this thing? He had wealth, position, a name; but was that any recompense for what she was giving him? He would listen to her gentle breathing, and place his fat face against the strands of her hair scattered between the two pillows. He loved the perfume of her hair; it had the tang of vital essences. Maisie? Peggie? yes, but those other women! Oh, he would give Barbara everything; he would make up to her in passionate solicitude, tenderness, self-sacrifice. Would she in time give him that love he so avidly desired? Barbara was fond of him, but he had at present no physical attraction for her. She was a little bewildered, frightened, almost disgusted and he had promised her that "love would come after." Well, why not? How horribly hot the nights were! George was not his best in the hot weather.

His mind ran on the arrangements he would make in town. He would be anxious not to take advantage of his position, not to trespass upon her freedom unduly, not to worry her. They would have separate beds in the same room. She would like that better. She should have a dressing-room of her own, and a boudoir, and a maid. She should have the best parts, the best songs in the revues. And then, one day perhaps, she would have a child he passionately desired a child. It must be a girl, an infant Barbara.

Barbara lived in a dreamland in which anticipation was perhaps a more imminent factor than realisation. The sun shone on the dancing waters of the bay. Fishing-boats crept lazily hither and thither. The people in this old-world village were friendly and good to look upon. On the other side of the Carrick Roads the low line of the Cornish hills forms a broad vista of enchanting beauty, in which the details were invisible and mysterious, like that bold vision of the life which was before her.

George was a dear. She had done something big in marrying him, and her heart rejoiced. Back in London, she would be a person of importance a power. She would help people Isabel, that little girl-accompanist she had met on tour, odd, pathetic characters who had drifted across her life. She would look after George's house, make him happier and more comfortable. She had learnt profoundly how "to look after herself." On tour she had learnt how to cook, and sew, and mend. She knew the value of things, and how to economise, get the best out of the domestic equation. She should suggest that they have separate beds. George was restless, humid and noisy in bed perhaps one day she would be able to get a separate bedroom, and a dressing-room, and a maid. She would try and not interfere with him and his mode of life. She would not take advantage of her position as his wife. Then perhaps one day she would have a child. She passionately desired a child. It must be a boy, and his name well, there was time to discuss that later.

You see, they agreed about practically everything. They had great fun writing to the lawyer about Barbara's sacrifice of her father's legacy. George had no objection at all. He was very amused, and said he would like her to write the letter herself, and let him see how cleverly she worded it. And this is what Barbara wrote:

DEAR SIR,

Re Thomas Powerscourt Estate.

I beg to say that re the above I shall not require my allowance any longer, neither do I wish to have any say in the disposition of it. The money is just to go back into the pool. You can do what you like with it.

Yours faithfully,

BARBARA (POWERSCOURT).

When George read this letter he slapped his leg and the tears rolled down his cheeks with laughter.

"You're a perfect little lawyer," he cried. "Oh, dear! that's lovely! 'You can do what you like with it" and then the bracket round Powerscourt! Fancy, Fancy, come here and let me kiss you."

They motored all the way back from Falmouth, stopping a night at Exeter, a night at Winchester, and a night at Oxford. It was all very thrilling and beautiful, but the most thrilling moment to Barbara was when the car glided over Westminister Bridge and she beheld the House of Commons, and Big Ben, and the dim profile of the Abbey, like official portents welcoming her to the city she meant to conquer.

XVI

During their absence the house in South Kensington had been re-decorated, and to Barbara's delight she found a little white-panelled boudoir upholstered in powder-blue silk. It was for her very own.

"Oh, George, how clever of you!" she exclaimed. "My favourite colour!"

"Is it? Well, now, that's lucky," he answered. Then he suddenly gripped her from behind and, pressing his cheek against hers, he whispered hoarsely:

"Do you think I didn't know your favourite colour?"

She thrilled with delight as she yielded to his embrace. He was a thoughtful dear.

The efficient housekeeper, Mrs. Piddinghoe, was early in evidence. The house was spotless and in perfect order. Discreet maids appeared. Her things were unpacked and put away in drawers. Fresh flowers were in all the rooms. The mellow sound of a gong announced the prelude to a dinner, which she had not even had the onus of selecting.

"I don't want you to be bothered about any of these domestic things, old girl," George explained. Well, she was not particularly interested in domestic things. In her father's house she had been unconscious of them. On tour, and when living with Isabel, she had been brought into abrupt contact with them, and she had mastered them fairly successfully, but they did not give her any particular joy. She did not want to meddle in domestic things.

If during the course of the next few days she sometimes felt a slight jar upon her proprietary sense, in the idea that she was living in an hotel, or rather that she was living in George's house as an honoured guest, she consoled herself with the reflection that well, George liked to arrange things like that, and, after all, it was the theatre which mattered, her art, her career.

Even if she had wished it, there was indeed little time to worry about domestic affairs. Rehearsals of the new revue started at once. They spent nearly all day at the theatre. George would lunch at the club with some important man, whilst she went out with some of the girls to a restaurant. Before they left in the morning and after they got home at night, the telephone would be ringing, all kinds of people calling with messages, and scores, and contracts, and estimates, and songs to be tried, and dialogue to be read over. So great was the rush and strain that she quickly realised how valuable was this smoothly working domestic machine.

It was the action of this other machine the theatrical one which absorbed her attention at the moment. As Mrs. George Champneys she inspired interest and respect from everyone; moreover all the members of the company liked her. But when the machine began to get into operation she found that Fancy Telling was not such an impressive proposition as she had imagined. George was nominally the producer, but actually the producer was a young man with raven-black hair and eyes like an eagle, whose name was Julius Banstead. He was a live wire, and he positively frightened her. Incredibly quick and clever, he cared not a jot for any man or woman. He would even bully George, and George would take it like a lamb, knowing that Banstead was supreme at his job. The broad outline of the entertainment was but sketchily conceived. They had a mass of material which they welded together, ruthlessly discarding some, extemporising some. The thing was built up gradually. The stage seemed to be crowded by a bewildering collection of authors, composers, managers, engineers, choreographers, to say nothing of actors, all trying to assert their own individual claims. And in the midst of it all Julius Banstead darted hither and thither, exercising an autocratic sway. By his side was an assistant stage-manager with the book, and Banstead would frequently turn to him and say:

"We'll have all that out, Thomson."

There appeared to be no appeal; a stylographic pen destroyed the fair anticipations of more artistes than Fancy Telling. Her own part, which at first promised to be voluminous, was whittled down and whittled down. A scene in which she was to play a Dutch girl was cut out. He did not like her parody of a forlorn heroine in a costume play, and gave the part to another girl. He cut out her song about "An Afternoon in Tennessee," and reduced a skit concerned with an hotel lift, in which she played the part of a country girl up for the day, to a three-minutes turn, whereas it was originally intended to occupy twelve. When the final rehearsals were reached she found that this was all that was left to her, with the exception of two rather sentimental songs, one of which concerned a Venetian night and the other a "Lullaby Among the Reeds."

Rather disconsolately she appealed to George about this. The great man said: "Never mind, old girl; we'll work it up big later. Better to start slow. Banstead knows what's best."

His own part had expanded rather than diminished. But then George was the show. The people paid to come and see George, and they expected him to be on the stage nearly all the time. Banstead knew what was best.

Another disappointment was that not by any means could she persuade George or Banstead to engage Isabel. Her old friend was now well again, but out of work and very hard up. The only thing Barbara succeeded in doing was to get money out of George to send her. She sent her fifty pounds. When she spoke to George about engaging her he said:

"It's all fixed up, old girl. We'll try another time."

Banstead said:

"Isabel Weare? No, she's slow in the uptake. Mrs. Champneys. Not enough pep for this show."

She realised the truth of this. The whole thing was a wonderful sample of "pep." There were no waste spaces or holes. Nothing was sacrificed to sentimentality of association. Everything was fined down, worked at, polished till there was not a phrase or a note that would not tell. She sometimes wondered whether she herself was not the only "sacrifice to sentimentality of association." Certainly if she had not been George's wife she would not have secured this part.

The position reminded her of that day when she had met her father being smuggled off to the House of Commons, and when she tried to stop him, and she had felt that she was opposing her will to the will of vast blocks of interests. George and Banstead were somewhat the same. They represented a tradition, a machine. They were the agents of a stern popular demand.

She felt a little envious of the other three girls, Rosie Ventnor, Polly Ravasol and Gine Sterne. They were so finished, so self-confident, so professional. Between this standard of entertainment and the tours she had been used to there was a great gulf fixed. Well, there it was. She would make the best of her small chances, and perhaps one day she would excel them all. It was something to be on at a leading London show and the wife of a leading London showman.

One Sunday night George took her to the Savoy to supper. She tasted for the first time the glamour of publicity. Opulent-looking gentlemen and gorgeously dressed girls glanced at their table and whispered. She knew what they were saying:

"That's George Champneys. And that's Fancy Telling, the young actress he has just married."

They drank champagne and her eyes sparkled with the gaiety of this new adventure. When they had reached the Peche Melba stage a tall, well-dressed societyish girl came up to their table and said:

"Excuse me, isn't it Barbara?"

Barbara looked hard at her and exclaimed:

"Why, it's Cicely! Oh, Cicely, what ages! How are you, darling?"

Dear her! Cicely had altered. A formal, slightly supercilious smile played round the corners of her pretty mouth. She held out her hand primly, as though afraid that Barbara might embrace her.

"Yes, it's Cicely, Barbara."

"Oh, how ripping! This is my husband George Champneys. Oh, of course you know him! This is Cicely Stradling, George. Don't you remember? We met at her house."

The two shook hands. George had forgotten her, and Cicely said quickly:

"I'm here with my husband, too Colonel Huskisson. We are sitting over by the wall. Shall we have coffee together, and then we can exchange news?"

The husbands were formally introduced and they all took coffee together.

Yes, Cicely had changed. The lines about her mouth and eyes had hardened. She spoke with a slight drawl. Gone was all the girlish abandonment of that summer day. Her husband was a thin, sunburnt man with a grey moustache; he must have been a good ten or fifteen years older than Cicely. He appeared a little disconcerted at meeting the large comedian a little uncertain as to whether it was quite the thing to be seen in the company of theatrical people. Barbara eagerly pumped her freind for news.

"Where is Jean, Cicely!"

"Oh, Jean is married, too, my dear. She is in India. Her husband is a Government assessor. He travels a good deal; Jean lives mostly at Simla."

"Is she happy!"

"Oh, yes, she likes the life. She gets crowds of parties, and picnics, and riding."

Jean! jolly little chubby-faced Jean! What a long way off she seemed! not only physically, but what sort of life was this: parties and picnics and riding in Anglo-Indian society? She had lost them both, these two girls. In our youth we dream of perpetual friendships; and then we drift apart, and when we meet again there lies between us the heavy barrier of unfamiliar experiences. It sounded so jolly parties and picnics and riding but who knew what tragedy might lie behind it? And Cicely, with her formal graciousness and her perfectly-coiffured hair no, she didn't look happy. Only she, Barbara, was happy. She was already a few rungs up the ladder of fame. She was married to a dear and famous man. She was rich and popular, and living in a world congenial to her. This society life inhabited by Jean and Cicely was alien, frigid and unattractive.

How they had drifted apart, indeed! The champagne had gone a little to her head, and she sparkled and chatted to Cicely, telling her many details of her new life, of the thrill of experience, of the fame and generosity of her husband. Two young men at the next table were devouring her with their eyes, and their attention added an elfish glamour to the narrative of triumph.

It was getting late when Cicely suddenly remarked:

"Sad about poor Billy Hamaton, wasn't it?"

Barbara felt a strange contraction of her heart. So absorbed had she been in the record of her vital experiences she had not even talked about Billy. She had forgotten Billy and the days when they four were all children together. And here was Cicely saying in the same chilling voice she employed for every remark: "Sad about poor Billy Hamaton." What did she mean? Barbara puckered her brows and could not frame the question.

Cicely continued in the same tones:

"Haven't you heard? He died three months ago."

"What?"

She wanted to scream. She wanted to cry out to all these well-dressed people.

"Leave off eating, and drinking, and flirting; oh, leave off! Billy is dead he died three months ago, and I was the cause of his death. And I never even asked about him. I was cruel and utterly callous. If the branch of that tree had not broken he would now be my husband not George. I can see his young, jolly, freckled face right up in the leaves against the sky, his brown hair all awry. I can hear his laughing voice: 'Come on, then, my flibbertigibbet. "And then he sat by my side on the branch, and there seemed to be no earth beneath, only this green fairway leading to the heavens, and he said, 'I love you, Barbara. "And then... and then....Oh, God!"

She looked around stonily at the festive scene. One of the young men at the next table openly smiled at her, challenging her with his eyes. George was smoking a cigar, and saying in his deep actor's voice:

'I tell you where you can get the best Napoleon brandy in the world at Fleuret's. It's in a little street just off the Faubourg St. Honore; I can't remember the name. I used to know old Fleuret very well. He won't part with it unless he likes your face, and then he charges twelve francs for a nip "

She rose and touched his shoulder.

"We must be going, George. I want to go."

He regarded her sleepily.

"All right, old girl. We won't be five minutes."

She shrank back in her chair, her impulses held in check by the heavy pressure of her environment.

XVII

The revue was called "Black and White" a title justified (the programme explained) by the connection of the costumes of the Pierrot troupe with the spirit of the age and it proved to be one of the most successful of the Frivolity productions. With various additions, excisions and slight alterations it ran for a year. Barbara's two songs went better than she had expected, and "The Lullaby Among the Reeds "was encored nightly, and made its appearance on barrel organs and in the vocal exploits of ambitious young ladies in suburban drawing-rooms. She sang both songs extremely well, and in an alluring black-and-white silk frock and ruffles she made a figure not unworthy of this distinguished group. She was disappointed that nearly all the Press reviews spoke only of George and Rosie Ventnor and the droll Mr. Ebbway, and that the best notice of herself only said:

"A song likely to catch on is 'The Lullaby Among the Reeds.'" It was charmingly rendered by Miss Fancy Telling (now Mrs. George Champneys), who promises to be a useful addition to the clever company."

Nevertheless she felt that on the whole she had no cause for complaint. She had been tested and not found wanting. All the company were charming to her. George was so excited on the first night that he kissed her every time she came off, and, not to seem too partial, he kissed all the other girls at least once. The novelty of this first-night excitement and enthusiasm thrilled her. But perhaps her proudest moment was when Mr. Banstead, the great Julius Banstead himself, came up afterwards and, gripping her hand, said:

"Fine, Miss Telling! Fine! You did splendidly."

And in the days that followed her cup of happiness was very full. The novelty of the situation kept her awake at night with nervous excitement. For a time rehearsals were over, and she had the leisure to put her world in order, to rearrange her rooms to buy additional furniture, and to go shopping in George's new car. And then the French maid arrived Was there ever anything so luxurious as a maid all to oneself! And being French added a queer piquancy to the luxury. Oh, the great day when Isabel came to tea in the powder-blue boudoir! And Barbara in a wonderful rest gown of a similar colour presided over a glittering silver tray. And the dark-eyed, pretty Annette, smartly attired in fawn and white, darted in at her bidding, and at every request exclaimed:

"Mais oui, madame." "Par fait ement, madame." "Jele fais tout de suite, madame."

Barbara hardly knew any French, but to be addressed like that raised her spirits heavenwards. And then the cosy chat with Isabel, recounting old times, discussing mutual friends, a dash of scandal, Barbara unable to resist a boast or two about her furs and their cost, her Sheraton writing table, the dinner at the Savoy, the run in the car last Sunday down to Burford Bridge, and the lunch at the inn; George's genius, what the Press said of him, how the company loved him, the parts she was going to play in the future.

Poor Isabel! She was still pretty and adorable. Certainly adorable, perhaps not quite so pretty as she had been; the little wrinkles were creeping round her eyes, her figure becoming a little sloppier, her movements slower. Well-dressed, of course, in a "managed" kind of way. She looked worried. A woman who relies on her talents, on her beauty, on her body, can't help worrying sometimes. Barbara was still helping her with money; there was vague talk of a tour in two months time. She examined all Barbara's things with interest, and loyally tried not to display jealousy.

"Does George make you an allowance?" she asked at one point. Barbara laughed.

"An allowance! Oh, no. Why should he? He gives me everything I want. I just order things, and the account is sent in to him. He always gives me any money I want. He has often said that everything of his is equally mine. "

"H'm, that's all very well," commented Isabel. "Don't you be a fool. You stick out for a settlement. He'd give it to you at the moment; later on well, you never know. Don't you see, while he talks like that and treats you like that, he's got a hold over you all the time?"

"Oh, but, Isabel, darling George He would never dream... I couldn't think of asking anything like that. It sounds so mercenary, so distrustful."

Isabel shook her head.

"I know it sounds so, but you haven't been round so many corners as I have. You haven't had so many pals married as I have. You never know. There was Meggie Farino married Reuben Jaikes like a couple of turtle-doves they were and then something went wrong one day. Meggie got mixed up with a boy at the Grand Hotel at Dieppe. Reuben had never made a settlement, and he chucked her out without a penny."

Barbara was highly amused.

"Then it's me you don't trust, Isabel, not George!"

"You never know, I say. It's always as well to keep on the safe side in a theatrical marriage. Look at Polly Patterson at the Gaiety, who got spliced with Lord Underwick. She got a settlement of fifty thousand quid, and when he went fooling round with that little Spanish dancer, after they'd been married a year, she just snapped her fingers at him. What did she care? She'd got the title and fifty thousand."

"You've got a nasty cynical mind, Isabel; I refuse to discuss the matter with you. Have another crumpet."

Barbara was not at all affected by Isabel's sinister warnings. Nothing could be securer or more roseate than her lot. As the months went by she adjusted herself more completely to her position. The physical aspect of marriage ceased to have any terrors for her. This was partly due to the greater freedom and the greater consideration George allowed her. His devotion increased. Although his time was so occupied he snatched every moment that could be spared to pass in her company. He appeared never so happy as when they were alone. He trusted her implicitly, and she gradually became to him more the mother than the child. His health was not always of the best, and at times when he became sorry for himself he loved to have her fussing over him. His large eyes would become moist with sentimental adoration. He would regard her pathetically, like a large dog regarding an intangible mistress. During the stress of his profession he was a little inclined to overlook her he seldom consulted her about the details of his productions, and even then in a rather preoccupied manner but when it was over and they were alone in the cosy security of their bedroom, and he was tired and worn out with the strain and triumph of the day, he would hungrily bury his face in her bosom and murmur endearments and appeals.

At such moments her heart would bleed for him, and she would suppress those little physical aversions to the contact of his embrace. In the morning there would always be about him a slight tang of yesterday's whisky and this morning's tobacco; in the evening the aroma of whisky dominated everything. George was not a drunkard, but for twenty years he had been in the habit of steadily imbibing, and he could not do without it. He seldom drank anything in the daytime, but he would have a whisky and soda before the show at night, another halfway through, and then several nightcaps when it was over. This was the one serious trouble she had to cope with. She detested the taste and smell of whisky. On one or two occasions she protested, but he was so upset by her reproval that she decided to say no more. She was astute enough to know that it was probably an ingrained habit, and that if he promised to give it up he would most likely break his promise.

"I suppose I must be thankful," she thought, "that he never drinks too much."

She eventually found a partial and not very satisfactory solution in having a tiny drop herself after the show. The taste was not so bad as the smell, and when she had had some she did not notice George so much.

As time went on and her ambitions were held in leash, she became vaguely conscious of a little slackening of moral fibre. It was a life of ease, and luxury, facile success, constant flattery and accumulating temptations. It was so easy and pleasant to lie in bed in the morning till twelve o'clock, reading a novel and smoking cigarettes, whilst the well-ordered household functioned below; and then to be dressed and coaxed and flattered by Annette; to drive down town and lunch with friends at a club she had joined in St. James' Square; afterwards to do a little shopping and join a tea party at Rosie Ventnor's flat, and then back home for a light dinner before the theatre. It was so cosy and jolly in her own well upholstered dressing room at the theatre, and the other girls would come in and laugh and joke and tell "the very latest." And then the show, the consciousness of singing to a packed house and knowing that you have "got them." Dim, mysterious faces above shirt fronts, their eyes glued upon her. The applause, the thrill, the easy intimacy of her fellow artists, where kisses meant little more than benedictions; and always the excitement of new friends, new faces, new people, movement and life. Afterwards home, the fire crackling in the oak-panelled dining-room; sandwiches, a siphon and tanalus on the table. George, sleepily communicative, still a little dazed by success. The bedroom, another fire glowing, rose coloured electric light shades, the two beds with the corners turned down, her creamy nightdress and George's pyjamas spread out invitingly. George, humid and adoring, asking to be mothered. An easy, luxurious, rather demoralizing life.

XVIII

"Black and White" ran for a year, and was quickly followed by another revue called "Fool's Cap." This new revue was to be Barbara's great chance. Rosie Ventnor was leaving, and she was to take her place. She arrived at the first rehearsals in a state of trepidation. Julius Banstead was again in charge.

At first everything seemed to promise auspicously. Her songs and she had a number were safe and tuneful. The parodies and skits were roughed out, and she had a principal part in nearly all of them. She rather fancied herself in the skits: little ideas, intonations, inflexions, and gestures occurred to her in bed and whilst walking along the street. But as the rehearsals progressed Mr. Banstead began to pull her up, and drill her at every line. Anyone who has not experienced it can have no idea of the degree of wretchedness to which a producer can reduce an actor or actress in this way. At first she struggled gamely, and tried to do exactly as he told her. Then she protested; but Julius Banstead was not a man you could argue with. He reduced her to tears, and one day there was a scene. It suddenly flashed through her mind that after all this was George's theatre; he had said that everything of his was equally hers. Banstead was only an employee. She turned on him angrily:

"I wish you'd let me do it my own way, Mr. Banstead. You don't know everything."

And Banstead quickly replied:

"My dear girl, it's my job to see that you do it right."

"I can't do it right if you keep on stopping me. I have my own ideas about it, thank you."

Then the tears started to her eyes. Banstead shrugged his shoulders and turned appealingly to George. The rest of the company shuffled and looked uncomfortable. George scratched his ear and said:

"Well, well, don't let's have any upset."

Don't worry, Fancy. We'll try again this afternoon."

She knew she had made a fool of herself. All the company and the stage hands and the composer and the librettist were looking on. The story would get around. Of course George couldn't openly take her side in a case like this; besides, he probably agreed with Banstead. Everybody agreed with Banstead; his position was impregnable. If she went to extremes she knew she could force George to get rid of Banstead. And then suppose the revue failed? What kind of fool would she look? It would be the talk of the town. Many well-known actors damage their careers by marrying incompetent wives who insist on playing leads. Oh, yes, it was quite true, she supposed, she was incompetent. And she had builded all her hopes on this revue. It was to be the turning point in her career. She dashed out of the theatre and drove home. In the sanctity of her blue boudoir she had a good cry.

Two hours later came George, looking distressed and flustered. He stood in the middle of the room, like a ruffled bear facing an unknown situation. He thrust out his large hands helplessly.

"I say, Fancy, old darling, I'm awful sorry. I'd no idea you 'd let Banstead upset you like that. Don 't you let him worry you. We'll make it all right."

Barbara only cried the more, and he snuggled his face against her damp cheek and mumbled consolations. Getting no response, he cried out desperately:

"Don't do it, old girl. I can't stand it. We'll get rid of the beast."

Then she got her voice at last.

"No, no, no, it's not that. You don't understand. You can't get rid of him. It's because I know he was right that I'm making a fool of myself. I thought I could act, and I can't. It's all right, George dear, don't worry; I'll be all right soon."

"Sensible little darling," thought George. Out loud he said:

"Of course you can act. What nonsense! There are only one or two points, Banstead thinks, and so does Paisley and some of the others one or two points could be improved. It's difficult for me. I don't know what to do about it."

"I know what to do. I'll try once more, and if it's no good you must get Rosie Ventnor back."

Well, was there ever such a reasonable, sensible little angel? Was there ever a child so fascinating in its wrath? He hugged her tight and buried his face in her hair.

"Fancy, you know I love you, darling? I'll do anything, anything you ask me. "

Was there ever a large man so gentle and so pliable? He coaxed her into a good humour and in half-an-hour's time she was laughing.

She attended the rehearsal the next day and tried again; but the rehearsal had not been in progress long before she realised that the great Banstead had altered his tactics. He was going through a process of freezing her out. He did not pull her up once; he just left her alone. He checked the others, but she was ignored. She went through the part like an unattached automaton; she had no criterion of its worth. Nevertheless, as time went on she began to be conscious of the telepathic waves of failure. In scenes that were meant to be comic no response came back from her fellow artistes not even George. In being frozen out she was freezing the others out. The thing went flat; George looked bewildered, the others uncomfortable; and Banstead chillingly indifferent.

At the end of the rehearsal she bit her lip and walked up to Banstead and George, who were talking together. She thrust out the typescript of her part and said:

"I can't do this part; I've no sense of humour. You must get someone else."

Banstead almost snatched the part, but he looked a little contrite and surprised. George stared at her pleadingly. What was he to do? The masterful Banstead was the first to speak. He took her arm.

"My dear Mrs. Champneys, I'm afraid I've been rude to you. Please understand there was nothing personal meant, anyway. We shouldn't get anywhere if we weren't candid in this profession. Quite honestly, I think you're wise. The part wants a more experienced comedienne. But look here, my dear, we 'll fix you up with a good singing part. You shall have a good show, I promise you."

Two days later Rosie Ventnor was back, rehearsing the lead. Barbara continued to sing coon songs and lullabies and to join in the choruses. She forgave her judges, but the incident affected her detrimentally. It was the first complete disillusionment she had experienced. The rich banquet was prepared for her and she could not eat it. Never, never, never would she be a great star. She had talent but not genius; she lacked just that elusive something which spells it. She sang charmingly indeed, almost too charmingly and subtly for a production like "Fool's Cap"; at the same time she had not the range of voice nor the musical intelligence requisite for grand opera. She fell between the two stools. She realised all this very quickly, and with an alert, protective instinct she decided how to act. She must keep her grip on George. As Fancy Telling she was of no account; as Mrs. George Champneys she was a person to look up to and respect. It was she who persuaded him to wire for Rosie Ventnor; it was she who took the rebuff philosophically. George was so upset at the time he seemed inclined to lose his head. Oh, yes, she was a wise, sensible, philosophical little thing.

But when the reaction came it found her drifting down the old channels of easy living. If the Muses would not reward her with bay leaves she would seek satisfaction elsewhere in the vineyards of Bacchus, for instance, or in the groves of Arcadia, listening to the pipes of Pan. In the months that followed she ministered to the wants of George. She was affectionate and tender, but their lives began to be lived apart. She discovered new aspects of him. His preoccupations were overwhelming, his conservatism impregnable. It was like being married to "a confirmed bachelor. His adoration had certain defined limits. He wanted her hungrily at special moments, but for his work-a-day life he preferred the society of men. In spite of his sentimental protestations, he was never able to conceal a kind of indolent contempt for her mentality. He lived in a groove, a large, cultivated, well-ordered groove. The fact that she had been admitted into it didn't make it any less a groove. He had passed the age when he could convert it into a sunlit meadow. In their association the comedian appeared a pathetic, almost a tragic figure, always appealing to her for the crumbs of passion she never felt disposed to give.

And so they gradually began to live their own lives. Frequently they would not meet all day. George would be working, rehearsing, lunching at his club, talking to the innumerable "old boys "who pass their lives round about Covent Garden and Garrick Street. And Barbara built up her circle of friends, too, mostly women, but she was not above mixing with the other sex also, and even lunching or teaing alone with one of the young "boys" so frequently referred to by Isabel. George gave her a small car of her own, and she flitted hither and thither, buying expensive frocks and fal-lals, dining at expensive restaurants and drinking expensive wines. And by these means she fortified herself against his caresses and endearments. He begrudged her nothing. He demanded nothing more from her only that she should not pity him. He even consented eventually to separate bedrooms.

XIX

The whispers of Eros were always about her ears, neither could she be unmindful of Isabel's prophetic warning:

"If you've ever been kissed properly it gets into your blood, and you can't do without it."

Within three months after the production of "Fool's Cap" she had been kissed twice "properly," and though in neither case were the wells of her inner being profoundly stirred, the experience left upon her the imprint of a bitter-sweet exultation.

The first occasion was with the great Julius Banstead himself. In the same way that George suddenly discovered her after knowing her for years, she became to Julius an identical obsession. He observed her one day in the wings, and in the depths of those masterful, restless eyes there flashed an insolent, savage desire. She was aware of him ever after that, following her with his eyes, prowling in her wake. She had no great love for Julius Banstead. She feared and almost hated him. And yet her heart beat flurriedly to know that the strong man desired her. It was insolent and characteristic of him to make love to the wife of his employer, to the wife of his great friend, to a girl he had been rude to. He spoke to her very little, but when near her he hummed under his breath phrases of impassioned song. He mesmerized her with his fierce assumption of indiscretion. In spite of her dislike she succumbed to the luxuriant image of his mastery. She would like this man to hurt her, to throw her on the floor and kick her.

She thrust the strange temptation back. She dismissed it altogether when he was not present, but when he came near her she was disturbingly conscious of him without looking at him.

Arriving at the theatre early one evening she met him going in. He said:

"Come up to my room for a moment. I want to show you something which may interest you."

She was fully conscious of the insolence of the command and the something which might interest her being a blind. The penetration of his glance had only one meaning which should have lashed her to a fury of revolt; and yet without a word she followed him to a room upstairs where the offices were situated. He walked ahead, and her eyes were glued upon the movement of that thick forceful back. She entered the room after him, and he shut the door and threw his hat on to a peg. She stood perfectly immobile in front of a gas stove, which was popping irritably. Without a word he came up and took her in his arms. She knew all this was going to happen before it did; her volitions were experimenting. She found herself enveloped in a fury of desires. She felt the thrust of his vibrant body as he crushed her to him, the lips upon her cheek and eyes; then suddenly his tongue between her lips. It was awful. She should have screamed and kicked, and not hung idly there, with closed eyes and a surrendered will. Instead of that, for some timeless period she was lost in a world of passionate response. When she escaped from that raging eternity she should have struck him and fled from the room. Instead of that she said in a drugged voice:

"Don't be a fool, Julius."

Banstead was not the man to fritter away an opportunity. He had succeeded already far beyond his wildest hopes. His voice came huskily and pleadingly:

"Darling, will you? will you?"

"Will I what!"

"It's you that's being a fool now. You know you know. Fancy darling, I love you. I want you. Will you?"

Oh, no, Mr. Banstead, the game can be carried too far. She pushed him away, rearranged her hair and, looking down at the stove, remarked:

"Your gas stove wants regulating."

"Damn the gas stove!"

She raised her voice to a note of passion for the first time:

"I hate that popping noise. It gets on my nerves!"

With a growl Julius bent down to readjust the screw. Like a flash she was at the door and through it. She never went into Julius Banstead's room again; neither did she ever report her experience to George or to any of her girl friends. When people afterwards asked her what she thought of him she said:

"Julius? Oh, he 's a queer fish." Sometimes at night she would lie with head on pillow, her body curled up like a little ball, and reflect:

"Crikey! George never kissed me like that! The second occasion was an aristocratic diversion. It occurred with the son of a lord. Geoffrey Vallance was the son of Lord Tremayne. He was a slim, elegant boy, just down from Oxford, with round Plantagenet eyes and an expression which clearly betokened: "For goodness" sake, don't say anything serious!"

She met him at a luncheon-party at Rosie Ventnor's, and he informed her within the space of the first five minutes that he had been to "Fool's Cap" twenty-three times, that he thought she was devilish clever and pretty, that he thought the whole show was top-hole, that George was a scream, that Rosie was topping, that all the girls in it were simply ripping, that his father wanted him to read for the Bar not much! The only bar he aspired to was the Trocadero! Ha, ha, ha! He told her that he liked all shell-fish except mussels, and that he never drank port after champagne. He played games, but they bored him. He only did it to keep fit. He liked squash rackets best, because it was so concentrated. "You sweat like a pig in five minutes."

The elegance of his outward and visible form was not enriched by any particular spark of inner and spiritual grace, and yet there was about him something rather charming. Perhaps; because he was so young and fresh, so redolent of a world novel to her, so different from even High Barren. She longed to tell him that her father was the great Thomas Powerscourt, the Chancellor, just to see what the effect would be upon him. But she wisely forbore and exchanged inanities instead. When he offered to drive her down to Pangbourne in his sidecar on the following Sunday she accepted. They lunched at an hotel, and afterwards went on the river. He behaved quite nicely, and delivered her safely to her door at Kensington in time for dinner.

Afterwards they met quite frequently, and flirted in a childish, playful manner. Sometimes she reflected: "It must be rather nice to be married to someone young and fresh like that. He thinks he's a gay dog, but he really knows nothing."

The kiss was the direct result of drinking too much wine. They had lunched together alone at the house; George was up west, as usual. Some rather heavy Burgundy had been served, and Barbara realised that it had suddenly gone to her head. The interplay of fustian emotions became accelerated. His face appeared lighted up with an added glow. He was really rather good-looking; he was really rather a dear. She could see the line of firm white little teeth between his red lips as he laughed. His face had the milky pinkness of a baby's; all eagerness and expectancy. Upon his upper lip was a thin down of golden hair. Abruptly she thought:

"I'm going to kiss this boy."

A laggard reflection tempered her resolution. "It can't make the slightest difference to George."

She stood up and said:

"Come and see my powder-blue room."

The consciousness of bespoken guilt merely quickened her impulse. What did it matter? Even the form of that mistress of discretion, Annette, vanishing down dim corridors, did nothing to distract her movements. Again she stood immobile before a fire, which in this case was not lighted, for the day was hot. He approached her from behind. "Let him kiss me; what does it matter? One can kiss better standing up."

He was more deliberate in his methods than Julius had been. He took her hand and pressed it gently. Then he doubled it up in his and kissed it. After pausing, as though expecting a rebuff, he put his arm around her waist. The pressure increased; he moved nearer and kissed the back of her neck, her ear, her cheek. Then she slowly turned and held him from her, looking deeply into his eyes. With a sudden firm movement she raised her arm and, placing it round his neck, she drew his lips to hers. They kissed properly, with the blood-inflamed, wine-inflamed, Aphrodisiac intensity which only youth experiences when it first breaks through the barrier of physical reserve. When it was over she could just see his flushed, almost bewildered face. He was trembling. She hid her eyes with a handkerchief, and said:

"Damn that Burgundy! It's gone to my head." He laughed self-consciously, and tried to approach her again, but she warded him off: "Don't be a fool, Geoffrey."

It was obvious that the boy was in a dilemma. The thing seemed so confoundedly serious, don't you know. He had probably never been kissed so seriously before, and the inexperience almost unnerved him. He desired amusement, but he didn't want to be a cad, and all that kind of thing, old girl. She could see him thinking that. Yes, he was rather a dear, and she had made him kiss her. He again laughed nervously, in the manner of a man who has committed an awful crime.

"You must go now, Geoff," she said.

He was contrition itself, but devoured by disappointment. Thank God he said nothing about loving her; neither did he make overt suggestions. There was something of the gentleman about him in spite of his devotion to inanities. There was something of the gentleman about him when he kissed her hand at the door, with a gesture which implied:

"Please don't think I have any disrespect for you on account of this. I assure you, it was all my fault, and all that sort of thing, don't you know."

She met Geoffrey Vallance on many future occasions after that, but never alone. The kiss was not repeated. After these two experiences she withdrew a little within herself, like a cat licking its wounds after battle, conscious that the wounds hurt, but fully alive to the fact that they are not incurable.

XX

Barbara had been married nearly three years. "Fool's Cap" had been replaced by a new revue called "Laugh and Grow Fat"—in which she still sustained an inconspicuous part when a disruption came to disturb the equanimity of the well-ordered house in Kensington. The affair concerned the competent Mrs. Piddinghoe.

In the luxury of being free from domestic worries Barbara had devoted herself to a life of comfortable ease and a ladylike disregard of the claims of household duties. But as time went on, and the theatre demanded less attention, she began to think more about her home. She began to take more interest in the details of its working. One afternoon she happened to be in one of the spare bedrooms at the back, which overlooked the passage leading to the tradesmen's entrance, and, looking out, she saw a boy standing at the back door with a large basket. She naturally imagined that he was delivering some goods. In an idle mood she watched him. Mrs. Piddinghoe appeared, and they whispered together. She retired, and in a few moments returned with a lot of parcels under her arm. They were wrapped up in newspapers, but sticking out of one she could distinctly see the frill of a ham.

"That's very queer," she thought. "I suppose Mrs. Piddinghoe is sending some things back."

And then suspicion began to work. She had never liked Mrs. Piddinghoe. She was altogether too plausible, too perfect, and too efficient.

For a moment an impulse came to the mistress of the house to go down and make direct enquiries as to the reason why this young man was taking these things away, and then a sense of caution prevailed. She would be further on the watch. A few days later she observed the same operation. She waited then till the following Saturday morning, when Mr. Toller, the secretary, was in the habit of making the weekly settlement with Mrs. Piddinghoe. When this was completed she went in to him and said:

"Excuse me, Mr. Toller, would you mind telling me what our household expenses came to last week? I should be interested to know."

Samuel Toller looked very surprised, but he smiled pleasantly and said:

"Certainly, Mrs. Champneys." He undid an attache-case and took out some papers. "Here we are. Fourteen pounds seven and threepence."

"What!"

"That's the amount, Mrs. Champneys. I have the details here."

Barbara; glanced at the figures and the items. Then she remarked quietly:

"I was home to lunch twice last week and George once. I dined here three times, and I think George did three times. On Thursday we had four people to lunch; there's been no more entertaining. There are four servants. Doesn't it strike you as being rather a lot?"

Toller blushed. He had often thought so himself, but it was not his business to enquire. He was a busy man, and the business of the theatre occupied most of his time. He said:

"Is that so? I didn't know. I thought you entertained a lot. Mrs. Piddinghoe said you did."

"Can you tell me is Mrs. Piddinghoe married?"

"Yes. She has a husband and a grown-up son. I think they keep a little shop somewhere." Then he added lamely: "She's very fond of George I mean Mr. Champneys. She's been with him ten years."

"I see. Thank you very much. Do you mind leaving the details with me?"

"Certainly, Mrs. Champneys."

That same afternoon the young man again appeared at the back door. Barbara walked deliberately down. Mrs. Piddinghoe was handing him a box full of eggs.

"What is this, Mrs. Piddinghoe?" she asked.

The efficient housekeeper looked flustered.

"Oh," she remarked perfunctorily, "we're sending some eggs back. They're not good ones."

Barbara opened the box.

"They look excellent ones to me. And are you sending back a shoulder of mutton to the same person? I thought one got mutton at a butcher's and eggs at a grocer's.

Mrs. Piddinghoe became dark with menace.

"If you please, Mrs. Champneys, I'm not in the 'abit of being cross-examined. I've done for Mr. Champneys for ten years, and there has never been no complaint."

"I'm not complaining yet. This is your son, isn't it?"

"He does errands for me."

"All right, only I should put those things back in the larder if I were you."

The following morning a Sunday after her bath, she went into George's room. He was sitting up in bed, with a dishevelled breakfast tray by his side, a cigarette in his mouth, and a copy of the Referee in hand. She sat on the edge of his bed and said:

"George, I want to speak seriously to you."

He put down the paper and blinked at her questioningly.

"Seriously! So early in the morning? Come and give me a kiss first. You look a little darling just out of the bath and your hair all wet "

She allowed a reasonable amount of "mauling about," then she said abruptly:

"George, do you think we ate five and a-half dozen eggs and seven pounds of butter this week?"

"Five and a-half dozen eggs and seven pounds of butter? Who? You and I?"

"No. I mean in this house?"

"In the house? Lord! I don't know. There are a good many of us. Is it a lot? Why?"

"Do you remember having a duck and two fowls?"

"My dear, what are you talking about? I can't remember what I ate last week."

"Do you remember having chicken at home at all?"

"I can't say I do. What are you getting at?"

"I'm getting at the fact that the Piddinghoe is an old thief and a swindler."

George's eyes opened wide, and an expression of troubled dread crept into them. He seemed to detect in his Fancy's attitude an outflanking attack upon his comfort and repose. If there was one thing he hated it was any kind of domestic upheaval. He laughed nervously and fell back on the same line of defence as that used by Samuel Toller.

"Piddinghoe! Nonsense, my dear. She's been with me ten years."

"Yes, and I suspect that for ten years she has been systematically robbing you. She has a husband who runs a little shop, and a grown-up son.

The son calls here nearly every afternoon and carries off the loot for his father to sell. I should think between them they steal four or five pounds worth of stuff a week. I can prove they've stolen a lot this week."

Now, George ought to have been very grateful to his Fancy for this information; he ought to have recognised that she was rendering him a great service; but curiously enough he was not at all grateful. He was distressed; he wished profoundly she hadn't done it. His voice was almost angry as he replied:

"Oh, no, I don't believe it. You've made a mistake."

There are some people whose nerves are always jagged early in the morning. Barbara's had not always been, but she was reaching that stage of development when they usually were. From her dressing-gown pocket she produced a bundle of tradesmen's bills. She struck them with her fist and her eyes blazed.

"If you like to come down with me to the kitchen and the larder, I can prove it. We've paid for all kinds of things which we've never had. Look here three tins of tongue. We never have tinned tongue, and there's none in the house

George became peevish. He picked up the Referee.

"My dear, I really don't desire to go down to the larder and hunt for tins of tongue. It's Mrs. Piddinghoe's business "

Then Barbara became really angry.

"You—men! It's the kind of thing you do. You go on encouraging people to be immoral—anything rather than disturb your comfort and, peace of mind—"

"Well, I after all—"

"If you won't do anything about it, I will. I won't have a thief in the place."

"Barbara, don't—don't—be in a hurry. Let's think—"

Barbara was already at the door. George got out of bed and tumbled after her. He stood at the open door, frightened and helpless. In a few minutes time he heard such a hullabaloo going on downstairs as had never before shattered the placid serenity of that well-ordered house. Two women's voices raised in shrill altercation, shouting each other down, and in each there was that note of commonness which invariably colours a primitive emotion breaking loose. The din went on for nearly twenty minutes.

At the end of that time Barbara returned, still ablaze with fury, still unapproachable, but just a shade triumphant.

"She's going," she said icily, and passed through to her own room and shut the door.

George groaned. This was a nice thing to happen! The Piddinghoe! The loyal and efficient Piddinghoe, who had served him all these years. What the devil did Fancy want to butt in for? He knew or in any case he had often shrewdly suspected that Mrs. Piddinghoe took a few things. But what did it matter? It was the recognised perquisite of her class. While the theatre was making a clear profit of five or six hundred pounds a week, and all his interests and energies were wrapped up in it, what did it matter if Mrs. Piddinghoe did take a few eggs or a tin of tongue, so long as she did her work efficiently and freed him from domestic worry? Women were impossible. He would like to explain to Fancy that one had to look at these things in a broad way. His experience told him that all the best and most competent servants were either thieves or drunkards. You allowed a margin for it. And what was going to happen now?

Barbara was unapproachable. She was aggrieved with him, even more with him than with Mrs. Piddinghoe, because he had not sided with her. And they had quarrelled yes, there was no getting away from that, they had quarrelled for the first time in their married life. Well, she was wrong; no doubt about it. She had no right to act like that without his consent. After all, it was his house, his money. Something began to harden in George. He would have to teach her a lesson. She was very silent in the next room now, probably crying women were like that their anger always had its reaction in tears. On such occasions it is better to keep out of the way. He lay back in the bed, conscious of his power. Babrara had not treated him as she ought. Did she realise her dependence on him? Did she realise that she was an unrecognised, penniless actress, an illegitimate child, and he had made her the wife of the great George Champneys? Perhaps it was a little unkind to look at it like that; he detested cruelty as much as a scene or a row. They would make it up later on of course, but in any case she must come to him, not he to her. He got out of bed and went into the bathroom. Having washed and dressed, he went downstairs and 'phoned for his car. He drove up to his club, and did not see Barbara again that day.

XXI

The row about Mrs Piddinghoe had consequences more far-reaching than either of them could have anticipated. She was something of a female Samson, and realising that the temple was to fall upon her own head, she did everything to embroil others in the crash. She did not leave till late on that Sunday afternoon, and then she took the cook with her, and an enormous quantity of mysterious luggage. Before she left she threatened legal proceedings, and called Barbara a string of names unflattering to her moral character and the integrity of her parental stock. The other servants were all out, except the boy who cleaned knives and boots. After she had gone, Barbara discovered that the basement was in a complete state of chaos. Things were scattered all over the floor; doors of cupboards and larders were locked and the keys missing; gas was escaping from the kitchen range; water dripped from some mysterious tank in the passage. It was Sunday night, and the chances of getting a plumber or a gas-fitter were remote. Fortunately Snowden, the boot-boy, proved a host in himself. It was he who detected what was wrong with the stove. Between them they strove to rectify the results of the disruption.

She had a feeling George would not come back till late, and she did not care. Over this business George had shown his worst side. He had behaved like a spoilt baby. He had been weak and unreasonable. He ought to have been grateful to her for discovering the robbery; instead of that he had practically told her to mind her own business. After all, wasn't the house hers as much as his? Hadn't he often said so?

They had quarrelled; no escaping that fact yes, quarrelled for the first time. Well, he was in the wrong, no doubt about it. He was too big and important to worry about tins of tongue and pounds of butter. He feared a scene or any unpleasantness, and so he ran away! Men were like that. If everything wasn't just right for them, they didn't try and put it right they ran away and hid. If George bought a thing, and when he got home he found it defective, he just grumbled, and then went and bought another. Catch him taking it back to the shop! Pampered fools! She was a little unstrung, but the occupation of putting her house in order steadied her. Her crust hardened. George had treated her badly. Did he realise that she had given him her youth? Did he not know that he was a puffy, elderly man? Perhaps that was unkind he loved her well enough in his way but he must be taught some sort of lesson. Of course they would make it up, but in any case, he must come to her, not she to him. She wasn't going to dine alone in an empty house, and cook her own dinner, so she telephoned to Isabel, and happened to catch her. The two girls went down to Romano's and dined extravagantly; and over the wine-glasses Barbara's eyes sparkled with malicious satisfaction realising that it was George's money she was spending.

The reconciliation was more difficult of accomplishment than might have been imagined. Indeed, it may be said that after the affair of Mrs. Piddinghoe they never quite got back on to the old footing. Two obstinate wills came into conflict: the man's defensive, cautions, and secure in its ultimate triumph; the woman's offensive, a little reckless, relentlessly logical and yet eternally conscious of exposed dangers. It seems strange how in this world of ours the test of our moral dissonances may be so often tried over matters which concern petty things like tins of tongue and pounds of butter. At the inception of this quarrel Barbara had not been unduly eager to follow up the attack on Mrs. Piddinghoe; she was a little sorry for her. It was George's attitude which inflamed her. In a flash she seemed to see epitomised in the incident all the turgid unpleasantness of his character his vanity, and weakness, his love of comfort, and above all the mighty claims of his possessive sense, a possessive sense which included her (body and soul) in its inventory of household goods.

On the Sunday night after it happened, they both got home very late, within ten minutes of each other. They were both a little scared about the quarrel, and both had had time to relent somewhat. At the same time, they had both determined not to give themselves away. George went to her door, and standing nonchalantly in the opening, he said:

"Did you get some dinner?"

She replied in an offhand manner:

"Yes, you bet I did. With Isabel. The place is in a nice muddle. The gas was escaping. That woman has pinched the keys."

All this, she implied, was George's fault. George was convinced that it was her fault; nevertheless he felt a little guilty about having left her to cope with the situation alone. He mumbled:

"Oh, well. We'll do something about it to-morrow Good-night."

"Good-night."

Not a word, not a gesture of real conciliation not an embrace, for the first time!

In the days which followed, the policies which the cumulative characteristics of those two married people embodied in themselves continued to sustain a silent conflict. A real good row, with passion and tears, would have tended to clear the air; instead of that, they continued to be themselves in a subdued form. Between them lay a barrier of unexpected, critical resentment. George was like and about as useful as a cat during a removal. He regarded the disunion of his well-ordered house with an expression which clearly implied: "There you are! What did I say? Interfere, alter, and things go to pot. It has taken me years to build this up, and you've destroyed it in a day."

Barbara, on her part, found like many other reformers that it is always dangerous to destroy an essential thing till you have found something to put in its place. George's valet, one house-maid. Annette and the faithful Snowden alone remained. Of these, the three adults refused to do anything beyond their normal allotted task, and even then under a kind of protest, as much as to say:

"We are not used to this sort of atmosphere. You must rectify it at once."

She found herself trying to do half the housework, cleaning George's boots, and cooking for the staff. On the third day she managed to get a housekeeper with an excellent character and her husband, an ex-marine. She also got a cook. Within twenty-four hours the cook was quarrelling with the housekeeper and refused to stop. A few days later the ex-marine came in one evening very drunk, just as she was going off to the theatre. He insisted upon going to sleep on a Chesterfield in the library, because he said that at last he was on board ship. It would be tedious to recall the changes, the quarrels, the complications which ensued in this household which had previously run with well-oiled simplicity. It was an undoubted triumph for George, the more especially as he made a point of only being there for bed and breakfast, the details of both of which comforts Barbara attended to herself. It was nearly four months before the place regained any semblance of ordered calm, and even then the standard was nothing like so high as it had been in the days of "the Piddinghoe." Many things were missing, including silver-backed brushes of George's, some carved ivory figures, a collection of Barbara's trinkets, and even a small clock. With all the changes it was impossible to bring the guilt home to anyone. Moreover nothing was just where it ought to be.

In one of his more agreeable moods George favoured her with a profound comment.

"A house," he said, "is like a State. It's got to be run on human nature, not high-falutin', ideals."

He left her to digest this apothegm at leisure. He had gone before she had time to reply:

"You mean to say it's got to be run by thieves and drunkards."

XXII

It was George, however, who eventually "came to her." He caught a chill and got very sorry for himself. It was at the time when things had improved.

A reliable Scotch housekeeper had been installed, and a cook who frequently cooked quite well, two new housemaids, and a char to do the unpleasant work for them a period of comparative calm.

George came home late after the theatre. He said he felt very tired, and his bones ached. He had his usual night-cap and went up to bed. She had retired, too, but in about half-an-hour's time there was a tap at the door, and he came in and shut it. She heard him stumbling towards her bed in the darkness, and mumbling, "Fancy! Fancy!"

He lay down upon it, on the outside of the eiderdown, and pressed his moist face against hers.

"I've been an awful cad to you, Fancy," he whispered.

He was humid and, at the same time, feverish.

"You're not well, George," she whispered back. "You'd better have some aspirin. I'll get you some."

He clung to her and would not let her move.

"It's not that. I've been worrying about you. 1 can't stand it any longer. I hate all this. I want you just the same as before. Forgive me, Fancy I love you. "

She lay there inert, and let him kiss her. When she could speak, she said:

"I'm sorry it happened. You'd better let me get you some aspirin."

"Afterwards, not now. I want to hold you like this, all alone in the darkness. Just you and I together-like we used to. Poor old George! He was sorry for himself. She put her hand at the back of his head and stroked his hair. She mothered him discreetly, shrouding her emotions in a genuine sympathy for his condition. This was married life, then perhaps as much as anyone dare expect fair days and foul days, and then a groping together in the darkness. This was marriage, then an institution, like a house or State, to be run on "human nature, and not on high-falutin "ideals." George had come to her because he wanted her, a warm and comforting niche in the structure of his domestic conception. Tomorrow or as soon as he felt well everything would go on just the same, but to-night. She felt the heave of his body hungrily restless for his traditional comforts.

"Get inside, then," she whispered again. "Only you must try and keep still. I'll go and get you the aspirin and some hot water."

On the morrow he was still feverish, and she sent for a doctor. It was only a chill, but he was obliged to drop out of the bill for three days. His part was played by an understudy. Barbara nursed him, controlling, meanwhile, with a firm hand her reconstructed household. When the fever had abated he sat about forlornly in a dressing-gown, bored by the enforced inactivity, the absence of glamour and applause. During the daytime he would be contented enough, but when it came to seven o'clock in the evening he would appear to shake with an ague of agitation. He should be in the dressing-room now, with Manners, and Banstead, and the others dancing attendance. He should be at the back, with callboys and property-men falling over each other, touching their hats: "Good evening, Mr. George." The agitated murmurs of the crowd in front, chattering over their programmes. Eight o'clock, and the orchestra tuning up people rushing hither and thither. "Lights, please, Mr. Winslow." Eight-fifteen "Beginners, please!" Eight-thirty, up goes the curtain; the roar of welcome at his familiar figure—

"There he is! That's George Champneys! Good old George!"

Oh, he had no use for Barbara during these vicarious exultations, only to say when the pressure became unendurable:

"I think I'll just have a spot, old girl."

So soon as his temperature became normal he drank a lot of whisky. He said it was good for him, and in a way she believed it was. The demand for it was in his blood, as was the demand for adulation and applause. During those days the true character of the man became vividly manifest, and she tried not to see it. His good temper, kindness of heart, and generosity were, to an extent, a combination of indolence and desire for popularity. It is easier and pleasanter to be good tempered than to be just and critical. He followed the line of least resistance in all things. Generous? Why shouldn't he be generous? He had abundance, and nothing so warmed and quickened the popular palate as lavish tipping and a reckless disregard for cost. Everything had come too easily to George, and the result had destroyed his moral fibre. He was wearing badly. His body was becoming loose and flabby, his face lined and puffy, his eyes dull and preoccupied. His dog-like attachment to her was of an unreliable kind. She was a necessary adjunct to his existence, and yet she bored him. She never knew whether he was really listening when she spoke to him. One thing was certain. If she told him anything overnight he never remembered it the next morning. This was a trait which irritated her almost beyond endurance. They would have a long discussion in the evening about, for instance, what was to be done with a certain bureau. The matter would be settled and disposed of, and then, the next morning, he would suddenly say:

"I say, Fancy, where shall we put that bureau?" Neither was his temper of that equable kind ascribed to it by reputation. It was one thing in the limelight of success to laugh and joke with everyone, to raise salaries, to tip extravagantly, to be hail-fellow-well-met with the humblest minions of his staff. All these stories got about. In the bars off Shaftesbury Avenue where the stage-hands congregated, in the clubs where the "old boys" foregathered, in green-rooms and agents offices, everyone would say: "Ah, you should get in with old George Champneys. He's a sport, if you like treats everyone alike gave young Cinders a quid for carrying his bag out to the car—"

All this was true, but it was she who had to bear the brunt of his sullen reactions. He would have moods of unreasoning irritability, when some trivial matter like cold toast would cause him to sulk and fume for hours. Sometimes he would appear to harbour some inexpressible antagonism towards her. He would regard her distrustfully, as though aware that she filled the niche he had designed for her reluctantly that she was an eternal challenge to the claims of his possessive sense. In short, he did not and never would possess her. The love which "was to come afterwards" had not materialised, and it was slipping farther from his reach.

Sometimes he would dismiss her from his mind altogether, and indulge in idle dreams the yellow sands of the little bay at Rapallo, the villa entangled with flowers against the dark trees, Maisie leaning over the balcony holding out her arms youth to youth, the unmatched beauty of unspoilt desire. And dark thoughts would flitter through his mind. He had gained the whole world and lost his soul. He became afraid of the darkness and the empty moments.

"I'll just have a tot, old girl."

And so the perpetual compromise went on, the eternal moving on and slipping back. And when he laughed the world laughed with him, and when he wept he wept alone, or into the husk of a stillborn love. And always there haunted him the recurrent premonition: "One day she'll get a lover what will I do then?"

It was characteristic of him that in that moment he thought only of himself. And he admonished himself:

"When it happens I'll have to keep my head. I mustn't kill her or the man, or I'll get hanged."

God! It might all have been so different! He tried to analyse the reasons, to locate the precise moment when everything had gone wrong. But he could not. The facile descent leaves few landmarks, and those which exist are usually invisible to the egoist. It was hard luck, just pure hard luck. If, now, he had a child a son? no, perhaps a daughter, a laughing, sunny girl, with all her life before her, flinging her little arms around his neck how secure he would feel with a love like that. No one can usurp a father's place or a mother's. But this other love that's like an open conflict with the world. He became watchful and jealous. He must be more careful with his darling Fancy in the future.

One day he came to the conclusion that Samuel Toller was a dangerous person to have about young and unattached, rather good looking, and becoming too free and intimate. He sent him away in charge of a tour and engaged Caleb Thirkettle as his secretary. Caleb Thirkettle was also young, but he was a plain, serious-minded young man, married to Grade Bard, the actress; and they had two young children.

XXIII

Barbara was only partly conscious of her husband's disorderly humours. After the revelation which had come to her during his brief illness, she preferred not to indulge in moral speculations, not to visualise dubious hypotheses. She had failed, her dreams had not come true; nothing was left but the ancient salve of making the best of a bad job. Direct compensation in the way of material things was easily accessible, and for a time she abandoned herself to it. She snapped the shutter on the little visions which had accompanied her through life. Only one still persisted in dancing before her eyes uninvited. It came at queer odd moments in the street, in her dressing-room, whilst singing, and when alone in the darkness if only she had a child a little daughter; no, perhaps a son, one who would cling to her and call her "Mummy" that would be a love that would endure through the inevitable fading and withering of the leaf. No one could supersede her. And he would grow up into a proud, strong man; not like his father, more like the knight of her dreams.

And so the tragi-comedy of this dubious alliance went on: nights of tunefulness and charm, and gay, mad laughter; applause and beauty, merry parties and extravagant feasts; fine clothes and motor-rides to the open country; wit, and company, and social interplay; meeting together and parting; spasmodic attempts to regain a thing which had never existed; pity and tears, and the groping together in the darkness; sullen realisations; and then back once more to dance to the tune of the piper.

One evening a strange thing happened to Barbara. The run of "Laugh and Grow Fat" had come to an end, and they were rehearsing a new revue; consequently; many of her evenings were free. Isabel had again got a small part at Daly's, and on this evening in question Barbara had arranged to go with her after the show to supper at a little cafe, frequented by "the" profession, near Long Acre. They arrived just before twelve, and the supper-room was very crowded. They eventually got seats at a table in the corner, where two old men obviously actors were finishing a meal. They were both drinking whisky, and were in that state difficult to determine whether drunk or sober. There are some old men who have the genius of appearing always drunk, although they 8 may not have had anything to drink for weeks. Their conversational methods are always ruminative, forensic and redundant. They bang on the table and say:

"Ah, old boy, you should have heard Florenzo—"

And then they give a convincing imitation of Florenzo, a performance which one should always allow them to do, because they enjoy it so much themselves. These two old blue-chins were of that kind. Isabel and Barbara both knew the type well, and were not unduly alarmed. Even when one of them said to Barbara:

"Mademoiselle, you have the face of a queen who ruled in Ascalon."

She only smiled, and said:

"Oh, do you think so! Might I trouble you for the O. K. sauce?"

The two girls had their supper in comparative peace. When they had nearly finished Barbara suddenly heard one of them say:

"Ah, old boy, there has been no one since Hannifan you take it from me."

For a moment the name Hannifan conveyed nothing to her; then she remembered, and her heart beat violently. Leaning across the table she said:

"Excuse me, sir, did you know Hannifan?"

The old actor's face lighted up with surprise and a joyous anticipation. Here was a chance, if ever there was one, to talk and air his experiences. And not, mark you, to old Bob Stepney, who had heard it all a hundred times and never listened once, but to a young and pretty woman, a stranger, eager to hear. He cleared his throat and thrust back his head.

"My dear, Hannifan and I were hand-in-glove for longer than your life. Hannifan and I were on the road together, in fit-ups, when these syndicate halls were unborn. Hannifan and I shared our crusts and bowls of gruel, when one had to serve an apprenticeship not like now. Hannifan! Ah! there was an artist for you "

"Yes, yes, I see. Excuse me, though, did you ever meet a singer called Kitty 'Bane?"

The old actor looked a little annoyed at the interruption. It had spoilt his periods. He might eventually have touched on Kitty O'Bane, but he had hardly launched Hannifan yet. He puckered up his lips.

"Yes, I knew Kitty an artist, too. She was out in the summer of '84. Hannifan said to me "

"Oh, please tell me anything you know about her."

Very well, then, if she wouldn't let him talk about Hannifan, Kitty 'Bane would serve almost as well.

"Kitty O'Bane might have climbed to the top of the tree. She had youth, beauty, and great talent. Her mother was Irish; her father—" He shrugged his shoulders. "Kitty O'Bane, when I first met her, was not unlike you, mademoiselle. She had the same dark eyes, the eager lips, the Queen of Ascalon air. She was taller than you, and she could ride. I saw her first in a circus, jumping through hoops. I was with dear old Larry, the best sand-dancer who ever put toe to board "

"Why didn't she climb to the top of the tree?"

The old man drew himself up, and took a deep draught of whisky-and-water. Then he said portentously:

"Because of the flesh-pots of Egypt."

"What do you mean by that?"

"I can't tell you exactly, my dear. Women have always been an unopened book to me. There was some scandal. She got mixed up in a love-affair in high society, I believe. She left the company. We did not see her for years. Indeed, I myself never saw her again. But Larry, I remember, told me that he came across her in Manchester. She was finished, broken, darting in and out of booths, cadging money any old way. She went down, and down, and down."

"Did she die?"

"This was twenty years ago, or more, my dear, and she was sliding down. The upward path is lined with thorns, the downward path is greased with butter. I cannot say. Why do you ask me about Kitty O'Bane?"

"Because she was my mother," said Barbara, and burst into tears.

BOOK III

I

In reorganising the details of her domestic world, Barbara found a certain element of delight. It was her first real taste of power. Having routed the redoubtable Mrs. Piddinghoe and triumphed over George, she took care not to let the reins of authority slip from her hand again. Aided by the Scotch housekeeper, she checked all the orders and supplies, and even went on pilgrimages to various stores to ascertain whether they were getting the best value for their money. It was rather a surprising streak in her, probably a by-product of the operation of having had a Chancellor for a father. Every Saturday morning she went into the library and spent an hour or so going over the accounts with Caleb Thirkettle, the new secretary. It was a source of satisfaction to her to realise the respect paid her by this rather solemn young man. He was the antithesis to the breezy Toller, who always treated the domestic finances of the Champneys' household with airy indifference. To Thirkettle it all seemed very important and interesting, and he supplied her with order-books, and receipt-files, and a wages-book for the servants. If anything went wrong with the electric light or gas, instead of writing to a firm about it, he would invariably rectify the trouble with his own hands. He was a competent young man, with a broad, flat, eager face, rather queer and frog-like. His grey eyes, which were set wide apart, were reflective and wistful. There was something about him which appealed to Barbara.

"He's unhappy, and he's taking it like a sport," she decided.

He was deferential and friendly, but not overfamiliar. It was always a pleasure to ask his advice. His face lighted up, and he had a way of twisting his head on one side and nodding it thoughtfully. Then he would begin:

"Well, what I would suggest, Mrs. Champneys, is this—"

He was essentially a person to be trusted and confided in, but a little difficult to draw out. Her affairs appeared to him of so much more importance than his own. He spent part of his time at the theatre and part of the time in the house. George liked him and found him incomparably more useful than Toller had been. He usually referred to him as "Frog- face" when speaking to Barbara, but to his face he called him "Thirk."

Thirk was in every way a great success. Apart from his executive efficiency, he acted as a kind of bridge between husband and wife. He had the confidence of both, and as the gulf between them tended to get wider and wider, so did this broad safe bridge became more and more valuable. Many a time when the tension became acute, when the conflict of wills threatened a crisis, by some adroit manoeuvre the young secretary would save the situation., Barbara's subversive inclinations towards material delights had not made things easier. She frequently went to suppers and dances after the theatre, and when she arrived home George would be asleep. She entertained more, and spent money lavishly. It was not, as she explained to Thirkettle when they were going through accounts, that she "wanted to be mean, but I do hate being done." And Caleb Thirkettle agreed that it was a very human and natural feeling.

Neither of them anticipated at that moment the part which human and natural feelings were to play in the immediate future. The welding of the links in that emotional chain which was destined eventually to circumscribe their united world of desires was a process which occupied some time. It began with the fellowship of a domestic inventory. It grew in the interchange of the most commonplace gestures of personal inquiry. It budded in the mutual recognition of unexpressed suffering. It came to flower in the unadorned confession of a failure to achieve. Barbara elaborated the full story of Mrs. Piddinghoe, and the quality of sympathy which her account evoked prompted her to ask Caleb Thirkettle 's opinion about the colour of curtains for a spare bedroom. Then she began to consult him about her frocks and hats. Queer, oh! so very queer. What could Caleb know about frocks and hats? And yet she felt that she had never had so sympathetic a consultant. Frocks and hats led to other things. As the days went on, she found herself more and more depending upon his quick opinion, and it was not his opinion only. It was that, in consulting him, the matter, however trivial, became of increased importance to herself. She looked forward to his visits, and saved up little things to tell him. Never before in her life had she met anyone to whom the barest detail became significant. Soon she had told him all about Isabel, and the affair of herself rehearsing for the revue, and then being frozen out by Mr. Banstead, and the return of Rosie Ventnor. These disclosures rapidly led to confessions of a profounder nature. She told him about her father, her life at High Barrow, about Billy Hamaton, and then the secret concerning her mother, her father's will, her life on tour. She only held back at the indecisions which obsessed her when George proposed.

Even this avowal, she knew, was only held in abeyance. And it gave her a certain joy to feel that one day she would tell Caleb even this. She could envisage the distressed expression on his face, the little, quick, nervous way he would shake his head, the movement of the eyes which seemed to absorb the vision of an experience almost before she had described it.

One afternoon she returned late from a tea and dance, and going into the library she found Caleb seated at the bureau with his head in his hands. The room was in semi-darkness. He looked up and made a movement as though to turn on the electric light. She waved her muff at him and called out:

"No. Don't turn on the light. Come and sit by the fire, if you're not busy."

He rose and walked obediently to the easy chair on the right of the fireplace. Barbara knelt on a tuffet. They looked at each other, and neither spoke. The fire crackled. Over in the studio two girls were rehearsing a duet. George, she knew, was in town. At last she smiled at him and whispered:

"What is the matter, Thirk?"

He, too, tried to smile, but the glow of the fire revealed a smile all twisted awry.

She repeated her question, and he answered huskily:

"I've no right to talk to you as I would like to."

The militant desire for revolt leapt to the forefront of the girl's mind. She flashed out:

"Damn it, Caleb; you have every right."

It was the first time she had called him Caleb, and the employment of the Christian name was part of the challenge she was flinging to the dark forces which always appeared to be imprisoning her desires. Why shouldn't she have a friend? Probably it was her own fault that she had so far muddled her life, but she had no intention of being cut off from every channel which might lead to a greater freedom. The young man did not appear surprised. He sighed comfortably, as though the impulsiveness of her interjection had steadied him. He shook his head and said quietly:

"What are you doing with your life, Mrs. Champneys? I've muddled mine."

What an odd question! What was she doing with her life? No one had ever asked her such a thing before. What was she doing with her life? Yes, of course, she. knew that Caleb had muddled his. She could tell it by his eyes. And she, too but no, she wasn't going to acknowledge yet that she had failed. She spoke defensively.

"I know I haven't done much. I expected to do more get on more quickly. I've married a successful actor-manager. I I've—"

She knew she was talking outside her subject, and when he replied:

"You're only speaking of material failures and successes," she answered humbly: "Oh! I know."

There was a silence in the room, emphasised by the distant sound of girls' shrill voices singing a song about "Casey's sold his sister's socks to Sue." The somewhat ironic contrast between this song and the sombre atmosphere of muffled confession was not lost upon Barbara. She could not hear the Words, but she knew the song quite well, and had sung in the chorus innumerable times. The ridiculous words kept jumbling through her head as she listened to Caleb's confession.

"You see, both the parents persuaded almost insisted. I had only just left school. The child was born before our marriage, you see. The trouble is, I never loved her, never, never. I lost my head. We met at a skating-rink in Whitby. I knew nothing. I could not even earn my own living at that time. The trouble is, Mrs. Champneys, she loved me. She still loves me in her way. I have no capacity for cruelty. Do you understand what I mean? At Charborough I won prizes for prose essays, and poetry also. I was mad about the drama. We were turned adrift. I tried to act, but it was a failure. Grade got small parts, but I couldn't sponge on her, could I? I have written two plays neither suitable for commercial production. If it had only happened later. I've had no chance of going through the mill. I'm an amateur. I want to do so much. I'm not exactly a fool. I'm a kind of intellectual handy-man. I can earn my living now. I could in all sorts of ways. I believe I could be a plumber. Don't laugh at me. But it's the terrible sense of not being allowed to do the work one wants

"Why don't you leave her?"

"How can I leave her? It would be unspeakably cruel. And there are the children."

"Do you love the children?"

"One can't help being fond of one's children."

Again a silence fell between them. Barbara's heart was beating fast. She knelt there in the firelight, a woman aglow in the luxury of the confessional. Clutching the beads at her throat, she whispered:

"I've mucked things too, Caleb. I expect you understand. It has taken me years to realise that I don't love my husband. He promised me that love would come afterwards...."

Her voice died away, and they were afraid to look at each other. Suddenly she said:

"Call me Barbara. We must be pals."

She did not turn her head, but she was aware of him rocking restlessly in his chair. His voice was almost inaudible.

"You see what it is drifting to. I must go away, Mrs. Champneys."

She could not account for it, but when he said that she felt a queer stab of triumph. For the moment the innate desires of her being were completely satisfied. They demanded nothing but repose for the purpose of reflection. She laughed softly and stood up.

"We're a queer couple, Thirk. You mustn't desert me. I've got to go and dress now for the theatre."

As she left she closed the door quietly, as one might on leaving a room where someone was at prayer.

II

That night Barbara slept but little. She was conscious primarily of a profound surprise.

"I've had some rum experiences," she thought, "but nothing like this has ever happened to me before. I've never met anyone before I wanted to tell everything to, regardless..."

Caleb, with his reticences and his restlessness had come like a prophet out of the wilderness. His almost incoherent implications had conjured up a vast sea of delight of which she at present only stood on the foreshore. His perfunctory dismissal of material failures and successes came almost in the nature of revelation. She was uneducated, neglected, already sickening of "the flesh-pots of Egypt," but hungry for more substantial satisfactions. What had Caleb to offer?

"It's damned awful being a woman," she thought at one point. It was less the restraints and inhibitions which the sex disability imposed upon her than the trend of outlook which the exigencies of her upbringing had forced her to adopt. Had she been a boy, her father would have educated her differently. Had she been a boy, she would have championed her mother's cause openly. She would have had the freedom to attack and reconstruct.

Caleb? Their cases were not identical. He had made his own mistake, and he was free to rectify it. She was a victim of the mistakes of others, and she had to work furtively, in the dark. She had to grope for the spiritual threads which others had snapped. Towering above her was the immovable mass of her father 's enduring shadow and she was by no means an irresistible force. Almost as though he had ordained it, she now staggered beneath the dominance of another man who exercised in the flesh somewhat similar prerogatives. A weaker character than her father, but with the same myopic conservatism of outlook. A little more human than her father indeed, in many ways far too human but equally egoistic, self-sufficient, and blind to another's particularly if it be a woman's point of view; and by these tokens carrying in his heart the infinite capacity for cruelty.

In that mood she postulated mankind as a wholly unbalanced discord of the sexes. Men were cruel. Her smattering of reading presented jumbled visions from Joan of Arc burnt at the stake to Tess hanged. Her own experience rioted with recollections from her father's injustice and silent tyranny to the little agents who mauled girls about, from George's almost unconscious grip upon her freedom to the arrogance of Julius Banstead. Strangely enough, this sense of inequality did not depress her; rather she felt stimulated and militant. St. George would never have been a hero if there hadn't been a dragon or two about.

She awoke refreshed and eager for whatever the day might bring forth. And the first thing that the day brought forth was a simple desire that her life might serve some useful end. She evolved this amiable ambition from her own inner-consciousness while having a bath, and she was extremely pleased with herself at the resolution. Caleb had said nothing about serving a useful end, but the influence of his benign disquietude prompted it. She resolved that George was frankly a materialist and to that hour she had been the same. "What were they doing with their lives but getting on, making money, chasing popularity, buying comforts, and worshipping luxuries? Never once had George hinted at anything more ennobling. He could be generous, kind-hearted, sentimental all within the ambit of these material considerations; beyond that the shoots of his ambitions withered and died.

The next thing which the day brought forth was distressing news. After the conversation with the old actor in the cafe, she had written to a lawyer in Liverpool and asked him to try and trace any record of her mother. A letter came by the second post. The lawyer had been successful in his search. Her mother had died nineteen years ago, in an infirmary in one of the suburbs of Liverpool. Having apparently no relatives or friends or money, she had been buried in a pauper 's grave. "When Barbara read that she cried out in agony. Annette came running into the room:

"Oh, madame! madame! qu'est-ce qu'il y a?"

But Barbara had no use at that moment for the decorative French maid. Her heart was bleeding. She must go and break the news to George. But George was in the studio, trying over some songs with Birtles; he would resent any interruption. Even if she told him she envisaged his large moist face looking rather scared and distressed; not distressed on account of her mother, but distressed because the news disturbed his own placid environment; it upset his dear Fancy and made her difficult and unapproachable. She had told him about the old actor, and that she had written to Liverpool, but he had never enquired whether she had heard any news. He looked upon the episode as unpleasant and unnecessary. Why couldn't she let sleeping dogs lie? On second thoughts she decided not to tell him. What was the use? She must tell someone. There was Isabel. Isabel would probably weep and hug her, but would she understand? Isabel had a way of sometimes just saying the wrong thing. She was as great a materialist as George.

No, the only person who would understand was her new friend Caleb, and he didn't come till four o'clock. She did not go out; but hung about the house in a fever of impatience. When he did arrive the ordeal became acuter still, for George commandeered the young secretary and they retired to the library. She went to the door and listened, and she could hear George comfortably sucking his pipe and droning.

"Er—you might write a line to Sydney Airedale and ask him if he's read 'The Gay Dog's Day." want to get his report in. Oscar Lemmon Doesn't think much of it. By the way, make a note, I promised Birtles 15 per cent, on the rake off we shall get from the sale of 'Mr. Percy's Pants Have Parted' Where are last week's returns from the B company on tour? 'Urn. I told Ledger that it would be no good north of Glasgow and Edinburgh. 'Um, 'urn, well covering expenses, anyway."

How trivial and vulgar it all seemed! And there was Caleb Thirkettle, who might be writing pros dramas or doing something great and worthy, wasting his time writing stupid notes about Mr. Percy s Pants! Caleb was trapped, and she was trapped, caught up in the machinery of social progress. Mr. Percy's pants! Social progress! Would George never stop talking? At last he drifted from business to social matters, and she heard him tell Caleb two of "the very latest," which he had heard at the Club yesterday, and Caleb laughed politely. Or, perhaps, he was really amused. Men were strange creatures.

With almost uncanny deliberation George came out into the hall and put on his hat and coat. On observing her he said:

"Hullo, dear. I've got to go up to White's to meet Joe Costing."

The temptation to say "All right. Well, hurry up," was almost unendurable.

When he had really gone she darted into the library, and, without any preliminary explanation, thrust the letter into Caleb's hand and said: "Read that!"

She saw the look of troubled concern steal over his face as his eyes scanned the letter. When he had finished it, he was really angry. He exclaimed:

"My God! What a damned injustice!"

Oh, it was just what she wanted, someone to express her own feelings, and to share the horror and the anger. Now that she had her victim there she did not mean to spare him. She stood with her back to the fire, and tears started to her eyes, although her voice was fairly under control.

"Think of it, Caleb. My father buried in Westminster Abbey, my mother in a pauper's grave. And at one time they must have loved each other. They shared the same house, the same bed. Do you think he could have known? Did they drift apart? If Father was so hard, so unjust as that why did he keep that packet of love letters? What could Mother have done that the lawyer said she treated him badly, 'after all his generosity'?"

She rattled out these questions, knowing full well that Caleb could not give any satisfactory answers, but comforted in sharing the anguish they provoked.

When she had quieted a little, he said reflectively:

"Your Mother could not have been a bad woman."

The remark surprised her, and she exclaimed "Why?"

"People have said that you are the spit and image of her."

Ah! She wanted him to know the truth of all things. She could not let that pass. She went up close to him and whispered fiercely:

"Don't be deceived, Caleb. I'm no bally heroine. I'm awful at moments. You'd never believe it if 1 told you what I'm like. I'm out for myself all the time. I've always been like that. As a child I was utterly selfish and spoiled. When I look back on it I feel convinced now that I only married George because it would help me on. Till you came and talked about 'material successes and failures. I believed my mission was just that to get on, and be popular and rich and successful. But now somehow I believe that it is something else—"

"Which goes to prove my contention. Fundamentally you're fine. They've never given you a chance Barbara."

"Thank you for calling me Barbara. You're awfully nice to me, Caleb, but, believe me, I don't deserve it. I know I'm not an out-and-out rotter like some of these women. But, oh! I have awful vicious, foolish impulses. I'm not only selfish."

"The tragedy is that a man may have vicious, foolish impulses, and be buried in Westminster Abbey. If a woman has them she goes to a pauper's grave."

"Then there is no God."

"Yes, there is. That's just what there is a God."

"Oh, Caleb, tell me what you mean."

The young man turned away from her and walked slowly up and down the room. The troubled look still haunted his eyes. He spoke disconnectedly.

"I am bad at explaining, Barbara. I can only say things as they occur to me. I'll tell you why there's a God when sometimes it seems there can't be. One has to look at the broad line. Man has sprung from an inferior mammal. What impresses me in this—in the big sweep of physical and spiritual evolution there is no such thing as retrogression. Sometimes things appear to be going backwards, but this is only because they are preparing for a spring forward. Individuals fail, races become decadent and die, but the thrust of humanity must inevitably be upward."

Barbara pondered these statements carefully. They went a little beyond her immediate comprehension, but they were charged with hope. She frowned at the fire.

"Do you believe in Nemesis, then?"

"I believe in a spiritual Nemesis."

Spiritual! Why did Caleb always talk about spiritual things, when no one else had ever done so except in connection with the Church or table-rapping!

Without turning her head she said eagerly:

"What precisely do you mean by spiritual!"

"That part of us which deals with ideas—"

"Ideas!"

"Yes. You and your mother are both victims of ideas. Those ideas will meet their Nemesis. Listen, Barbara; we are all so apt to regard the ugliness and injustice which surround us that we overlook the greater ugliness and injustice from which they have sprung."

"Do you really believe that mankind advances!"

"Mankind can 't help advancing."

"It didn't help my mother much."

"The physical existence of both your mother and your father is at an end. Their spiritual story is not yet complete. That is what I believe."

"Oh! I would like to believe that so much."

"Moreover, the ideas which they individually embodied will work out to an equitable solution."

"I would like to believe that, too."

"Perhaps that is why you are conscious of sometimes feeling like an instrument. The forces are working through you and through your—"

The young man hesitated, and Barbara buried her face in her hands.

She groaned aloud: "O God, I wish I had a son!"

III

George was quite right. Love did come afterwards to Barbara Champneys, but it was not through her husband that she plumbed its mystic depths. It came suddenly, tempestuously, and with a radiance which illumined the dark corners of her soul. It was there before she knew it, with gossamer wings fluttering against her window pane at dawn. It filled her crowded day with a thousand tokens of rapture. For the first time she saw life as it was, and as it might be, and as it had never surely been before to anyone. And the magician holding the key to this enchanted world was the queer little "Frog-face" secretary, whom George had substituted for the dangerous Mr. Toller.

Her love was cradled in his enveloping sympathy, which quickened as it warmed. She flew to him like the bee to the clover. She rose to him like a drenched flower to the rays of the sun. He became an indispensable, inevitable salve to her aching wounds of moral duress. She listened for his footsteps, lulled her senses to an ecstasy of comfort in the warm timbre of his voice, in the exaltation of his words. The idyllic connection rapidly followed the normal evolution of "human and natural feelings." She realised this one morning when he was packing a despatch case. He was leaning over the table, vigorously tucking a sheaf of contracts into the case. The lines of his mouth and nostril were accentuated. Around his eyes were tiny wrinkles as he frowned at the job in hand. Abruptly she thought: "Good God! I love him." She wanted to laugh, but at the same time she thought: "There will never be anyone else."

She felt no idle desire to kiss, as she had in the case of the lord's son. It was an overwhelming desire to possess. She wanted Caleb for her very own, always always. She knew at that moment that fate had mocked at her; her life with George was a travesty. What was she to do? And Caleb? The action of packing the bag was symbolical. Every day he determined to pack his bag and go away. He knew that this was the right and proper indeed the only thing to do. And every day he put it off. He was an idealist whose idealism was temporarily suspended in face of a stupendous temptation. A married man with two children making love to his employer's wife! It was in vain that he persuaded himself that this statement gave a false account of the situation, that he was not "making love to her" he loved her, which was a different thing; he was helping her, in a way he was necessary to her. His conscience mocked him. Her image was never for an instant absent from his thoughts. He knew the hour would come when he would have to declare himself or die. This was no ordinary intrigue of the senses; nevertheless, the senses insist upon playing their part in such a communion. He had never attempted to kiss her, or even to press her hands unduly when they met and parted. He rather went to the opposite extreme, knowing that any such action would mark the approach of crisis. But their eyes were not idle, and the message of eyes cannot be muted or misunderstood. For the rest, everything dovetailed with a satisfying perfection that appeared pre-ordained. The playground of their dawning passion seemed specially prepared. Caleb had every reason to spend several hours every day in the house, and George was frequently not there. Barbara had every excuse for visiting the young secretary in the library. Was it not natural for the manager's wife to talk about the affairs of the theatre? In the evening she would frequently see him again behind the scenes or in one of the offices. Frequently they would drive down together in her car.

Barbara, moreover, was not unschooled in the science of intrigue; her conscience was a little dulled by the hazards of her theatrical career. In every instance it was she who made the advances, she who was the more obstinate in the acceptance of the established fact. Blinded as she was by the sudden glare of this new revelation, she nevertheless realised the need for caution. So far he had not had time to focus the eventualities and possibilities of the position, but she was instantly aware of its dangers and penalties. Her one absorbing impulse was not to let it slip away, to hold this precious visitation and make the utmost of it against the buffets of the world. To this end she quickly realised that circumspection would be essential. She must be cautious and watchful, and not shatter the spectrum of this heaven-sent light by any rash or foolish act.

Caleb at first was for doing the wise and proper thing, but by the more pervading force of her reliance upon his strength she gradually gained the ascendancy over his resolves.

"So long as it doesn't go any further," was the rampart of defence upon which he constantly fell back.

At the same time, he knew in his heart of hearts that the day would come when it would be bound to go further. He adumbrated visions of Platonic gestures, but the central fact of passion was graven with no uncertain markings. She was at that time -a beautiful and desirable woman, in the fullness of her development. In her presence his idealism became a thing of dusty theories. Life is a reality which springs surprises upon us every day. Even what we think and believe and pin our faith to today may be on the shelf to-morrow, accumulating the dust. Oh, he could argue himself out of it well enough, but what of the morrow? If he should awake to find himself beyond the sound of her voice, away from the perfume of her hair, shut off for ever from the welcome of her eyes, what would brook the noblest theories of the noblest theorists? Let Plato rage in hell, and Aristotle, Luther and Marcus hug their precious sophistries in what dim corner of the universe the gods had placed them! He was alive, in Kensington, with an April sun warming the spring buds in his employer's garden. And soon she would be there.

Above the passion which obsessed him his mind brooded like a mother alarmed at a recalcitrant child but unable to check its unexpected humours. He analysed and introspected, and wavered hesitatingly before the apparition.

Barbara had no such misgivings, or if she had they were buried in a sub-conscious plane, momentarily shelved by the urgency of more pressing affairs. She was like an animal recognising an atavistic tendency, and blindly consumed by an uncontrollable desire to preserve it, believing thereby to serve the primal instincts of its type. What thinking she die was directed by her sense of cunning and self-protection. In her presence Caleb found himself a vast compendious philosopher, with the heart of a child Oh, it was a joy to tell her little things, to watch the eager parting of her lips, the eyes hungrily absorbing his most trivial impression. Banalities became important, generalisations a delicious adventure, the hard facts of daily experience a tender chronicle of mutual regard. And then the confidences which swung backwards and forwards whither did they expect them to lead?

The crisis came in a very commonplace way. One evening, after tea, she went into the library. She was dressed for going out. Caleb had his back to her and he pretended to be absorbed in his work. She crept up on tip toe and in a sudden whim put her arms round his head and her hands over his eyes. Then she laughed, and glanced at the desk. On it were books and papers connected with the theatre, but in one corner was an open copy of Browning. She exclaimed:

"Oh! so this is the way you pretend to do your work! The sack for you, Mr. Thirkettle."

The boy seized her two hands firmly and pulled them down upon his breast; but he did not release them. By this action her cheek was very near his own. He replied:

"Please, madame, I was only reading about you."

What was he reading about her? The question was not immediately answered, for their cheeks touched. He felt her hair tickling his temples, and it was more than he could endure. He swung round on his seat, put his right arm round her neck, and pulled her face to his. He kissed her cheek, and mouth, and lips, and she did not protest. When it was done they both laughed self-consciously. It was she who spoke first.

"What were you reading about me?"

He found it necessary to kiss her again in a rather more prolonged manner before he replied:

"You shall read it yourself."

And he handed her the book opened at "Porphyria's Lover."

Neither made any reference to the sudden expression of passion. Barbara took the book away and went and sat in a corner seat. She did not look up until she had finished the poem. Then she said:

"What an extraordinary poem? Why does it make you think of me!"

Caleb stood up and walked towards her stealthily. He sat down by her side and took her hand.

"I don't know. I always think of you as Porphyria."

"What does it really mean, Caleb! Why does the man strangle her!"

"For the same reason that I want to strangle you."

"Oh, you mustn't do that. It would seem so, so ungrateful, after we had been such good friends. Besides, I should hate it. I don't want to be strangled. No, no, not again—"

She darted away from him with the book in her hand. When some distance away she read aloud the last two lines:

And all night long? we have not stirred,

And yet God has not said a word.

"I like that. It's so—graphic, isn't it. Of course God never does say a word. He wouldn't have said a word, whether the man strangled her or not. Do you know what God does, Caleb? He sends messages to our door by a messenger, and the mess ger hands them in and says, 'There is no answer There never is an answer to God."

There were tears, born of a fierce excitement on the brink of her eyes. Suddenly she thrust out arms and said in a changed voice: "What are we going to do about this I"

Caleb sat there staring at his feet. He was ashamed, perplexed and profoundly stirred.

"It's got to be faced," he answered, not looking up. "It's been coming on so long. I'm a cad, Barbara a cad, an utter cad. I must go away. "

Like a flash she was upon him, her arms round his neck, her lips pressed to his.

"No, no, you can't do that. I want you, Caleb. I love you."

From that moment they became lovers, lovers without a plan or a policy, loving secretly and furtively, without shame or misgiving, content that for a few hours each day the world rewarded them with the light of each other's presence.

IV

The Frolics still played to packed houses. At that time a revue was being done called "The Baker's Dozen," the company having now swelled to eleven people. The judicious sometimes murmured that "George Champneys and his company are nothing like they used to be in the old days, when they did the whole show in pierrot dress and practically no properties or change or raiment," but George knew the taste of the groundlings, and he was out to please them. He spent thousands of pounds on elaborate sets, properties, illusions, and tricks of lighting. The performance more closely resembled a pantomime than an entertainment by a pierrot troupe. Rosie Ventnor had gone, and her place was now taken by the famous May Mendelssohn. In other respects the cast had also been strengthened But as it happened, Barbara made an unexpected hit with an Apache dance, which she danced with an actor named Leonard Greer. The scene was a dingy attic with weird lighting effects, and the music, which had a haunting lilt, was by an Austrian named Szolt. Greer was an excellent 'dancer, and there was something about the combination which excited Barbara indescribably. With a red scarf round her head and a loose black ulster over her pierrette frock, she threw herself into the interpretation of the dance with great abandon. The actions were extremely violent and exhausting to the performers, Greer in the finale picking her up and throwing her across his shoulders; but the dance always brought down the house, and had to be repeated.

"What has happened to Fancy?" queried the other members of the company. "She seems to have found herself."

George was frankly delighted and proud. He went about saying to everyone:

"I say, have you seen Fancy's dance?"

Even the Press bestowed a measure of praise upon the performance, and "Day by Day" said: "In the Apache dance in the last act Miss Fancy Telling and Mr. Leonard Greer proved themselves artistes considerably above the average British terpsichorean standard." Could enthusiasm go further? To Caleb her explanation was this:

"When I do that dance I think of Porphyria. She was like that. She had a dolt of a husband, and she got fed up. One night she just went mad. It was music or something which got her. Music's a queer thing, the way it makes you sometimes feel you are yourself, only seventeen times more so. You see, she was very keen on that poor, lonely man and his cheerless grate." She went to a dance and danced like mad, but she couldn't get the thought of him out of her head. And so, suddenly, late at night, she just sneaked out when no one was looking her husband was probably having a whisky and soda in the smoke-room she rushed through the rain and the sullen wind to the poet's house, where he lived all alone. She knew it was an awful thing to do. She burnt her boats, you see. But it was worth while, perhaps."

"Perhaps it was," replied Caleb. "It may be we are only to take the strangling as a symbol, suffocated by popular disapproval, eh? All the same, I can't bring myself to like your Apache dance."

"Oh, but why, Caleb?"

"I don't know. It's somehow you, and yet, as you say, seventeen times yourself. It's the savagest thing I've ever seen."

They were in the library at the time, and she went up to him and pretended to bite the lobe of his ear.

"I am a savage," she retorted.

He pulled her down on to his knee and kissed her.

"This is getting horribly serious, darling," he groaned. "What are we going to do?"

"Be circumspect," she replied, snuggling her cheek against his.

"This is a good demonstration of it. Anyone might come in at that door at any moment."

"George is in town. There is no one else likely to."

"It's the unlikely thing one has to watch. I love you terribly."

Barbara left him and went to the window. In the little garden clumps of panises and tulips were revelling m the April sunshine, a lilac bush was a-bud Suddenly she turned to him and said:

"Where are your rooms?"

"In the Fulham Road."

"Why shouldn't we go there?"

"My dear, what were you saying about circumspection?"

"There's no harm in my calling on you at your rooms, is there?"

"I have a landlady."

"Well, what about it? She wouldn't think I'd come to murder you, would she?"

"No no, I suppose she wouldn't, We might be seen going in. You're famous, you know, Fancy Telling."

"Nobody lives in the Fulham Road."

"All right, my dowager duchess. You'd be shocked, though. It 's an awful little hole."

"I'd be happier there with you, Caleb than in any dowager duke's mansion."

"You darling!"

And so, the following day Barbara Champneys called on Caleb Thirkettle at his rooms in the Fulham Road, and no one saw them go in, and no one saw them come out; neither did anyone know what transpired in the rooms. They were dingy. There was a small sitting-room, overcrowded with heavy mid- Victorian furniture, and the room connected by a folding-door with a bedroom slightly larger.

V

In talking of "spiritual Nemesis" Caleb soon became aware that he was submitting himself to the position of being hoist of his own petard. His conscience was on the rack. Every day he became more deeply in love with her, and the more he loved her the more troubled he became. He was a cad to George, a cad to his wife, and an unspeakable cad to his two young girls. Somehow the latter case affected him most. He had no particular regard for George, not a great deal for his wife; but the children who were at present in the charge of a sister-in-law were dependent upon him and his good name. Moreover they adored him, and although they were too young to understand any marital complication, they were old enough to hug the illusion of a devoted mummy and daddy. If he left Gracie in the lurch it would bring unutterable distress upon all three. The grim question of money had also to be considered. Barbara had no private means, and he was entirely dependent upon his salary. If they ran away he might find it very difficult to get another situation, and Barbara had been accustomed all her lfe to every luxury and refinement. He could not possibly desert the children, or leave Gracie to keep them.

The position was impossible. The love which had come to them both at last, ablaze with the fine flowers of idealism and true passion, could never be anything other than a sordid intrigue. In this respect the attitude of Barbara surprised him. She gave no evidence of the slightest shame or remorse. She was a complete intriguer. She brought to bear in the matter a degree of cunning which astounded him. Down at the theatre she was just friendly and a little formal. In the house, when others were about, it was the same. But when they were alone he could have verified Isabel's comment:

"You're a passionate little devil. A man could have a good time with you."

They ranged through moods of playfulness and passionate disputations. Although her mind was less tutored than his, he found her easy and companionable to talk to, probably because she had tasted the stuff we call real life. She made shrewd and surprising conclusions, and would sometimes jump an obstacle which baffled him by the aid of her intuitions. In reverting to the culpability of their unholy liaison, she always adhered to the primitive excuse.

"We're not doing anyone any harm. It's our affair. Something tells me that love like ours can't be wicked."

Caleb found it difficult to answer this satisfactorily, particularly as the solution would involve the honour and the character of Barbara herself. And so he compromised, and the summer months slipped by. Every day he came to the house, and two or three times a week she visited him at his rooms. Sometimes they would take the car and dash down into the country, for a few hours ramble over the Surrey hills. And they would sit in the bracken, and talk of God, and life, and poets, and the mystery of sex, nations, personality, destiny, restaurants, stage-chatter, books, love and so back to God again. And except for restaurant and stage-chatter, Barbara appeared not to have talked of these things before.

She was a spiritual opportunist, making a religion of her own as she went along. The more she yielded 'to the claims of this illicit passion, the more alert did she appear to religious suggestion. She wanted to know all about God, and the why and wherefore of existence, and in this regard, Caleb was as much an experimenter as herself, except that he had covered more ground, j He described himself as an agnostic, with a sneaking regard for theosophy and a confirmed belief in reincarnation. When she asked him the value of reincarnation, he replied:

"Because it confirms my faith in there being no such thing as retrogression. If you believe in physical evolution, you must believe in spiritual evolution. Everything is emerging going forward."

"But," said Barbara, "how about when you see a man start decently and then go to pot?"

"He has emerged from a lower type still. The fact that he started life decently may show that he is improving. In the next reincarnation he may hold as a decent chap to the end."

Barbara shook her head. She was not enamoured of reincarnation.

"It seems to wipe out such a thing as heredity, for instance."

"Wouldn't you have it wiped out?" quickly retorted Caleb. "We are too apt to look at things in terms of duality, whereas everything is a trinity."

"How do you mean?"

"There is action and reaction, and then the spirit it evokes. If you study mathematics, you find that everything is in threes."

"The Father, the Son, and the Holy Ghost."

"Precisely. You cannot talk of the Father without first postulating the Son, and so the Spirit is produced."

"Now, come down to earth, Caleb darling Assuming that my father treated my mother badly, are not his sins visited upon me?"

"Nothing is visited upon you except physical attributes, and even these only by suggestion You are an independent spirit, with an independent existence to work out."

"That's rather jolly, but it sounds so lonely. Nature seems beastly cruel."

"Nature is, but nature and God are not the same thing. God is rather a reaction against nature. Nature is a kind of wild profligate. It is picking up the pieces and putting them in order which is God."

VI

In those days she was studiously charming to George. The large comedian had arrived at a position of static security at the top of the tree, both professionally and socially. His popularity had never been greater, his wealth more soundly invested, his home life more comfortable and satisfying. The staff had settled down, and his dear Fancy was always there in the niche he had designed for her. He had only to whistle and lo! she answered his bidding. For the rest, his days were filled with pleasant activities, in which universal adulation of himself played a conspicuous part. He sometimes drank a little more whiskey than was wise for him, and in the morning his pulmonary organs were invariably congested and wheezy; but for the most part his health remained good. Moreover, his affection for Fancy increased. He observed that during the last month or so she had been much more tractable and friendly, much less touchy, and less ungettable; he was proud, too, of the success she had made with the Apache dance. George had never found her so adorable. He cherished a supreme hope that perhaps, after all, his Fancy was going to fall in love with him. As to any suspicion concerning herself and Caleb, he never gave the matter a second's consideration. Banstead said to him one night in the dressing-room:

"I say, old boy, that young Thirkettle's sweet on your wife."

Not even then did he feel the slightest apprehension. He laughed and said:

"Oh, is that so! I hadn't noticed it. Poor Fancy!"

He did not even enquire upon what Banstead based his suspicion, but the producer not without reasons of his own followed it up.

"You've only got to watch his face when he's looking at her. It's my business to read faces."

George smiled indulgently and dismissed the matter from his mind. Certainly, later in the evening, he did detect Caleb regarding his wife with an adoring, dog-like expression. Instantly he glanced at Barbara. Her face was tranquil, almost cold and expressionless.

"Poor old Thirk!" he reflected, and prepared for his cue. It was nothing. These little wayside infatuations were common to the whole order of his experience. "Why, even he yes, even since he was married happily married he occasionally.... It meant nothing, nothing at all unless the attraction was reciprocated to the full. And look at Barbara! Not much chance of that. In three minutes time he was singing:

"Oh, my! Hold me down!

My wife's gone away till Monday!"

In spite of Barbara's extreme circumspection and George's obtuseness, the lovers did not, however, escape the breath of scandal. It would have been a miracle if they had. Annette had her shrewd suspicions, and one of the parlour maids had entered the library at an unfortunate moment. And the long arm of coincidence was stretched forth by the call boy's aunt, who lived a little further down the Fulham Road, and on two occasions saw Caleb and Barbara coming out, recognising Miss Telling at once through the good fortune of having, on occasions, had free seats given her. Thus was Barbara's contention that "no one lived in the Fulham Road" completely discountenanced. The call boy's aunt told the call boy, who told one of the stage hands, who passed it on to the assistant stage manager. From there the story passed by easy stages to the whole company, increasing a little in force at every repetition. Everybody began to know that there was an affair going on between Fancy Telling and the Chief's secretary; everybody except George. You have to be on very intimate terms with a man to hint to him that his wife is unfaithful. No one was in this position except Banstead, who foresaw the possibilities of a little sexual blackmail. His attempts in this direction did not, however, meet with the success he anticipated. He ensnared her into one of the offices by a subterfuge, and then tried to put across the strong, masterful stuff which had almost succeeded before. But on this occasion he received a violent slap on the mouth. It hurt him, and he winced. Drawing back, he growled:

"Hold on, you little wildcat! I suppose you think it isn't known about you and young Thirkettle."

Barbara was staggered. She certainly had no suspicion that it was known. She turned pale, and blurted out:

"What are you talking about?" Banstead saw that the blow had gone home. He shifted his ground a little.

"Come, be decent. I have no wish to tell your husband."

The implied threat stung her to a fury. "Tell and be damned to you!" she snapped, and she raised her hands like a kitten's claws, ready to strike. Her eyes blazed. She strode with tense deliberation towards the door. Gripping the handle she hissed at him:

"Get out of the theatre, you dirty cad!" When she had gone Banstead whistled. "Didn't come off, old boy," he said to himself. He was not, however, unduly perturbed. She had no authority to turn him out of the theatre, and he knew that she would never report the matter to George. If she started stirring up mud of that description, even George might become suspicious. On the other hand, he had warned his Chief, and he could go no further. There was no proof, and George would only resent these insinuations. For the moment it might be considered a drawn battle. He had frightened her, and hurt her feelings; but she had given him a jar to his vanity and a swollen lip.

From that day greater circumspection than ever was employed; on the other hand, they were both under a closer scrutiny. At the theatre they avoided each other entirely, but in the house they felt fairly free when George was out, but a little nervy of sounds and knocks. Not having the personal acquaintance of the call boy's aunt, and not being aware that the first rumour came from that direction, they were less circumspect regarding the visits to the Fulham Road. Once there, they felt perfectly safe and free. George did not even know the address, and Caleb's wife was on a summer tour in the North. Love laughs at locksmiths and even landladies, and is seldom down-hearted at anything except deliberate frustration. Barbara did not tell Caleb about Banstead, but she hinted that there were rumours going about, and they must be more careful. Caleb by this time had subdued his moral misgivings. In the light of his mistress' eyes all was right with the world. The position was tragic but inevitable. He would get on, and by some means or other make money, and then they would run away. They would both get divorced, and then one day he would be the lawful husband of his darling Barbara. But of course he would always continue to keep the two children, and would compensate Gracie in some way or the other. Gracie was warm-hearted but shallow-minded. She would soon adapt herself to the new conditions probably marry again. Oh! it would be all right in the end. If only one were not eternally haunted by the element of crisis.

Some shadow of it came to Barbara one wet evening in July. It was Sunday, and she had been forced to spend the evening at home, as George wanted her to help entertain a party of his friends. They had left early, as they came from a distance.

When they had gone she went up to her dressing-room and changed into a peignoir. She was feeling tired, and a little anxious. She looked at herself in the mirror, and noted the pallor of her cheeks and the little rings beneath her eyes. For some reason or other, she put some lip-salve on her lips, sighed and then removed it. She walked across the room and rang for Annette. When the French maid arrived she said:

"Annette, will you go and ask the master if he will come and see me for a minute? I'm going to bed. I'm rather tired."

"Parfaitement, madame."

The mirror had a curious attraction for her. She turned her face this way and that, and sighed again. "I shall have to tell him. I might as well get it over."

George came into the room, puffily solicitous.

"Well, old girl?"

"George, I'm afraid I shall have to cut that Apache dance."

"All right, old girl; as you like. It's been going some time. Weather too hot for you?"

"It 's not that."

"What is it, then, dear?"

"I'm going to have a child."

The earth rocked under the clamour of this calm, terrific statement. She had done it, and there was nothing to dread except the humidity of his acceptance. She saw his large, somnolent face suddenly alive with the signs of startled vitality. It shook like a pink blanc-mange. His eyes expressed amazement, fear, joy, and worst of all adoraton. Then then seemed to melt and die away, as he murmured:

"Fancy darling thank God!"

The fool! He was blubbering the worst thing that could have happened. A big man blubbing and blubbering like a child! What did he want to blub for? What had he got to thank God for! Who was God? What was God? Caleb had said that it was picking up the pieces and putting them in order.

Nature was a profligate. Quite true. Oh, but she couldn't stand this. He was advancing upon her, holding her in his arms. His tears were wetting his cheeks. He was murmuring:

"Fancy darling, this will make all the difference. We shall be so happy. You shall come out of the bill and rest. You shall have the best of everything: nurses, specialists a lovely place to go to everything; nothing shall be spared."

She choked hoarsely:

"I shall be all right. I don't want all that."

Everything he did made it more difficult. His sentimentality would kill her, and she couldn't afford to die yet. So difficult to keep one's head. She assumed uncontrollable fatigue and eased away from him.

"I must go to bed now."

"Yes, yes, yes, of course, of course. I will help you; lean on me dear old girl."

Would it never be possible to rid herself of his protestations, all this while, all these months to come? In bed she hung limply, and turned away, was only her demand for Annette which finally brought about his departure. When he had gone she set her teeth and said: "I will not cry. I hate him. Why did he want to go on like that?"

Sternly she thought of Caleb, and of their love of the days to come. But she was tired, very, very tired, and a little unstrung. George had looked so big, and helpless, and babyish, and appealing, standing there, so pathetic and pitiable. Oh, it was cruel, horribly cruel; and she did not want to be cruel, not even to George. Suddenly the tears came, whipped into being by the torture of her husband's image.

VII

The appearances are always with us, the riot and the record of chronicled events, the unctuous pronouncement of ordered authority, the awards and penalties of standardised codes, honours for the worthy and the lash for the unsuccessful, virtue and vice clothed in fustian, strutting before an audience hidden by a glare of light, the big band playing, with the crash of cymbal and the beat of drum.

But real life moves onwards to a muffled beat, paying little heed to the appearances. Action and reaction and the spirit evoked, its roots buried deep in the illusion of time. The child unborn is building the temple which the workmen have deserted. The tears which a woman shed long ago are watering the flowers of to-morrow's celebration. It is the tyrant who forges the chains of freedom; the outcast who instructs us in the precise interpretation of civic laws. Memory, like a withered leaf, is lightly blown away; but through the twisted years the horror and the ecstasy come tumbling upon us, and we know them as our own. That life we call our own is not a chronicle of events, but an interaction of conflicting periods. The metallic records of a king are as brittle and unreal as the coloured baubles on a Christmas tree. The nearer we get to life, more muted become the strings, more elusive the word upon the tablet. All the tenderness and sweetness is a heritage we pass along; all the bitterness and anguish is a mortgage upon our spiritual estate. We share it with these others stretching out their hands to us through the darkness. The profligacy of nature is so great that its very abundance would defeat its own ends, but for the fact that there is a force always at work checking it, demanding more sharply defined contours to the specimens evolved, more closely woven fibre to the material produced. And this force demands not merely growth but a definiteness of form, with crisis and accent; as though it were obeying a Draconic law that ordains all things to be made in the image of something, or in a reflection of that image. Our consciousness pivots upon the recognition of our propinquity to the form we are ordained to complete. A buffalo is not conscious of the clumsiness of its form, nor does its conscience smart when it has stolen a choice root from a weaker brother. Man, being nearer to a more perfected form, is conscious of it. He sees himself, and the nearness and the littleness of his perfections. Moreover, he sees above him and beyond him, the solidity of his development, with its accents and crises.

The crisis which came to Barbara was the inevitable chisel-mark of the sculptor who had been preparing his form for just this accent. That she had contributed to its fashioning goes without saying, but that it was only a contribution who shall deny? The conception of absolute free-will is the pleasant illusion of moral policemen. It is the negation of man's place in evolution. It dismisses all complexes and physical reactions. The appearances demand it, but the heart denies it; and the human heart has always been surer in its touch than the human brain. In short, man is not yet far enough advanced to have free-will.

Barbara's early life had been an obscure passage of inhibitions, with their violent reactions. Her natural impulses had been thwarted, less by decrees than by implications which bewildered her. From the very first she was conscious of being spiritually starved, of having to build her own world furtively, and without assistance. No one told her anything. The discovery of the truth about her mother poignantly wounded her. She turned to the world with open arms, asking for pity. It seemed to her the moment for pity; but the world shrugged its shoulders and labelled her a social pariah. Then she became a little heady and reckless. The gay allurements of the theatrical world, which had been her mother's, attracted her. Even here disillusionment dogged her footsteps. She learnt that everything has its price, even beauty. She became embittered after that, but still hungry for she knew not what some inner satisfaction, perhaps. Then one day she met George. She liked him, and he was rich. Inexperienced in the values of love, she plunged into the desperate experiment. Had he not promised to teach her all there was to know of love? She realised with him only what love might be. And she realised that it not only might but must be the most wonderful thing in the world, and she had missed it! Missed it, and cut off her chances forever!

She was young, and she did not utterly despair; but she became less fine. Pleasant compensations were easily to hand, and the years drifted on. It was always her heart which cried out for finer things; her brain which said:

"Don't be a fool. Have a good time."

She observed George becoming more and more material, more and more repulsive. There were times when it was almost impossible not to express her physical loathing of his contact. Beyond that, he realised that he was an empty husk. His ideas were centred on himself, his theatre, his money, his wife. She saw her life in perspective, its past and its future, and she began to be desperate. A child might have saved her, but no child came. Everything was dark and finished, and melancholy stalked in the gay appearances.

And then, just when everything was blackest, came Caleb, offering her everything which the lessons of her experience had taught her to be of value. Can it be said that she did more than contribute to the crisis which she herself knew to be inevitable from the very first?

Blinding in its suddenness, horrible in its effect, and enduring in its result, she nevertheless nurtured a sneaking welcome to the first sounds of its coming. She had reached a position that was intolerable. What part Julius Banstead played in the careful staging of the denouement it is impossible to say. Beyond a known interview with the call boy's aunt, nothing is known of his personal machinations. Being a clever producer, one may assume that he did not rush the action of the tragedy, and that he chose the actors best suited to their parts. Doubtless he enjoyed the subtle construction of his design, and rejoiced in the sure sense of his technical equipment. The complete success of that culminating crisis must have thrilled him.

The last week in July Caleb had gone away for a fortnight's holiday. He went with laggard feet, for the interruption took him from his love. Gracie was then in Ireland, and her sister and husband were taking the two children down to Swanage. There was no excuse for his not joining them. He was fond of the children, and he had neglected them of late. His first letter was couched in this strain:

DARLING,

I am seated in a little garden looking down into Swanage Bay, where white sails flitter hither and thither in an opalescent haze of sea and sky. Hollyhocks stare at me over the low, stone wall, and the tender green of tamarisks fades away into the yellow sands below. The sun is always shining, and at night a pale moon looms disconsolately above the sea like a wistful mother. And it is all hideous. At least, I don't mean hideous I mean empty. It is beautiful and adorable, but empty and meaningless. Oh! my dear, my dear. I sit here at night, all alone in the empty garden, thinking of you, wanting you, aching for you. It is all a setting and no more; an empty stage. It is only love which brings it all to life. How beastly it is pure luck. It makes one feel that the fall of man was a matter of inexperience rather than conscious wickedness. We were both unwise, but, God in Heaven! we didn't mean to be wicked. We both yearned for beauty, and because we had not seen it, we took the reflection for the reality. And now that we have seen the reality and hold it within our grasp we are paralysed by the cruelty its acceptance may bring to others. I play with the children on the shore, and their love and trust shame me, because I am always thinking of other children yours and mine. Getting through the days is a torture. In town one does not feel it so much. Even when I do not see you I know that you may appear at any moment. Barbara, I love you and nothing can ever take that from me.

Your own,

CALEB.

Barbara replied in a similar but brief strain, and these letters passed two at a time every day for the week. On the Saturday Caleb received a telegram.

G. going away Sunday morning till Monday evening.

On Saturday night Caleb arrived home at his rooms in the Fulham Road for the week-end. At eleven o'clock on the Sunday morning he rang Barbara up. Yes, Mrs. Champneys was at home; he should be put through to her. Barbara's dear voice. Everything satisfactory. George had just gone off with Ebbway in the car to Walmer. They were going to play golf; would not be back till just in time for the show the next night. Well, where should they meet? Oh, Barbara would call for him. She was there within the hour. They lunched somewhere, neither was quite sure where, and in the afternoon they motored to Pangbourne, and went on the river in a skiff. They would have preferred a punt, but neither knew how to punt, and so Caleb rowed and they tied up under the willows, and five hours slipped by before they had had time to recount all the important things that had happened during the week's separation. The river was rather crowded, and a rowing boat is not the most comfortable thing to lie in, and so, shortly after six, they returned to town.

"I feel extravagant," said Barbara. "Let's dine somewhere jolly. I 'll pay."

She laughed, and Caleb laughed. Money was such a contemptible thing in the scale of their love. They were always candid about it, and Barbara was so much richer than he.

They dined at an expensive but rather secluded restaurant in Vigo Street, and drank champagne.

They sat for a long time over their dinner, exchanging eternal intimacies, and flashing messages with their eyes and hands. At last Barbara said:

"Well, we must go."

He nodded. "Right you are. I'll see you home."

They went out and hailed a taxi. Caleb looked at her meaningly and repeated: "I'll see you home."

She nodded, and Caleb turned to the driver and said:

"I want you to drive to the Fulham Road. Go straight down. I'll tell you where to stop."

They got into the cab, and Barbara remarked:

"You are a little devil!"

VIII

The mise-en-scene for the climax was not chosen with any regard to aesthetic considerations. Caleb's rooms were dingy, badly lighted, and not even too clean. Smells of ancient cooking pervaded the staircase. In other respects the place was suitable enough.

In the first place, the landlady and her husband had gone out to a supper-party, and some lodgers who lived on the top floor were unknown to Caleb, and seldom visible. To all intents and purposes they had the house to themselves. They entered the sitting-room, and Caleb turned on the light and locked the door. Then he took her in his arms. The embrace was of the prolonged, silent kind. When it came to an end Barbara sighed and took off her hat. In the corner by the window was a box ottoman, with some cushions. Caleb said:

"Come, let's sit down."

She sat a little timidly on the edge of the ottoman, and he sat by her side. Suddenly he remarked:

"I don't think we need the light."

He went and turned it off, and then returned to her, and they made themselves more comfortable in the darkness. There had been no indecision in all these actions. Each seemed to know that everything was predetermined. Even that which followed, the passionate manifestation of mutual desire, was deliberate, as though conceived in an impatient presentiment. Swanage Bay was a poor place compared with the dingy room in the Fulham Road. The possessive sense was soothed. She dozed at last, in a sweet luxury of fatigue, and Caleb listened to her gentle breathing.

Suddenly she started. He felt the white chill of fear about her.

"What's that?"

There was a sound on the stairs outside. Quite true. It was his business as a man to calm her.

"It's nothing, darling. The people upstairs, I expect. "Then he added in a whisper: "The door's locked, anyway."

There were footsteps in the passage. Somehow the terror was contagious. Of course it was only the people from upstairs. Barbara must not be alarmed; that was the first consideration. But, God! what was this inevitable premonition of horror? Why did it seem such a vivid and foreboding fatality that, although he had locked the sitting-room door he had forgotten to lock the bedroom door, and the folding doors between the two were open? Why didn't he dash across even now and lock it? and frighten Barbara? No, no, it was all foolish. In another second he would hear the sounds dying away.

The handle turned. Someone had entered the bedroom. Barbara was sitting up, clutching him fearfully.

"What is it, Caleb? Who is it!"

And still he could not move. The crisis had come and he lay there, as in a coma, watching its development. There was no electric light, but a match was struck in the next room. Two figures appeared at the opening of the folding doors.

They were George and Ebbway.

Someone said: "My Christ!" and the match went out.

They had all seen each other. Ebbway struck another match and advanced into the room to light the gas. His face was white and he was trembling like a leaf. George remained by the folding doors. Barbara was still seated, making ineffectual dabs at her disordered hair. Caleb stood with his back to the window, looking like a murderer condemned to death. The incandescent gas cast a cold, greenish light over the room, and made all their faces appear ghastly. The atmosphere of guilt swathed the actors with a weird mantle of inertia. There was nothing to be said or done.

After lighting the gas Ebbway drew back and stood near George, as though following his traditional habit of giving up stage centre to his chief. It was a position which the famous comedian appeared unable to take advantage of. He put his hand to his heart; his breath came with difficulty.

He gave a kind of whimper: "Fancy" and then stopped. His face shook, and tears started to his eyes. He appeared to grow suddenly old, all the purposes and desires of his being mangled by a glance. He was a finished man, broken and pitiable.

Barbara saw all this, and a profound pity for him crept into her eyes. Poor old George! She could not have controlled the feeling, whatever the circumstances, but almost instantly she remembered his saying:

"The one thing I won't have is your pity. When a man wants love, and he gets only pity, it drives him mad."

The words danced through her memory as she saw his face change. Her pity robbed him of the last shred of hope. He was no longer a man, no longer a lover, but a madman. He who was, by nature, a possessor was robbed of his greatest possession. Into that one moment there crowded all the spoiled impulses of his life, multiplying self-pity. As happens with a weak man in a crisis, his egotism was the controlling force. He was blinded by the cumulative disappointments and disillusions, and this last disillusion of all acted upon him a he had predicted. It fired him with a gleam of insanity. For a second he rushed at her, as though about to strike her. He raised his arms above his head, then stopped and shivered: saliva oozed around his lips. He screamed at her in hoarse, rough accents, in which the Lancashire note was evident:

"Get out of it ye bloody prostitute" Barbara slunk against the wall, and whimpered. Her terror was entirely physical. She was prepared to duck and flee if he attacked her. And it was not her own life which this instinct prompted her to protect. She had got beyond all that. She must get away, somehow anyhow, before he destroyed that other life for which she was responsible. She slunk by a sideboard, watching him alertly. At the same instant she heard Caleb's voice:

"Oh, no, not that, not that!"

The distraction caused George to turn away, and she reached the door. Another moment and she would have been through it, when her progress was stayed by the sounds of a falling chair. George seemed to have observed Caleb for the first time the man who had robbed him of his most precious possession. With a growl he lurched towards him and grabbed at the other's throat. In a normal fight the odds would have been about equal. George was heavier, taller, and stronger, but on the other, Caleb was nimbler and in better condition. One blow over the heart would probably have crumpled the older man up. But George was fired with the fury of a maniac, and Caleb was defending himself with the nervelessness of a guilty man. In Caleb's eyes George's anger was justifiable, and he could only protect himself. The confined space and the congested furniture played their part in the brief struggle. George fell over a chair, but in falling he managed to grip the other 's throat, and they both crashed against a cabinet on which were china vases. Ebbway was crying out:

"Don't! Don't! For God's sake!"

Before he could get near to part them they had fallen in a heap amongst smashed vases. Blood was let on either side, and there was a feral growling and groping for primitive weapons. It was impossible to see exactly what took place in that ugly minute. By the time Barbara had reached them, Ebbway was pulling George away, and Caleb was coughing in a queer, unnatural way, a kind of inside choking cough. Ebbway exerted all his strength and managed to pull George back on to the ottoman. He continued to shout:

"For God's sake! For God's sake!"

George fell among the cushions, which a few minutes earlier had been the playground of a different passion. His passion being sated momentarily, the wave of insanity also passed. His hand was cut, and he groaned aloud:

"Throw the—into the street."

But Ebbway was kneeling over the fallen boy, about whose neck was an ugly gash.

"My God!" Ebbway was saying, "get someone—a doctor, quick!"

Two scared people appeared at the door, the lodgers from upstairs. It was Barbara who dashed out into the street, calling out to the first person she met:

"A doctor! quick! Where 's the nearest doctor?"

It was nearly twenty minutes before a doctor was found. When he arrived with Barbara, there was a crowd outside the house, and two policemen were in charge. The doctor, a quiet, elderly man, went calmly to work. He knelt upon the floor, and the only remark he made was:

"This is a case for the mortuary."

Barbara screamed, and Ebbway put his arm around her.

"Courage, Mrs. Champneys. It's all right! it's all right!"

He patted her hands, and coaxed her. George's interest in her had subsided. He was lying back on the ottoman, nursing his bleeding hand. His large eyes were transfixed, staring obliquely at the huddled form upon the floor. Suddenly he exclaimed:

"By Christ! they 'll hang me!"

It was again Ebbway's mission to act as comforter. He patted the big man's shoulder.

"No, no, old boy. Don't you be frightened. It was an accident. I saw it all. You never meant to kill him. He felt on the vase"

Then, as a masterly after-thought:

"A man is always justified in defending his wife's honour."

The scene became an unwieldy phantasmagoria. Strange faces came and went, unreal people with notebooks and solemn, official manner. Questions were asked, and incoherently answered. She and George never looked at each other.

"I can't stand this any longer," she suddenly thought. The desire to escape became an obsession. She crept out of the room and went downstairs. There was a policeman in the hall. She drifted by him to the kitchen stairs, as though waiting for someone. When he was not looking she stole down into the kitchen. The basement was deserted. She let herself out into the side passage, which connected with the tiny front garden. She walked calmly through the crowd of people outside the gate. When she came to the first turning she ran. She was whimpering like a dog that has been thrashed. Where was she to go? She had no money, not even her hat. She would never, never go back to George's house at Kensington. Perhaps they would put her in gaol.

What did it matter? Suddenly she thought of Isabel. Isabel was living at that time in lodgings at Netting Hill. She walked all the way there, too preoccupied to be conscious of the concern her dishevelled appearance caused. To her relief she observed a light at the window of the first-floor room, which was Isabel's sitting-room. She knocked, and a woman let her in. She went upstairs and tapped on the door. There was a sound of laughter and the clink of glasses. Her knock had not been heard. She opened the door. Isabel and four other people were sitting round a table, playing cards and drinking beer. They were all in high good spirts, far too good spirits to be concerned at the appearance of a dishevelled girl. Someone called out:

"Hullo! here 's Fancy. Come on, Fancy, and take a hand. They've got all my money."

She looked beseechingly at Isabel and said: "Can I have a word with you in the next room?" Isabel detected trouble, and she rose at once from the table and went out with her. They both went into the bedroom. As briefly as she could she described what had happened, but before the narrative was completed she had fainted. Isabel put her to bed. "When she came to, Isabel was bathing her temples with scent and murmuring:

"It's all right, my lamb; you stop here. I expect you've exaggerated the trouble."

IX

Isabel's conclusions were usually laconic and frequently shrewd; but on this occasion they proved wide of the mark. Barbara had not exaggerated the trouble; she had rather understated it. On that night and during the weeks that followed, her sanity was only preserved by a concentration on one central fact. It simplified the issue considerably. Everything was lost and finished, except that one reality which it was her mission to vitalise. She was unable to focus the disaster which had overwhelmed her. The loss of Caleb and his love was the dominant calamity. By comparison, the loss of her position, her public disgrace in the law courts, and the question as to what would happen to George, seemed trivialities.

A few days later a letter came from a lawyer to state that his client, Mr. George Champneys, was "prepared to take her back on certain conditions." She tore the letter up. A week later a letter came from George himself, imploring her to go back, on any conditions, when he was released after the trial. She tore that up also. On that point her mind was definitely made up. Under no circumstances would she ever go back to the man who had murdered her lover, for murder him he had. In the witness-box she averred that she did not see what happened in the struggle. She suppressed the fact that she saw George stab at Caleb with a broken vase. Her accusation did not seem worth while. What did it matter now? She was not vengeful. She did not want George to be hanged. He would be a very bad condemned man, probably go mad. It would be horrible to contemplate. Caleb was dead, and it didn't matter what happened to George; but she would never live with him again. Neither would she ever take a penny of his money. She had wronged him and betrayed him, and to accept money from him would be placing her in the position of the thing he had called her. All that was finished between them Of course George would get off. He would be worried and harrassed, and spend some time in a comfortable gaol, having his meals sent in; but clever lawyers would see him through. Ebbway had sworn that he actually saw the deceased strike his head on the broken vase as he fell! She also had lied for George, and the lawyers would make a great deal of the "defending of his wife's honour."

His wife's honour! Well, she had not denied her guilt, and she was vividly alert to the "sensation in court" when, in reply to the question: "How long had this been going on?" she had replied: "About four months."

All theatrical London was there, in its best hats and frocks, and there was a kind of hiss of delight. Oh, yes, she was finished all right, so far as that went. The climax had been thorough. But the central fact remained her mission was not yet fulfilled. She had to go on living. What was she to do? She was a fool not to have retained her father's dole! Four hundred a year now would be a fortune. When Isabel, not tauntingly but maternally, remarked: "I told you, dear, you were silly not to ask him for a settlement just after you were married," she could not be angry, for she was living on Isabel's charity, and that she could not do for long. After her disgrace theatrical managers would fight shy of her, neither would she ever be in the mood again to sing and dance. In a few months such a thing would be impossible, anyway. She had no other accomplishments.

At last she bethought her that at George's house were certain pieces of furniture and a few trinkets which had been hers before she married him. She wrote to the lawyers about this. Negotiations went on for several weeks, but eventually they were sent to her. She sold them. The result realised one hundred and twenty pounds, and she breathed again. With economy that would keep her till the end of November the fateful month. And afterwards? The future did not bear thinking about. Caleb had said she must not always be thinking about Caleb. The tears started to her eyes as she snapped the little shutters on recurring memories.

"Anyway, it will be Caleb's child. His, when he was young and unspoiled. Mine, when I was at my happiest."

And she became alive to the necessity for placid contemplation and calm hope.

Isabel was angelic. Materialistic and thriftless, she was yet prepared to share her last crust with her downfallen friend. Neither did she make any great attempt to influence her attitude. "You beat me, darling," she said once. "You've only got to stretch out your hand and you can get it all back, or nearly all. Instead of that, you prefer to pig it along with me. When the kid comes, it's going to be precious difficult, old girl."

One night Isabel came in very late, and found Barbara awake. She undressed quietly and got into bed alongside Barbara. They whispered together, odds and ends of subjects, and then Isabel said:

"I suppose you know, old girl, you could stop this if you liked?"

"Stop it? What?"

You know what 's going to happen. "For a moment Barbara could not grasp her meaning. Then she said eagerly.

"Oh, no, no. I'm not going to do that." Isabel sighed and remarked:

"Oh, well, it's your business. I know what I'd do."

Barbara did not answer, and Isabel thought to herself:

"This child beats me. I can't see what her game is."

Bleak autumn months closed in. The great Frolic tragedy ceased to hold public interest. George had been released; but it was said that he was broken in health and had gone abroad. He had made five attempts to see Barbara, but she always managed to avoid him. He sent emissaries offering her money, and any terms she liked, and she rejected them. He called himself, but instructions had been left with the landlady to say that she was out, whenever this occurred. At last, apparently, he gave up hope and went away. The theatre was closed, and the house in Kensington let to another tenant.

London is an excellent place to hide in. In the comparative obscurity of Notting Hill she managed to avoid all her theatrical acquaintances. She never went up to the old haunts. Many of her friends sent her sympathetic letters, and Ebbway was kindness itself; but her great desire was to sever herself from that side of her life. The association was too bitter, the record too humiliating, the wound too fresh.

"I must do some work," she said to Isabel, after a fortnight's idleness. She ran her eye over the whole gamut of women's unskilled labour market and the prospects loomed appalling. She would have gone as nursemaid, but for the dread of meeting people who knew her. She could not type or do shorthand, and she was ignorant of clerking. Even a mother's help or a shop-assistant requires some knowledge and a "character" from a responsible person. At last, through the intervention of a friend of Isabel's, she did obtain work of a kind. It was as an assistant to two women who strung pearls, and who had a little establishment just off New Oxford Street. They were quite pleasant women, and the principal was French, and her name Madame Guillard. She worked there seven hours a day, and they paid her fifteen shillings a week. The amount seemed pitiable after her inflated experiences. In any case, it would help her to eke out her small capital, and above all things it would help to distract her mind.

"Barbara Powerscourt is dead. Fancy Telling is dead," she said one day to Isabel. "The third person is suspended like Mahomet's coffin. Caleb always said that everything was a trinity. I'm beginning to understand what he meant. "

"The pity is," replied Isabel, "that you can't go and have a good time, and forget about it."

Barbara smiled and shook her head. She fully appreciated her friend's meaning. It had often been her own solution when she was person number two, but even if she were a millionairess it did not fit in with the aspirations of person number three. No, in the meantime the little room off New Oxford Street served her purpose. The work she was given to do was purely mechanical, tying knots, checking, even running errands and making tea, but the work itself was interesting, and the expert knowledge displayed by Madame Guillard and her friend surprised her. When she first went, one pearl looked like any other, but these two ladies were able to detect the subtlest quality and gradation, and she gradually began to recognise differences also. Isabel was performing in a sketch at the Victoria Palace, and they did not see much of each other.

One afternoon in the middle of October she was at work at Madame Guillard's when a charming woman came in about some pearls she wished reset. She was in the early thirties, of medium height, with a distinguished pose of head and wistful, sympathetic eyes. Barbara had never heard a gentler voice or seen a more ingratiating manner. She talked for some time to Madame Guillard, and then Barbara became aware that the good lady was looking at her with interest. Others were also in the habit of looking at her with interest at that time, and making her feel uncomfortable, but one could not resent the peculiarly kindly and sympathetic glance of this customer. When the arrangement about the string of pearls had been finally settled, she walked slowly towards the door. As she was passing Barbara's desk, she turned to Madame Guillard and smiled.

"Perhaps this young lady will bring them to me when they are ready?"

"Parfaitement, madame."

Barbara smiled back at her and nodded her head. When the lady had gone she felt all a-flutter, as though something very important had happened to her. She was to learn afterwards that it had.

The voluble Madame Guillard returned to the room, exclaiming:

"Oh, but she is charming, distinguee and so rich! Haul"

"What is her name, Madame Guillard?" Barbara asked.

"Her name? She is Mrs. Myrtle, wife of what he is? Some big man in Government and the ships, an old familee. Veree rich, a nice man, but too old for her, I t'ink. She is so sad, isn't it? You see her face, a sad, sweet face. They entertain at their beautiful bouse in Sout' Street, and they have a big, big place in Yorkshire old very old mansion. She is veree kind, a veree nice customer."

Four days later Barbara appeared at the house in South Street by appointment, and was shown into a white-panelled morning-room, with Chinese curtains and red lacquer furniture. A small clock above the fireplace whispered the velvet beat of indestructible time. There was about this room an atmosphere Barbara had never encountered before, a quality which wealth alone could not buy. The furniture and curtains spoke of that security of cultivation which had outlived the very meaning of its production. These seemed not to be chairs and cabinets and tables, but a spiritual atmosphere in which these things dumbly reposed.

Within a few minutes Mrs. Myrtle entered the room, wearing a dress of black crepe de chine. Immediately the room seemed to respond to her pervading presence. Everything took its place, and even the caller seemed a part of an unstudied perfection. Mrs. Myrtle shook hands and thanked her for coming. Then she opened and examined the string of pearls, with which she was delighted. This business over she said to Barbara:

"What is your name?"

The girl was expecting this, and she answered promptly:

"Barbara Power."

"Barbara! a pretty name; and so is Power." Then she turned to the fire and said in a low voice:

"When is this going to happen?"

This question was also expected, and the reply was:

"About the third week next month."

The presiding genius of this tranquil retreat now approached more difficult ground, and it was with the gentlest pressure of the arm and the most kindly insinuation of voice that she enquired:

"Your husband!"

"My husband has left me."

"Ah!"

Mrs. Myrtle was toying with a long chain of cornelians and regarding the fire intently. When she looked up her eyes were overflowing with sympathy.

"You live with friends?"

"I live with a girl-friend in rooms in Notting Hill."

Mrs. Myrtle nodded. She appeared to be finding difficulty in framing a suggestion. At last she said:

"I'm afraid you'll think I'm very impertinent asking you these questions. Only I don't know how it is. I felt drawn to you when I first saw you at Mme. Guillard's. You see, I'm very fond of children I have none of my own. I wonder whether whether you would let me help you, Mrs. Power!"

Barbara's eyes narrowed. She had had a presentiment that some such proposition as this might be put before her, and she had not, so far, been able to frame a reply. What was the motive? Her somewhat bitter experience taught her that people seldom acted without motives. Certainly Mrs. Myrtle was different from anyone else she had ever met. She could not believe that this good lady could have any ulterior motive in an act of simple kindness; at the same time, it was as well to be cautious. She regarded her new friend watchfully as she replied:

"It is extremely kind of you. But, really, there's no necessity. I shall be all right."

The elder woman suddenly put her arm around her and pleaded.

"Oh, please, do let me help you. You see, I—I had a little child of my own, a girl she died. It would make me so happy."

After all, what was the real objection? It wasn't like taking money from George. This woman was a stranger, just a kindly stranger, and she could afford it. Barbara lowered her eyes and repeated:

"It is extremely kind of you."

X

She had little idea at that time of what was to be the surprising extent of Mrs. Myrtle's kindness. She imagined it would amount to gifts of chicken jelly and, perhaps, an offer to pay the doctor's fees; but a few days later Madame Guillard came to her and said: "Barbara, zis charming lady, I tink she lofs you.

"She has spik to me of you, and she wants to take you away. You are a lucky leetle girl. Come, now, you are to go to see her zis afternoon."

And that afternoon Mrs. Myrtle put her project before her. She said that her husband was away on business in America, and he would not be back till the end of December. She had what she called a week-end cottage up on Leith Hill in Surrey. She wanted Barbara to go there at once. There were two servants there, and later on there would be a nurse and a doctor. She was to go out for gentle walks every day, and was to feed up. Mrs. Myrtle herself would come down now and then and stay a few days. This rapid and unexpected change in her fortunes almost unnerved her, and she wept in Mrs. Myrtle's arms.

Two days later she packed up her traps, bade an affectionate farewell to Isabel, and set off for Leith Hill. The week-end cottage proved to be a charmingly-appointed small Georgian house, with central heating, bath-rooms, and every modern convenience. The bedrooms were large and airy, with glorious views across commons and pine-woods. There was a grand piano and a library full of boojss. Mrs. Myrtle went down with her, and directed that everything was to be done for her comfort and complete satisfaction, and Barbara quickly realised that on this score there would be little cause for complaint. Between the sheets on that first night she thought to herself:

"Well, this is the rummest go of the lot. this is where my son will be born or will it be a girl? No, I've made up my mind it will be a son, and I shall call him Caleb. I shall tell him about this in after-life just where he was born, and about Mrs. Myrtle's kindness. Its wonderful a kind of predestination as though the way is being prepared. Oh, I'm so tired."

The weather was wet and stormy, but every day she tramped through the rain, and returned home to drink glasses of rich milk. She began to feel well and strangely elated. She took books down from the library shelves, thumbed them, read a few pages, and then sat there dreaming. And the past had no significance, and the future did not concern her. And one day a nurse arrived, a brown-eyed, sympathetic little person, who was friendly without being too intrusive.

The crisis came a week before it was expected. When the agony came upon her, she grit her teeth and said to herself: "This will pass."

In the middle of the night the doctor came, grey-haired but athletic of frame. His calm presence helped to fortify her. But the grim battle had to be fought alone. The agony increased, and the next evening became so unbearable they gave her morphia. She swam off into a vague unconsciousness, during which the earth seemed to be ripped asunder. She knew at one time she was groaning, and could not control it. A voice came through an indeterminate mist of time.

"Yell, you little devil!"

It was the doctor's voice, and she clutched at the sheets and tried to speak. The nurse was leaning over her, and at last the whisper came through:

"It's all right, my dear. You're all right. It's a boy. He's all right."

Again she drifted away, but this time the darkness was sanctified. When next she came in contact with the conscious world, she managed to say:

"Where is he?"

The nurse was smoothing her pillow. She said quietly:

"You can't see him yet, dear. You must wait a little while. He's quite all right. Don't fret."

When at last she saw her son, it was the most moving hut the most tranquil moment in her life. The nurse allowed her to kiss him once, and then took him away.

It was many hours later before she could say:

"Why did they call him a little devil?"

Nurse laughed. "Oh, that was Doctor Pollen. We couldn't make him cry. We thought at one time he was never going to."

The morning brought Mrs. Myrtle, all eagerness and joy. She kissed Barbara, and said:

"Oh, my dear, I congratulate you. He's a splendid baby."

Strength and vitality slowly returned, and: consciousness of the wealth of her achievement. Mother and child did well. She lay there idly regarding the deft activities of the nurse and clamorous protests of the babe. Sometimes she was allowed to have him in the bed with her, and she anxiously scanned every line of the little body

"You can't say he's particularly like anybody, can you, Nurse?" she once remarked.

"Oh, I don't know, my dear," the other replied encouragingly "He has blue eyes at present. often Slough. I think the chin is like yours. Of course, I—"

"You mean you never saw the father, Nurse. He had blue eyes."

"Ah!"

It is, nevertheless, always rather sanguine to detect likenesses in a few days old baby. Barbara was perhaps a little disappointed in this. She seemed to expect a speaking likeness of Caleb, with all his characteristics and quaint manners clearly developed.

"What a long time to wait," she thought. But still, there would always be the interest of this development. Every year a little more and a little more.

Development! As the days and then the weeks progressed, and she was able to sit up and then to move to another room, to walk slowly, and to feel the old vitality returning to her limbs, the practical consideration of development was beginning to grow on her. The mission had been fulfilled, but its further direction had yet to be determined. The intervention of Mrs. Myrtle had been like an act of God, but she had no intention of taking advantage of it further than was necessary. She and her son would not live on charity. It would mean, then, when well enough, a return to Netting Hill and to the pearl- stringing business. Fortunately her hundred and twenty pounds remained untouched. They would manage somehow.

In any case, Mrs. Myrtle had not even given any hint of an indefinite state of charity. She had only said:

"Now, my dear, you are to stay here as long as ever you like."

A remark which plainly hinted that a day would come when she would expect the mother and child to turn out.

On a December day, when the snow was festooning the pine-trees and the wind was blowing bitterly, she would regard the view from the warm security of the library, and her heart would be filled with misgiving. Not for herself, oh; dear no; she had met the buffets of the world before, as her mother had but this boy, this son of predestination; this ought to be his world, midst books, and culture, and wise counsels, away from the ugliness and terror of sordid strife. She would lie awake at night, shuddering at the forbidding future.

"You 're getting soft, Fancy," she said to herself. "You've been pampered and spoilt for too long. Even now you get moods when your soul cries out for the 'fleshpots of Egypt,' as the old man said."

At Christmas Mrs. Myrtle went away to stay with relatives in Yorkshire, but she gave Barbara permission to ask any friend down to stay with her, and so she naturally wrote to Isabel. The sketch that Isabel had been playing in having come to an end, her friend came down and stayed a week. Isabel was much impressed with the house and the baby and the food and the servants. But on the second evening she said:

"Don't we get anything to drink here, old girl?"

And Barbara had to acknowledge that they didn't. Mrs. Myrtle was a teetotaller, although she had made no objection to Barbara 's daily glass of port, which the doctor had prescribed.

"Do you mean to say," persisted Isabel, "we can 't get a bottle of fizz on Christmas Day?"

Barbara felt a little uncomfortable about this. She knew her friend would expect to celebrate this important day in her accustomed manner; so she arranged that they should send down to the inn in the nearest village and make a few purchases on their own. She was now walking again and almost feeling her old self.

She then became aware of a curious aspect of her friendship with Isabel. In the scurry of town, with plenty of excitement and social change, their brief chats about each other and current events were entirely satisfying. But in this isolated spot, in the pure clear air, amidst the solemnity of pines, these two actresses became distinctly bored within a few days. The evenings were long and dark and dull; and, curiously enough, Barbara noticed it more with Isabel than when alone. And the result was, they sent down to the inn and made more purchases. They kept Christmas Day royally. In the ordinary course of events this fact need never have come to the ears of the lady of the house; but it happened that the cook was an extremely religious and abstemious person. She was a Seventh Day Adventist, and when Mrs. Myrtle returned a week later, she felt it her duty to conduct her to the larder and show her an array of bottles, the contents of which her two guests had consumed in her absence. There were three champagne bottle, three port, and a dozen and a half empty stout bottles. And the spectacle saddened Mrs. Myrtle's heart. Isabel had by that time departed, but she went straight to Barbara, and said gently:

"I'm afraid, dear, your friend has been leading you into bad ways."

Barbara did not at first grasp the purport of this accusation. She looked perplexed until Mrs Myrtle added:

"All those bottles in the larder."

Then she knew that the truth had been detected. At the same time she was not willing to throw all the blame on Isabel, and she replied a little sullenly:

"It was Christmas-time I have unhappy memories."

And Mrs. Myrtle thought:

"Good heavens! this child is the responsible one, then." And she answered:

"It's so bad for you, my dear. One cannot cure unhappy memories in that way."

The incident created a definite chasm between the two women. Mrs. Myrtle was disappointed. Simple and abstemious in her mode of life, the sight of those bottles conveyed to her the record of an unbridled orgy. It was a thing she could not understand: but what made it worse was that the affair had been conducted behind her back. Barbara was not to be trusted. Could a woman like that be trusted to bring up a child properly?

Barbara on her part felt a half-savage resentment against her hostess. She was annoyed at the discovery. Of course, she was in the wrong, but oh, it was all very well for Mrs. Myrtle; all the influences of her life had been towards refinement and restraint. She hadn't come up against the experiences of Isabel and herself. They were indeed as the poles asunder. The reflection hardened her decision to depart as soon as possible.

Mrs. Myrtle returned to town during the second week in January, and the day following her departure Barbara wrote to her as follows: MY DEAR MRS. MYRTLE,

I do not know how I can thank you for all your kindness to me. You have been one of the few real friends I have ever met. But I feel that the time has come when I must get back to my own life, whatever it is to be. Baby and I will therefore be leaving here to-morrow, and we shall be going to my old address in Notting Hill. Please, dear Mrs. Myrtle, accept my best thanks for all your loving kindness. Your friend,

BARBARA POWER.

Having sent this letter, she went upstairs and kissed the small Caleb on his smooth skull, and whispered:

"Old son, we've got to go back and face it. This is all swank, you know, us living here. I wish you could stop, old boy. I love you so; but it can't be done. We're poor folk."

A ten o'clock the next morning, a telegram came from Mrs. Myrtle:

Please wait till I arrive coming this morning very urgent.

"What's all this about?" thought Barbara. She decided to wait, but she continued her packing.

XI

When Mrs. Myrtle came into the hall, it was apparent that her normal air of calm assurance was ruffled by some inward agitation. She found Barbara packing in her bedroom, and for the first time Barbara's presence slightly unstrung her. She smiled graciously, and asked her to come downstairs to the library. Once ensconced there, she sat rather rigidly on the edge of an easy-chair, and said:

"Barbara, I want to make a proposition to you, and whatever you think of it, I want you to believe that I am thinking of the best interests of us all."

Us all! Then she was coming into it herself! "Please don't be angry or shocked till you have heard me out. Briefly, it is that I offer to adopt your son."

"What!" Barbara almost screamed the word, and her eyes blazed. Before Mrs. Myrtle had had time to qualify her appeal, she was having shouted at her:

"Oh, so you—you too, even you had an ulterior motive."

The little burst of anger steadied the elder woman. She said calmly:

"I assure you, the idea only germinated after my return at Christmas. I only came to a decision when I received your letter this morning."

Barbara searched her face keenly. Yes, she was speaking the truth all right. Well?

"Of course I know it is a stupendous suggestion to make to a mother. It is also idle to deny that I am thinking of myself, too. Oh, my dear, I want a child so much. I would do everything for him. He should have the best of everything: training, education, choice of career. He should lead a clean, healthy life in the best surroundings. He should travel and have friends chosen from the wisest and best. He should have opportunities and large horizons—"

"Yes, yes, that's all very well!" shouted Barbara. "But what about me?"

"I should, of course, compensate you, my dear, to my fullest ability. On the other hand, since you talk about yourself do you think that you

"I know, you think because I've got no money, and because I because you found some champagne bottles in the larder you think I'm not a fit person to bring up a son."

"My dear, I'm not criticising you. But you can't deny it's going to be difficult. You're a dear little person but you are what I should call unstable. Even the child, you have confessed to me, is the son of a man who was not your husband. He starts with rather a handicap. I can at least launch him into the world with an honourable name."

"Name! You mean to say you would adopt him, and pretend he was your own son!"

"That is the proposal I make. I do not wish to coerce you. It is for you to decide, and please take your time over it.

"I don't want any time. I can tell you now. I'm damned if I 'll do it."

Mrs. Myrtle smiled sadly.

"Please don't be angry with me. I'm so sorry. Let us say no more about it, then."

And the two women kissed affectionately.

That afternoon, however, Barbara returned with the young Caleb to Netting Hill, and the grim struggle began. Isabel was "out" again, and not in the best of tempers. When Barbara told her about Mrs. Myrtle's offer, the two friends nearly quarrelled for the first time.

"You do throw away your chances," Isabel grumbled. She was not particularly enamoured of the idea of having a two months old baby in their congested lodgings.

"Chances!" retorted Barbara. "Would you sell your baby?"

"It isn't selling it. It's giving it a great opportunity which it's otherwise going to miss. Besides, it doesn't really know you yet ""It does!"

"No, it doesn't. As long as someone gives it its bottle it doesn't care. If it was a year or two older it would be different. Did she say how much she'd give you?"

"No; I never discussed the matter."

"She might have offered you a thousand a year. They say her husband's nearly a millionaire."

"I wouldn't take ten thousand a year."

Isabel sniffed, and repeated her accustomed formula:

"You beat me, Fancy."

The immediate difficulties were manifest. To return to the pearl-stringing industry was an utter impossibility. A two-months baby requires the constant attention of at least one person. It prefers two. If she hired a woman to look after it whilst she was at the business, she would have to pay her as much as she herself was paid by Madame Guillard. Isabel was already in debt. The hundred and twenty pounds was intact, but when that was gone, what was to be done? With the utmost economy they could -not expect it to last more than a few months.

It must be said for Isabel that, after the first unpleasantness, she behaved well. She curbed her natural extravagance, and every day she went round to the little agents and waited patiently for interviews. And when Barbara became fretful, she always cheered her with:

"Never mind, old girl; I'll get a shop soon, and then we 'll be all right."

But theatrical things were in a bad way just then, and Isabel was not so young as she had been. The baby was a source of delight and terror. Sometimes when he cried she thought she would go out of her mind. Of his upbringing she was profoundly ignorant. The landlady was consulted, and proved a mine of comfort. The only trouble was that she had forgotten most of the details of baby-craft, because, as she explained, "she buried her last sixteen years come Easter Sunday." Barbara was always in dread of doing the wrong thing. The marvellous organism of his structure was so delicately adjusted, she became convinced that his hold on life was slenderer than it really was. His cries sounded protests against her ignorance and irresponsible motherhood.

No word came from Mrs. Myrtle. One evening Isabel said:

"At a pinch, I suppose, you could always touch that Mrs. Myrtle for a bit."

"Oh, no, I wouldn't do that," Barbara snapped. "It would be like backing down. I was rather rude to her, you see. It would be an awful climb-down."

Another evening Isabel came home and said:

"I've heard news of George. You can get a divorce if you like."

"What is it?"

"He 's come back from Italy. They say he 's living at a private hotel in Knightsbridge with Queenie Myland, a flapper in Covent Garden pantomime."

Barbara shivered, but she said quietly:

"I don't care. What's the good of a divorce to me?"

"You might want to get married again."

Barbara laughed bitterly, and put on the kettle for the baby's bottle.

Two months slipped by, and the funds were reduced to less than forty pounds. They could not be as economical as they ought to have been. At times conditions became unendurable, and Barbara would send down the road for a bottle of red wine or whisky. At other times she would leave the baby in charge of the landlady, and she and Isabel would penetrate to a restaurant in Soho, where they could obtain hot, rich, and uncommon food, filleted herrings in oil, coquille of sole with cheese, braised chicken, savouries and peche Melba.

"Damn it all," Barbara would say, "one must live."

On one of these occasions they ran into Julius Banstead. He was dining with a fair girl at an adjoining table, and they didn't notice him till the meal had been ordered. When he caught sight of Barbara, he came deliberately across to her, and in his round assertive voice exclaimed:

"How are you, Miss Telling! We haven't met for a long time."

Barbara felt her personality dwindle under his gaze. She replied limply:

"I 'm all right, thanks."

"I'm running the Charing Cross Theatre now. Won't you give me a call one day?"

He fixed her with his searching glance. Yes, she had heard about that. Banstead had got hold of a rich man, a sleeping partner. He was now a power in the theatrical world. The temptation was obvious, and the more dangerous on account of its abruptness. And yet some instinct prompted her to say:

"You never used to think much of my performances."

Banstead laughed and displayed his fine teeth. He suppressed the idle temptation to say: "My dear girl, I hadn't thought of offering you a part."

Instead of that, he answered:

"Oh, come now, you misjudge me. I know we used to quarrel, but I never underestimated your abilities."

Isabel, who had drunk two cocktails, exclaimed:

"Oh, Fancy, do go. I'll look after the baby."

Banstead already had a diary out and was remarking:

"What about Tuesday at three?"

Then Barbara felt angry with this importunity of fate. She was, perhaps, unfair to Isabel. Julius might offer her a part at twenty pounds a week, and she could keep a nurse and live in comfort. But no, she knew her Julius too well. She had no illusions on the score of his attitude towards her. He thought he had her easily trapped. She tossed her head, took a sip of claret, and said firmly:

"No, I'm not doing anything like that now, thanks. I have a baby to look after. I've given up the stage."

"Well, then, just as an old friend."

"I don't recognise you as a friend, either ancient or modern. "

This might be called the retort conclusive. Banstead grinned superciliously, snapped his diary to, and returned to the fair girl without a word.

"God! you are a one. You do chuck things away," whispered Isabel tearfully.

But Barbara's jaw was set. She was like a besieged animal that still has ground to defend.

XII

The day was rapidly approaching when the last bulwark would fall. Forty pounds, thirty pounds, fifteen pounds and some bills owing. In that dark hour Isabel suddenly got a small engagement in a musical comedy at Hammersmith. Her salary was to be three pounds ten a week, but from her jubilation and high spirits it might have been going to be thirty pounds.

"We'll be all right now, Fancy."

Poor dear Isabel! Her loyalty was pathetic. Somehow this insignificant stroke of fortune added fuel to the flames of Barbara's despair. "Was she going to sponge on Isabel she and Caleb's son!

One night she met a rich man from the Midlands in that same restaurant. He was to all appearances a decent, healthy animal, probably with a wife and children in some busy Midland town. He made love to her in a straightforward gentlemanly way, without pretence or vulgarity. He complained of his loneliness, and appealed to Barbara rather sentimentally for help. He gave her his card, and said his name was Theodore Moffat, and he owned terra-cotta works at Tamworth, and rented a flat in St. James. He was obviously probing to see whether the two girls were members of the demi-monde, and yet he did not treat them with disrespect. He explained that he had to spend three months every winter in London, and he had few friends and was frankly bored. Would they take pity on him and visit him at his flat? Barbara made it quite clear that they were not members of the demi-monde, but they liked his face, and that they would come and call on him together if he promised to behave himself.

They went one afternoon, and Theodore made no attempt to conceal the attraction which Barbara had for him. He badgered her with questions, which Isabel answered. It was easy to worm out of Isabel the state of the two girls' finances, and when the story was told he leaned towards Barbara and said:

"I wish you'd let me help you."

"Why should you!"

"I like you, and I can afford it."

"No; it's not done. Why should you give something for nothing?"

"Well, you could—"

"Yes, I know well enough. I could be nice to you."

"No-o, I don't insist. I'm really not that sort."

"It can 't be done, old boy. Besides, I 'm not free."

"What do you mean, you're not free?"

She couldn't exactly explain. She was a desperate woman. Here was the easiest way in the world to secure some sort of protection. But could she keep Caleb's son in that way? The man from the Midlands nodded.

"A deal's a deal," he said, "and a bargain's a bargain. You have my card. Come and see me if you're in difficulties. I've never forced a woman against her will, or let in a friend."

"I think you're a decent sort," commented Barbara, and the two girls went away.

By the time Isabel's rehearsals were over, their united resources amounted to twenty-three shillings in cash, and eleven pounds odd in debts. Moreover, clothes were getting shabby, and holes in stockings unmendable. The baby cost fifteen shillings a week in Allenby's, beyond incidental expenses at the chemist and the hire of a pram.

"Never mind," said Isabel; "I shall get three quid and a half next Saturday night."

When Isabel said that, Barbara knew she was beaten. Tears swam in her eyes, and she went to bed.

"I've been undermined somewhere," she said to the darkness. "I haven't the grit to stand a life of poverty and begging. I've seen you through all right, though, little son. Thank God! you won 't remember me."

The next day she wrote to Mrs. Myrtle, and asked for an appointment. A telegram bade her to go that afternoon. She found her patroness in the morning-room at South Street. Barbara's face was tense and set. She said sternly:

"I've come to give in; to offer you my son."

The elder woman's face lighted with a quiet exaltation, tempered by pity for her visitor. It was a situation which required all her tact and restraint. She solved it by kissing Barbara affectionately and whispering:

"Oh, my dear you will allow me to compensate you handsomely?"

She was surprised by the passion of protest this offer evoked. Barbara almost pushed her away, and cried out:

"Oh, no, no. That is what I will not have. Do you understand me? I haven't come here to sell my son! I've come here to hand him to you as a sacred trust. Not a pound, not a penny will I touch. I've come to you because I'm beaten, not only financially, but morally. I'm a rotten woman and you're a good one. I have nothing to offer him but cramped poverty, the influence of vicious nature, narrow friends and outlooks. But you—you talked to me of wide horizons, of great opportunities of the pure sweet air among the pines. That is what I give him for, because—because I somehow believe he will be rather fine."

Her voice broke over this last statement. Then she continued excitedly:

"I am a kind of instrument, do you see? of some dumb fate. A friend, a very dear friend of mine spoke of a spiritual Nemesis. Perhaps that is the end, in my poor way, that I am serving. I wanted a son more than anything in the world. He has the best of everything that is in me. Where my mother and I failed, let him succeed. Where my mother and I suffered, let him rejoice. This cannot be done without the true environment, the wide horizons, as you call them. This is a sacred trust I offer you, Mrs. Myrtle. Do you accept it?"

"I accept it, my friend."

"Say to me, 'I swear to adopt your son, and to educate him, and to make it the passion of my life that he shall be a good man."

"I swear to adopt your son, Barbara, to educate, him, and to make it the passion of my life that he shall be a good man."

"There is only one thing more."

"Tell me, my dear."

"You shall call him Caleb."

"He shall be called Caleb."

She wept then, and Mrs. Myrtle put her arm round her and said:

"Oh, my dear, I had no suspicion that you had so noble a soul. You wouldn't I suppose you wouldn't sometimes come and see him?"

"No, no, I couldn't do that. I couldn't stand it. The gift is absolute. Whilst I live I shall watch you and him from afar. He will never know his mother."

That afternoon a nurse arrived in a cab, and Master Caleb was taken away to South Street. And Barbara lay alone in the darkness, murmuring:

"Oh, my son my son my little son!"

And Isabel came in late, and moved softly, knowing of her friend's anguish.

"It all seems damned unfair," she said meditatively. "Men can have no end of a good time. It's always sugar or dirt with them. It's sugar, they share a little with us. If it's dirt, they throw it to us and run away. I had an awful job to-night with young Stephens

"And God sends a messenger to our door, murmoured Barbara, "and says, 'There is no answer.' That amused Caleb. I remember—"

"What's that, dear!"

"I was talking in my sleep, darling."

Isabel turned out the light. And these strange bedfellows, who had drifted together and formed so great an affection for each other, and yet with so little they could really share, wandered apart in the darkness, each occupied with her own thoughts.

Isabel was thinking:

"Poor darling old Fancy! It must be a blow to her. It 'll make it much more comfy, though, having the brat out of the way. I do hope she gets a shop soon."

And Barbara was thinking:

"O thou God, who are you? What are you? Have I done right? Oh, please protect him and make a fine man of him."

XIII

The morning brought a condition of utter lethargy. She was worn out. The child's crying echoed through her tired memory. He would be crying now. Who would be looking after him? Wouldn't he miss her? Wasn't there something which would always tell him? Three times she started up to go and get him back. She couldn't stand it. Mrs. Myrtle would be bound to give him back if she insisted. She had signed nothing.

Her limbs ached so, she could hardly move. The meagre room became a dim tabernacle of remorse. Isabel was breathing heavily, her hair all frowsy, scattered on the pillow, her mouth open. And she once was beautiful. The long hours trailed by, unbroken 'by anything except -Isabel's 'snoring, 'the cries of tradesmen, the clatter of milk-carts It must have been past ten when Barbara suddenly lost control. She screamed out:

"Oh, damn you, Isabel, wake up! Get up!"

Isabel opened her eyes in amazed surprise Barbara was hysterical, laughing and swearing and crying at the same time. Isabel became alarmed She dressed quickly and ran out to find a doctor. The doctor happened to be starting on his rounds, and he came at once and examined the patient.

"What's she been doing?" he said a little impatiently. "There 's nothing wrong with her except hysteria. Her nerves are all unstrung. She ought to go away for a few weeks to get a complete rest and change."

"Yes?" said Barbara. "Where do you think? Madeira or Monte Carlo?"

Before he had time to reply she flung herself on to the bed, and laughed and cried alternately. Isabel put her arms round her and wept also. The doctor shrugged his shoulders, wrote out a prescription, and went away.

After he had gone she quieted down. For two days and nights she lay in a kind of coma, completely oblivious to her surroundings. Isabel waited on her, but she was unaware of it. Everything was finished. She was slipping away into a welcoming darkness. In dreams she visited unfamiliar places, talked with unfamiliar people. She could not see the people, but she could hear them. They were not unkind, only strange, bewildering. They wanted to be kind to her, and they talked eagerly in low-pitched voices.

Hands touched hers, lips were pressed against her brow.

Then, suddenly, she was a child again, playing with dolls in the large nursery at High Barrow. Miss Ridde was there. She could see her face above the fire-guard. Her eyes glued upon a novel, she was saying:

"I see, dear. So Mrs. Wilkins is coming to have tea with the postman."

Miss Ridde said that, but she wasn't thinking about what she was saying. She was too immersed in the romantic story. Poor Miss Ridde! With an unromantic figure she appeared, with her thick spectacles and broad, flat nose. And yet why shouldn't she dream of knights and ladies and gallant deeds?

Miss Ridde had closed her novel with a snap. She was wiping her eyes.

"Come now, dear," she was saying. "Get your little cape and the brown fur bonnet. I'm going to take you down to the House to hear your dear father. Your father is a very great man, a very great man indeed. He is the Chancellor of the Exchequer. He has all the money of the country in his charge. Think of that!"

They were driving in a carriage through the streets of London. It was a dim winter afternoon. The pavements were wet, and they reflected the lights of street lamps in perspective. And there was the river, and the lights on the other side, and barges feeling their way along stealthily. There were large policemen, and big, official-looking men looking her up and down. And she wanted to nudge Miss Ridde and say:

"Tell them about me and who my father is."

But they were already in the hushed hall. There were the rows and rows of elderly men, just as she had seen them once before. There was the man in the wig a kind of umpire; and there was the brass mace. A mace! Yes, yes, she remembered about the mace the symbol of ordered authority. And there they were all listening intently to her father. But no, that was a queer, funny thing. They were all listening intently, sure enough, but it wasn't her father they were listening to. The speaker was a young man and he was talking about "shibboleths." He had them all right, as theatrical folk say. He had gripped them.

"Surely the honourable member does not expect us to return to the shibboleths of the Powerscourt tradition?"

Eh? What was that? Powerscourt? Shibboleths? She wanted to ask Miss Ridde, but queerly enough Miss Ridde was no longer there. Instead, by her side sat an old lady with a gentle, distinguished face, and she smiled at Barbara and said:

"Well, my dear? Are you satisfied?"

Of course Barbara knew her. It was Mrs. Myrtle. Mrs. Myrtle! Well, what did she mean when she said: "Well, my dear, are you satisfied?"

She looked again at the young man speaking, was tall and loose-limbed, with a broad, strong face, the blue eyes widely set, the brown hair ruffled. There was about him the atmosphere "wide horizons."

She knew then.

She wanted to scream out: "Caleb my son! my son!"

But she could not scream or cry; she could only sit there, clutching—clutching.

He was speaking again:

"Those of us who passed through the great war, which happened long ago, hardly need reminding of the horrors of it. Its physical record is set down for eternity to read. But, may I ask, did nothing come out of it? Men and women pass away, but ideas take their revenge."

Yes, yes, that was it! That was what Caleb would say. What did he call it? Spiritual something spiritual—spiritual Nemesis! Not only in wars...

The House had vanished. She was all alone on the top of a hill amongst the bracken. Her feet were bleeding and her limbs ached. She had walked far and the day was closing in. And yet she was not unhappy; neither was she entirely alone. Her thoughts were always responded to by a large, comforting voice:

"I am weary, broken, at my journey's end," she said.

"Journeys do not end," said the voice. "Nothing ends. Everything flows on irresistibly."

"Yes, I see that," replied Barbara quietly. "And yet I am a wicked woman. I cannot escape my own weaknesses. Oh, listen to me, stranger, I gave to the world a son. When I say gave, I mean literally. I gave him away to a better woman than myself as a sacred trust. I have seen him in the long hereafter. With my hair greying I looked down into the hall where he stood. I was a stranger a distinguished stranger. Think of that! Did you ever hear of a woman being a distinguished stranger to her own son? He will never know his mother

There was a short silence, whilst her thoughts ran riot. Then the voice capped her reflections:

"So, you see, my dear, the pauper's grave in Liverpool becomes the centre round which a new world now revolves. Ideas take their revenge."

The hill was aglow with the amber light of the sun or bracken and sand.

"God is watching you," said the voice.

"Who is God?" she asked calmly.

"When everything has been given, and everything taken away, God is the pity which remains."

A strange sense of comfort stole over her. She was not alone. One is never alone, perhaps. Her body relaxed. She passed into a dreamless sleep.

XIV

It was early morning of the third day after her collapse Her mind was perfectly clear, nakedly f of illusions. The cold morning light, the ugly wallpaper, Isabel snoring noisily. Well! She had visited strange places and she had come back.

She was still Fancy, Fancy, with all the weight of calamity upon her; still Fancy, with her restlessness and weakness, still Fancy—broken free, though, buoyed up by a comforting secret. Things happen deep down within us.

She dressed quietly and went out.

It was late February, and there was a faint touch of spring in the air. Crocuses and snowdrops were already raising their modest heads in neighbouring gardens. She drifted idly down the streets, and her limbs responded to the movement. She reached Hyde Park, and sat upon a seat, the opposite end of which was occupied by a blotchy-faced woman fast asleep. Sparrows quarrelled amongst the beds. Suddenly her heart was touched with pity as she regarded the blotchy-faced one down and out, old and finished. But, after all, wasn't she the same? Down and out yes, but not yet old or blotchy. She had her youth. Nothing was left her but her youth. Well, was youth a thing to be idly disregarded? Free: she was free, not a responsibility in the world. A curious thing, freedom, the possession only of irresponsible people. Decent people weren't free. They were tied hand and foot. Something inspiring, though, about freedom. After all, one might as well go on living.

She ambled back to the rooms in Notting Hill, and found Isabel making tea, and looking anxious. Barbara gave her the first smile for three days.

"I've been for a walk, old girl."

"Oh! are you feeling better, Fancy?"

"Yes. I shall be all right."

"I do wish we could afford to send you away for a bit."

Poor Isabel! she had not yet received her first week's money!

"It isn't necessary, darling. It's work I want."

"Will you go back to that pearl-stringing?"

"Oh, I expect so."

But she did not go back to the pearl-stringing. She felt that the association of that room with Mrs. Myrtle and her tragic connection would be too much. She idled the days away. Her health became normal. But she was hungry, hungry for the good things. She wanted to dine out, and they had no money. "It's in my blood," she thought. "It's like Isabel said, 'If you've ever been kissed properly' I shall never be able to work, not this ordinary, drudging kind of work that decent people do."

On the night when Isabel got her salary they spent a third of it within an hour on a carouse. During the height of it Barbara reflected:

"Who was it I kept saying I was not free tot I am free I am free."

She parted with Isabel at the stage door. Then she took a bus to Piccadilly and walked briskly through St. James' Square. She found the flat occupied by Theodore Moffatt. The clean young animal was dressing. He had dined in the City and was going to a dance. A man showed her into his sitting-room In a few minutes he appeared looking rather handsome and astonished. He cried out:

"Hullo, Betty"—she had told him that her name was Betty Broadhurst—"This is a delightful and unexpected surprise. "

Barbara stood a-quiver on the hearthrug her immobile, but her bosom heaving rapidly.

"You said once that a bargain was a bargain, a deal a deal; and that if I came to you—"

Moffatt was even more astonished, too astonished to rush the position. He replied questioningly:

"You would like me to help you in some way? Come, tell me—"

"I'm hard up and desperate. Yes, I want you to help me."

"All right, old girl. Come now, sit down; let's talk about it. Have a drink."

She sat on the Chesterfield, and he poured out two drinks. They silently consumed them, as if in need of encouragement for the crisis to follow. Yes, there was a touch of the gentleman and the sportsman about this man. She could believe that he had never taken advantage of a friend or an enemy. Suddenly she broke out with:

"You understand, Mr. Moffatt, I'm not one of those women, don't you? Neither I nor my friend. Only I'm desperate. I shall soon be hungry and one might as well go on living. When you spoke to me I was not free. Now I am free. I haven't a shred of responsibility in the world and very little conscience, I'm afraid "

The significance of her visit was now clearly patent to him. The good fortune almost tongue-tied him. He whispered:

"You mean to say that if I help you, you—"

"A bargain's a bargain. A deal's a deal. I'm not going to take your money for nothing. Only one thing if I remain straight with you, you must promise to remain straight with me."

Very solemnly he repeated: "I'll remain straight with you. I promise."

He went to take her in his arms, but she repulsed him gently.

"Not yet, man Listen to me. I want to talk first, fairly and squarely as one human being to another. A bargain's a bargain, a deal's a deal. You will keep me in comfort and make me an allowance, eh?"

"Yes, yes."

"I want something more from you than that. I shall be a kept woman, old boy. Is it possible to make it a reasonably decent life! Come, you are acting dishonourably in keeping me. I ani acting dishonourably in coming to you. We are both pretty low down; but don't let us sink altogether. We mingle our virtues and our vices. I know myself pretty well now. I'm a miserable compromise. I can neither be entirely virtuous, nor entirely vicious. I have made myself like that. There are a lot of women like me. But I don't want to sit around in this flat, idling and drinking and smoking, waiting for you to turn up and demand your rights. I want some sort of companionship. I want work, and interests, and distractions."

"You shall have all that, Betty. I also am not all Cither virtuous or vicious."

"My name isn't Betty. It's Fancy Telling. I -was an actress, but that's all over. We've got to be dead straight with each other. I hate these women of the demi-monde, not because they're vicious usually they're not but because they're damned le~ The people I like are the kind of people you meet lunching in an A. B. C., little clerks and typists, with ordered lives and an eager intentness in all kinds of insignificant things, walking about in the sun after a cup of coffee, looking in the shop windows ripping!"

"You're a queer girl, Fancy. If you feel like that why don't you go and get a job- I could get you a job instead of coming to me?"

"Because I'm Fancy Telling. I can see it all, but I can't do it, if you know what I mean. I should break out one day and destroy the whole thing. I altered Barbara Powerscourt, but I can't alter Fancy Telling. You can alter what you are, but you can't alter what you make yourself. I've made myself that. Crudely speaking, you want me for certain animal satisfactions. Perhaps I'm the same. I shall never love you. I shall never love anyone again—"

She walked to the window and listened to the distant roar of traffic. Suddenly she remarked:

"I like to have things straightforward. Doesn't it seem queer! There's you and I making our bargain here quite decently together, with London roaring all around us. If they knew, they would I don't know what they'd do. They'd certainly say we were very wicked. They have to have labels for everything. And yet they're all very much the same. London is a kind of clearing-house of the emotions. Some belong to one company, some to another, and they have to be sifted, and sorted, and labelled. But underneath it all lies the great pity."

"By gum, you 're a strange kid! There 's only one thing I'm frightened about."

"What's that?"

"I'll get too fond of you."

"Do you love your wife?"

"In a way yes."

"Why do you do this, then?"

"You're candid with me. I'll be candid with you. The kind of thing you and I the reason why you're here, I mean that kind of thing bores her. I don't believe she'd even mind very much if she knew about you. I'm made differently. That's all."

"But if you fell in love with me?"

"Golly! There 'd be hell!"

"Then you mustn't. Another point, friend."

"What's that?"

"No children."

"I should be as anxious as you that that shouldn't happen."

He went across to her and passionately put his arms around her shoulders.

"Is it a bargain, then?"

"Yes."

"Fancy, I'm not going to that dance to-night."

XV

And so she went to live with Theodore Moffat, and within the limit of their code he played straight with her, and she played straight with him.

"One day he'll tire of me," she thought. "Well, when that day comes I shall look out for another if I'm not too old."

Old age! No, she didn't fear old age. Nature has a way of forcing us to adapt ourselves. And when everything has been given, and everything taken away.

She was quite happy in the young man's flat, singing quietly as she went about her duties. If the day was cold or wet there was always the morrow when the sun would shine, the busy streets, people hurrying hither and thither. Dear people! every face with a different story to tell; music stealing through open doorways, glitter and movement, pity and pathos, and that almost unbelievable courage. A long way ahead it would all come right "the pity which remains. "Isabel would come to tea. She would come up the stairs, puffing, sloppy, and a little bewildered.

"Fancy, you beat me, darling. I never thought you'd do this!"

Darling Isabel!

She was not frightened. She went to South Kensington Museum and made a real study of old lace this time. She started making lace. She kept accounts. She mended the poor man's linen, darned his socks, ministered to his wants, read a little "Shibboleths," eh!

A long way ahead...

Stacy Aumonier – A Short Biography

Stacy Aumonier was born at Hampstead Road near Regent's Park, London on 31st March 1877.

He came from a family with a strong and sustained tradition in the visual arts; sculptors and painters.

In 1890 the teenage Aumonier attended Cranleigh School in Surrey. Although he would later write critically about English public schools (with articles for the London Evening Standard and New York Times) in how they tried to impose conformity on students, records indicate that he integrated well into Cranleigh. Aumonier was a passionate cricket player, belonged to the Literary and Debating Society, and, in his final year, became a prefect.

On leaving school it seemed the family tradition of the visual arts would be his career path. In particular his early talents were that of a landscape painter. He exhibited paintings at the Royal Academy in 1902 and 1903, and 1908. An exhibition of his work would later be held at the Goupil Gallery in London in 1911.

In 1907 he married the international concert pianist, Gertrude Peppercorn, at West Horsley in Surrey. She herself was the daughter of a landscape painter (Arthur Douglas Peppercorn, occasionally cited as 'the English Corot'.) A son, Timothy, was born in 1921.

A year after his marriage, Aumonier began a brief career in a second branch of the arts at which he enjoyed outstanding success—as a stage performer writing and performing his own sketches.

The Observer newspaper commented that "...the stage lost in him a real and rare genius, he could walk out alone before any audience, from the simplest to the most sophisticated, and make it laugh or cry at will."

In 1915, Aumonier published a short story 'The Friends' which was well received (and voted one of the best short stories of 1915 by the Boston Magazine, Transcript).

Despite his age being 40 in 1917 he was called up for service in World War I. He began as a private in the Army Pay Corps, and then transferred as a draughtsman in the Ministry of National Service.

By now he had four books published—two novels and two books of short stories—and his occupation is recorded with the Army Medical Board as 'author.'

In the mid-1920s, Aumonier received the shattering diagnosis that he had contracted tuberculosis. In the last few years of his life, he would spend long spells in various sanatoria, some better than others. In a letter to his friend, Rebecca West, written shortly before his death, he described the debilitating conditions in a sanatorium in Norfolk during the winter of 1927, where the dampness was so severe that a newspaper left beside the bed would feel "sodden to the touch in the morning."

Shortly before his death, Stacy Aumonier sought treatment in Switzerland, but died of the disease in Clinique La Prairie at Clarens beside Lake Geneva on 21st December 1928. He was 55.

Whilst Aumonier's works are now slowly coming back into circulation at the time of his death his works were extremely popular and his loss was a profound tragedy for literary society.

The chief fiction critic of The Observer, Gerald Gould wrote: "His gifts were almost fantastically various; they embraced all the arts; but it was the charm and generosity of his personality which made him—what he unquestionably was—one of the most popular men of his generation." It went on: "The things he wrote will be remembered when the company of his friends (no man had more friends, or more devoted and admiring) are with him in the grave; but just now, to those who knew him, the thing most vividly present is the charm and wisdom of the man they knew."

Of his general appearance and manner Gerald Cumberland gives us this interesting set of observations: "A distinguished man, this—distinguished both in mind and appearance. Self-conscious. Perhaps. Why not? His hair is worn a trifle long, and it is arranged so that his fine forehead, broad and high, may be fully revealed. Round his neck is a very high collar and a modern stock. When in repose, his face has a look of shy eagerness; his quick eyes glance here and there gathering a thousand impressions to be stored up in his brain. It is the face of a man extremely sensitive to external stimulus; one feels that his brain works not only rapidly, but with great accuracy. And at heart, he takes himself and his work seriously, though he likes on occasion to pretend that he is only a philanderer."

In literary terms Aumonier was amongst the best short story writers these shores have produced.

The Nobel Prize winning author John Galsworthy called him "A real master of the short story. The first essential in a short-story writer is the power of interesting sentence by sentence. Aumonier had this power in prime degree. You do not have to 'get into' his stories. He is especially notable for investing his figures with the breadth of life within a few sentences." Galsworthy asserted that Aumonier "is never heavy, never boring, never really trivial; interested himself, he keeps us interested. At the back of his tales, there is belief in life and a philosophy of life, and of how many short story writers can that be said? ...He follows no fashion and no school. He is always himself. And can't he write? Ah! Far better than far more pretentious writers. Nothing escapes his eye, but he describes without affectation or redundancy, and you sense in him a feeling for beauty that is never obtruded. He gets values right, and that is to say nearly everything. The easeful fidelity of his style has militated against his reputation in these somewhat posturing times. But his shade may rest in peace, for in this volume, at least he will outlive nearly all the writers of his day." In summing his up Galsworthy suggested that, through his stories, he would "outlive all the writers of his day."

James Hilton (author of Goodbye, Mr Chips and Lost Horizon) said "I think his very best works ought to be included in any anthology of the best short stories ever written." He cited 'The Octave of Jealously' as his favourite short story for the March 1939 edition of Good Housekeeping saying it was a "bitterly brilliant tale."

Rebecca West said of his writing in 1922 that his ability to blend reality with the imaginary was "the envy of all artists."

Stacy Aumonier – A Concise Bibliography

More than 87 short stories in more than 25 magazines, and in 6 volumes published during Aumonier's lifetime.

Among more than 20 other magazines, his work appeared in Argosy Magazine, John O' London's Weekly, The Strand Magazine and The Saturday Evening Post, as well as being anthologized, and adapted for film and television.

Short Story Collections

The Golden Windmill & Other Stories (1921)
The Friends & Other Stories (1917)
Miss Bracegirdle & Other Stories (1923)

Novels

Olga Bardel (1916)
Three Bars Interval (1917)
Just Outside (1917)
The Querrils (1919)
One After Another (1920)
Heartbeat (1922)

Other Works

A volume of 14 Character Studies: Odd Fish (1923)

A volume of 15 Essays: Essays of Today and Yesterday (1926)